da bushes

Rich Kisielewski

Steve,
Hope you enjoy Harry & da bushes.
Rich Kisielewski

PublishAmerica
Baltimore

© 2003 by Rich Kisielewski.
All rights reserved. No part of this book may be reproduced in any form without written permission from the publishers, except by a reviewer who may quote brief passages in a review to be printed in a newspaper or magazine.

First printing

ISBN: 1-59286-309-4
PUBLISHED BY PUBLISHAMERICA BOOK PUBLISHERS
www.publishamerica.com
Baltimore

Printed in the United States of America

Thanks to PublishAmerica for giving me, and Harry Mickey Shorts, the opportunity to be heard and enjoyed; to everyone in the WritersAnonymous group for being there – especially the original gang from the Writer's Subgroup days; and a very special thanks to my technical assistant and favorite daughter, Tara.

Chapter 1

Eighteen years old. Eighteen fuckin' years old. What could a little snot-nosed kid of eighteen (well, maybe six foot five inches and 225 pounds ain't so little) know about hitting and pitching and catchers calling pitches etc., etc., etc.? We got him right where we want him; Barney's gonna get him with the next pitch, and we are outta here.

Maybe I should jump back a few steps and let you in on what's going on here. My name is Harry because I'm told an aunt promised to lay some bread on me if my mom named me Harold. I don't believe it one little bit because I don't have a pot to piss in and never have. Don't ya think I'd still have at least a couple of bucks from that rich aunt's donation to my future? Nah – drugs, booze, broads and the horses or any other fuckin' thing you can think of would have gotten it long ago, just like any other money I've ever put my hands on.

Oh yeah, it's Harry, or should I say Harold Mickey Shorts, which wasn't my given name when I was ushered into this wonderful world of ours. My original name bit the big one in my opinion, and the Mick, Mr. Mantle, is my all time favorite. Plus, my original last name was way too long. Wearing tee shirts and shorts is how God intended us to dress, so that's how I came up with my new and improved name Shorts, which just happens to be a great conversation topic for the ladies.

Some people say I ramble on too much. I hope you won't agree with them. There is some logic to the smattering of brilliance that originates in my brain and exits through my mouth. Or at least after our little trip down reconstruction lane, you will know me to a T and can't possibly agree with those know-it-alls. I just like to tell ya what's on my mind so you won't be confused.

I'm getting to the point of this whole story if you are getting just a wee bit impatient by now. By trade, I guess you could call me a private investigator. But I'm not your run of the mill, everyday private dick – and in my opinion all dicks should be kept private. That TV show where the guy pretends to be someone else, cleverly named *The Pretender*, I do a little of that too. Something's going on and you can't figure out what it is; you need help but don't want it to be too obvious. Out of nowhere I appear on the scene to save the day for you. Fortunately for me and my bank account, it usually takes a bit longer than a day in most of my cases. This happened to be one of those cases. Remind me to give you the *Reader's Digest* version of some of the other trips I have been on. I'm counting on ya 'cause my memory slips every once in awhile…like yours doesn't?

One thing that irks me when reading, which I do quite a bit, is having to wait forever for the chapter to come to an end in a book. Just a little quirk in my otherwise fabulous personality. Anyway, you have to keep peeking to see if the next page is the end of the chapter. Not here, kiddo – get used to it, I call everybody and his grandmother kiddo – so end of chapter period

Chapter 2

I don't know how to come up with names for chapters the way some people do. They can produce cool and catchy names that give you some idea what's going to happen in that chapter. I am clever, but the pressure to come up with a new title every chapter would take way too much brainpower. I need to conserve as much of that as possible. Anyway, I'm not writing this book, I'm just talking and you're just listening, so they aren't really chapters, I guess. If I did, though, this one might be where I explain what happened and call it "What Happened?" That way I could tell ya why I'm a used-to-be, once-was, or could-have-been catcher, in what appears to be a down and out Double A minor league team in Bayport, New York. That's towards the end of Long Island, which makes great tea, by the way. That's why it's called Long Island Iced Tea, a drink with enough punch to knock you on your ass pronto, quick. But as always, you'll have to remind me to tell you a doozy of a story about Long Island Iced Tea, and me and two other guys from my younger days.

So, I'm in my office in Manhasset in the back room I rent at Top Line Realty from my ex-brother-in-law. It really isn't a room, but more like a desk we share, because he owns the place and I use the phone and the address for mail deliveries. Happens to be real convenient and we used to live in the town for what seemed like a lifetime awhile ago. The we is me and the ex and a coupla kids. It's a few miles from the Long Island parking lot, or Expressway as it's actually called, and the Long Island railroad gets you into midtown New York City in a jiffy.

Did I mention the ex-brother-in-law rips me off on the rent with some outrageous number each month, and I only stay 'cause he's one of my favorite three brothers-in-law? I'll get to that "phrase" later when I rant about the dumbfuck sports writer/announcer who did away with RBI's as an incorrect use of the term. It is now RBI, as in Runs Batted In. You will of course agree with me and start a vicious write-in campaign to change it back. But you guessed it – I digress.

So, as I was about to tell you before I rudely interrupted myself, I'm sitting in the back and the phone rings, which of course wakes me up from a sound sleep. I knock the coffee cup off the desk and onto the floor. No problem, it hits the same spot the other ten or so cups have hit before. Ex-bro-in-law will find out some day, but fuck him till he does. Cost of doing business and well within the rip-off factor included in the rent.

"Kizmet Incorporated," I proudly announce in a sleep-induced, semi-awake voice. "May I be of some service on this beautiful fall day?" I said as I tried to get my sights centered on some object to correct the double vision caused by my blistering hangover. As a somewhat expert on this sort of physical malady, this one could conceivably be classified as a "category 4 brain-smashing, stomach-tumbling, body-shivering, eye-bleeding doozy of a morning after a very long night before" hangover. Wonder if I could get one of those copyright things on that phrase, like the slick-haired coach from Miami did on Three-Peat. Slight digression, back to business.

"Is this Mr. Harry Short?" my caller asks. I immediately see "paying customer" tied to the Mr. before my name. If he is calling me Mr., he obviously doesn't know me, and far be it from me to educate him before I get a few of his hard-earned dollars.

"It's actually Shorts with an S," I say, leaving out my normal "just like in-your-shorts" explanatory declaration. Smart little critter and dumbfuck in the same sentence. I do have a way with words on occasion.

"Just call me Harry, and what can I help you with?" The spot that was helping me center my vision and inner being at that instance was the most delectable rear-end (ass to the crude ones in the crowd) of the 21-year-old secretary my Ebil, ex-brother-in-law in shortened version for sake of brevity, hired about two months ago. Business is either good, or he likes looking at delectable rear-ends the same as I do. Your

da bushes

choice, but don't forget he is male and breathing.

My senses were starting to return to me all in a rush as I began to smell the coffee, and the urge for a cigarette hit me with an overpowering rush like a sledge-hammer to the side of the head. Small problem – I quit smoking not two days ago. Question – why? Answer – I'm getting older, and stupider, and clearly forgot moments like these. Solution – just bum one from sweet Bunny Malone, the secretary (I couldn't make that name up if I tried for a thousand years) and quit the next time I feel guilty. By the way – you were just subjected to your first classic Question/Answer/Solution combination from Harry Shorts. More will most definitely follow in the time travels we will enjoy together.

If I weren't 31 years old I'd swear I was ready for the Old Age home. What's left of the old mind gets off on some weird tangents and I need Scotty to beam me back to reality.

"Sorry for the error, Mr. Shorts, ah Harry, but I secured your name from a distant relative who was in need of your services some time ago."

He was turning into my kind of guy with each passing minute, and before it was too late, I figured it would be good to know who this prince of a guy might be. My mouth opened, but words were blocked by the sound of that infectious high-pitched giggle coming from the general direction of Ms. Bunny. It could stop a world war dead in its tracks when she really gets it in gear. Try to concentrate numnuts and pay some small attention to business instead of the wiggle in your pants. Finally the fog began to clear slightly and I remembered the telephone.

"Are you still there Mr. ah…." I mumbled, trying not to sound too space cadet worthy. My kingdom for a name!

"My name is Trundle and I hope I'm not inconveniencing you by catching you at a bad time, Mr. Shorts. My niece spoke very highly of you and assured me your talents were quite evident in your mutual dealings. She can be somewhat naive at times, but I was aware of her problem, and I believe it did come to a satisfactory conclusion. But if this is a bad time, I can attempt to contact you at some later date."

The light bulb flicked on directly over my pained head. Trundle, as in bed, as in Connie the niece, and that's a story and a half that you are gonna have to be real good for me to divulge the details. Some cases are better left as privileged information and that one fits the bill to a T.

Repeat after me – end of chapter period

Chapter 3

Back to the beginning of the story...

Barney was the third best pitcher on the Schooners, but today he couldn't throw a strike if his miserable 24-year-old life depended on it. My knees were fuckin' achin' like I had been crouched behind the plate forever, and it was only the top of the 4th inning. Trundle's phone call began running through my brain as I gave Barney the sign for the deuce low and away. We set big boy up for it and the 2-2 pitch was the one we wanted. Pretty good breeze on a hot Saturday afternoon when a 6 foot 5 lug goes down swinging while looking like the kiddie fool he is.

Best laid plans, my ass!

The fuzz-faced kid called time to adjust his cup before he succumbed to our trickery and struck out, which allowed my mind to wander back to last fall, and the telephone call that got me in this mess to begin with. Trundle turned out to have more money than God and somebody had fucked with his favorite toy of the moment. He purchased the Bayport franchise in the Minor League Baseball Eastern League for more money than I could dream of and built a stadium better than half the Triple A teams played in. Three years in the making and their first year turned out to be a Freddie Kreuger nightmare. Let's see if I can run it down from the exhaustive research that I conducted:

Daddy Warbucks the 2nd decides to dabble in minor league baseball – probably a frustrated mediocre college has-been.

Buys a franchise at top dollar, starts from scratch and builds a state of the art stadium in Bayport Long Island. QAS Time – why Bayport? League needs a Long Island franchise. Uses the land he already owns!

Recruits talent from other teams in the league, raids the lower minors and adds a few choice, very overpaid free agent kids.

Signs a few good coaches and gets a top drawer manager

Makes his son the general manager even though the putz couldn't spell baseball with the help of a dictionary.

All in all, your typical beginning to a minor league team with a bazillion bucks to back it up. Give him credit for being bright enough to go out and get some baseball talent to run the on-field show while numnuts (Warbucks Jr.) parades around playing baseball exec-for-a-day. And that fuckin' bimbo attached to his arm known to be able to suck a golf ball through 20 feet of garden hose. All right, I stole that one from an Eddie Murphy movie, but it is a good one, and since I can personally confirm the possibility, take it as gospel and believe it. Amazing how much info/gossip/bullshit bitching you can gather from one phone call to a friend in the business. I owe him a big one, but it's not the first, and I'm sure it won't be the last.

Now, let me get this pain in the ass kid out of the way so I can go on with my story. Barney throws a beaut of a curve on the outside corner an inch below the knees and dickhead hits it 400 feet to right center over the Mountain Dew sign. Give a kid a million dollar bonus and Boom! – he can hit. As I said, I'm a private investigator and not a baseball player for good reason, though I did set him up perfectly. Gotta find out that kid's name – he could either be a good one some day or lucky as shit. Either way, he owes me one.

Did I mention his real name is Danny Rubble and I immediately nicknamed him Barney first time I met him? Nicknames are a hobby of mine

After that titanic blast into outer space, the schmutz of a new pitching coach jumps out of the dugout; so it's a good time to say end of chapter period

Chapter 4

Scootch, the pitching coach, could be mistaken for a top-notch #1 flying asshole. Now follow along with the class and do as you're told. Take your pointer finger and touch the end of that finger to the end of your thumb on the same hand. Makes something like a circle or an O for the slow members of the group. Raise your hand in the air and wave it around while moving the other three fingers up and down in a fluttering motion. There you go – a flying asshole. Don't tell anyone I taught you that one, or they may think I'm a little nimble-minded. But don't forget, you were the one with your hand in the air making like a flying asshole. Just hope nobody was watching.

Now Scootch is dynamite with the young pitchers and perfect for this level of minor league baseball. He understands the mechanics like he got a Ph.D. in pitching, and most importantly can teach what's inside his head. His problem is that he doesn't have a ball (or testicle, if you prefer) in his body. Not a one. The following exchange is typical mound conversation when old Scootch wanders out of the dugout and ends up at the mound.

I normally beat Scootch to the pitcher by about two steps whether I run out or crawl. He is always two steps behind me.

"How you feeling, kiddo?" I ask.

"That last pitch was right where we wanted it and the big prick goes and launches it just south of the can." Scootch looks from me to Barney and can't figure out what fuckin' can Barney's talking about.

"The Mountain Dew can, Scootch, on the fence, and I'm pissed as all hell. That was my out pitch the fuck hammered into outer space, but I'm still feeling pretty good for a 75 degree day this early in the year."

Yep, Scootch looks at me as I tell Barney we can get the next guy, hit the dugout and cool off for awhile. "Alrighty then" is all he says and turns to go back to the end of the dugout where he sits till coach sends him out again, if needed. Thanks for stopping by, Scootch – nap time.

I should tell ya that "Scootch" was another one of my gems and the damndest thing, too. His real name is Herbert somethingorother and he was always called just plain Herb. He had this annoying habit of using the word scootch for absolutely everything. That reminds me, I need to replenish the supply of Absolut at home; and yes, you guys from Absolut should be throwing some major bucks my way for all this free advertising. But, as I am wont to do, I digress.

So, old Herb would sit down next to you and say "scootch over just a bit, will ya," and constantly say "let's throw just a scootch harder to this guy, and get just a scootch more over the top on the table deuce" to the pitchers. I'll explain table deuce later for you non-pitching experts who are reading along only because I enthrall you so. I'm sure you'll be able to struggle along till then.

I'm hanging out in the bullpen one day before the game watching our ace of the day get ready for another gem. It just pops in my head, which was about a half-size too big from the long evening before, and I say "Hey, Scootch, how's he look?" The guys look at me and all at once they get it and fall down laughing. Herb just shakes his head and walks toward the dugout, and the damndest part is he never said the word scootch again. You guessed it, though; it stuck to this very day and even got into the back of the sports pages of *Newsday* once.

Since I occasionally find myself with some unintended free time on my hands between international espionage, secret spy stuff and the occasional "get me pictures of the rat bastard cheating fuck of a husband," I have been able to do some coaching on the local front. I try not to go deep undercover during early season or the playoffs. I have to tell ya, it's the real kick in being involved with coaching sports on any level. When you can work with a particular kid and get him to improve and see the joy in his face, it really is a rush. Be sure and appreciate the good coaches out there who are doing it for the kids and

da bushes

not to relive their own past failures. In case you dozed off there a few times, Absolut is my poison of the moment if you happen to live in Manhasset and your appreciation is about to be coming my way.

And no, I wasn't just running off at the mouth as usual – there was a point to all that. Scootch spends every waking hour giving of his time and unusual ability to get inside a know-it-all dumb shit kid's head and make him really see what and how and why. He transmits the picture into their brain and wills their body to do the mechanics, and there is nothing prettier than a kid walking off the mound after finally getting the big hitter with his new pitch for the first time. Look down the bench and there's Scootch knowing and smiling. No CEO or brain surgeon could do it any better, and I'll never forget him for it. Now if we could only perform a testicle transplant he would be a saver.

The dumb shit kids that don't get it just get sent back to Single A, and if Scootch can't get to them, say so long, 'cause they ain't coming back.

Oh man, too heavy for me, so end of chapter period

Chapter 5

You will probably notice that at times my concentration level leaves something to be desired, and my attention span is relatively short. I skip around from one time and place to another fairly often. I'll try to keep you on track, but you're gonna have to use your imagination on occasion. Let's go back to my office.

I moved my concentration from the fabulous "Bunny butt" to the potential live one on the phone. Quick now – let's get some info and get a hook into this guy somehow. Here comes the brilliance:

"The Connie problem was a tough one and I was quite pleased to have it work out as well as it did. Confidentiality was the key, along with sensing the far-reaching ramifications if the outside world was to get wind of her 'predicament,' shall we say. My firm specializes in working where we aren't expected to be and getting results when most others would be stymied. My personal assistant is available on all cases and the most difficult ones I try to handle personally. May I assume the same requirements exist here?"

Go right ahead – I can wait until you're done applauding the masterful way I drew in my prey and hooked him with absolutely no means of escaping.

Trundle slowly began his tale of woe, sounding like a kid whose dog pissed on his favorite teddy bear. I almost felt sorry for the poor guy till I realized he was describing a scenario with real people getting hurt, and some unknown scoundrels doing the hurting. Brilliant detective minds sniff out details even when incapacitated by the remnants of an Absolut and Bud overdose.

I'm not gonna bore you with the half-hour story from Trundle, whose first name by the way turns out to be M. Randle, which I guess is really an

da bushes

initial and middle name he uses as a first name. Why the hell do people do that? Somebody gave you the M. and wanted it to be your name but it just isn't good enough, so the old middle name switcheroo pops up. At least I kept Harry. That's right – I digress.

To save your sanity, here's the shortened version of the story. Seems all was going along just ducky, the team was up eleven games at the halfway point and the park was jammed for almost every single game. Junior was like a side-show hawkster with more fuckin' gimmicks you'd think he was Bill Veeck or something. But give the little bastard credit, the fans ate it up and Mr. Beer Man was keeping the kids in shoes with all the suds he was selling. The players were having the time of their lives, and the major league clubs were starting to roll around to see what was up with this new team in BumFuckEgypt, Long Island.

Life was like a bowl of cherries! Unfortunately, these cherries turned out to have pits.

The second half started out with more of the same until the team got home from a road trip in early July, ten games up and riding high on the hog. Slowly but surely the home runs they had been pounding up till then started ending up on the warning track, and the pitchers lost a foot on the old hummer. Nobody could figure out what the hell was going on; the lead diminished, and the players were just tired as hell. All but three of the regulars needed time off, and most of the subs just didn't have any energy when they came in to hold down the fort. The team went into the shitter and never came out. They barely had enough healthy players to finish out the season and wound up in third place seven games behind the champs. A swing of 18 games and a bunch of questions with no answers.

So, there you have it. Trundle was having gobs of fun until the wheels came off and he wanted his toy fixed. Cogitate on that one a minute while I get a cool one for myself, which I am wont to do on occasion, as it's end of chapter period

Chapter 6

    Harry Mickey Shorts has not exactly glided through life for the 31 years he has inhabited this earth. Seventeen years old, had the whole world by the balls, and I wasn't planning to let go any time soon. High school baseball phenom setting all kinds of school boy records and the college of my choice just around the corner, not to mention every scout in Queens and the metropolitan area sniffing my butt every time I moved. What could possibly go wrong? Baby! Marriage at 18. That QAS was the end of the fairy tale and the beginning of the self-imposed trip to shitsville for Harry Mickey Shorts.
    It was my senior year and the numbers looked something like this: batting average of .679 with 14 dingers, 51 RBI's and 21 stolen bases for a catcher with a certified gun for an arm on the soon-to-be city champs. Two more playoff wins and "we be champs" with an undefeated season. You get in a groove and you just know everything thrown your way is gonna get stroked with authority. The hard stuff looks slow and the breaking balls are as big as beach balls on a sunny day. Even the outs are smoked right at somebody. Don't dare pinch me 'cause I'm on cloud nine floating up to baseball heaven.
    Sherry told me on Friday night. We were gonna get to the finals after beating Holy Cross, or somebody the next day, then on to Fordham University next Saturday to finish out our storybook year.
    When you're the stud it seems like the girls are all over you before, during and after every game. I played the field like the champ I was and kinda liked Sherry more than the rest of them. As it turned out, I guess that was a good thing since we became a "we" on that Friday night. A coupla months late was not a good fuckin' sign, and the "am I gonna have a baby?" kit confirmed it as fact the following Monday.

da bushes

We won the two damn games in romps and life should have been perfect. But shit happens. Funny how the scholarship offers dwindled and then disappeared altogether after we got hitched at the end of June. Sherry stayed with her folks, which was good, since we didn't have anywhere else to go. I didn't know what else to do, so I signed with Tampa Bay and headed to Florida to become a star.

"Baseball been berry berry good to me!" to quote a famous *Saturday Night Live* star.

Let me ask you all a question – how many "stars" are there in the sky? To save you the problem of counting them, I'll give you the answer. They are equal to the number of "stars" that exist in high school baseball throughout the United States, and numerous Latin American countries and/or islands, that all end up in the minor leagues together. Picture a school of minnows with a gazillion of the same little itty-bitty fish, and you would know exactly how I felt. Just one of the many high school All-Americans tossed together waiting for the strong to survive.

Starting off "the man" and fading into oblivion sends thousands home to their mommies to cry about what might have been. The big bad world of baseball business is so far from the high school game. It catches you by surprise, knocks you to the ground and steps on your nuts for good measure. No room for missing anybody and no room for Mr. Nice Guy. Long periods of nada to do except work at your new trade or fuck-up. I grabbed a chunk of each and went at both as hard as I could. Unfortunately, I did real good at both with a bit too much emphasis on the second choice. I should have chosen the curtain instead of the box.

And a one, and a two – end of chapter period

Chapter 7

Let's get back to the phone call in my office.

When Trundle finished his rap, I was just a wee bit curious and saw the opportunity to do what I love to do more than anything else in this world – play baseball. Being too many years out of real game shape, and several hops and barley fields down the road was no problem. Absolutely no problem – poor choice of words as it turned out. The Absolut part seems to have taken its toll somewhere along the way as well. But, first things first.

To make sure I didn't get myself in deep before I needed to, I suggested we meet to discuss his problem in depth and hammer out a game plan. The exchange of greenbacks may come up in the conversation, but the thought of getting back in the saddle was probably enough of an incentive for me.

"How about tomorrow for lunch?" was my brilliant reply when my brain finally managed to direct words to my mouth. I have a tendency to be thinking about four sentences ahead of where you might think I was at the time.

"Sorry, but I missed where you are calling from." Always let the customer pick the spot so they are on familiar turf and comfortable. Lets them feel free to let go and give you the details you need and saves you time trying to fit pieces together later on.

"I'm currently in the air, but I'll be back in New York later tonight and could arrange to meet you tomorrow for lunch. I'll have to maneuver a few things, but that shouldn't be a problem. This is important to me, if I'm making myself clear, Mr. Shorts."

I love a guy who listens and gets the "s" in my Shorts. That didn't come out real clean but you get the picture. If you don't, you will.

da bushes

"If I send my car for you at about 11:00, we can have something at my office around noon and spend the rest of the day discussing your assistance in this matter. If that suits your schedule, that is?"

Never jump when you can let them hang just a tad. "Let me confirm my schedule for the remainder of the day tomorrow. Can you hold a second, Mr. Trundle?"

Luckily, Bunny was out of typing paper and Ebil's placement of said paper in the bottom drawer of a strategically placed filing cabinet kept me busy for the few seconds I needed. The idiot that tried to do away with short skirts and go ankle-length need only to have spent the past few seconds in my shoes to know he fucked up big time. Thank you, Ms. Malone, and the pleasure was certainly all mine.

"Sorry for the delay, Mr. Trundle, but I was rescheduling a client conference and it worked out satisfactorily. The day will be all yours. Where might I say I will be as there are several current matters nearing fruition and I may need to confer in an emergency?" Truth is things are deader than three-day-old shit, but you gotta look and sound booked to new clients. And if Bunny goes into one of her giggling fits, Ebil can call me to brighten my outlook on life. How one treasures the smaller things that bring such joy.

"I apologize, Mr. Shorts, for my selfish approach to our communication so far. I get wrapped up in my problems and neglect to give adequate details on occasion."

I assured him we were all guilty of that at times – some of us don't really give a shit though. When I get to it I'll tell you what you want to know. That's why you pay me the big bucks. It did come out sounding like "No need to apologize, Mr. Trundle, I'm sure you were about to get to it any minute." Diplomacy pays Ebil's rent ticket and fills the fridge with aluminum-encased essentials.

"Charles will be there at 11:00 a.m. as I said to bring you to the Trundle Building, my downtown office on Madison Avenue. I'll have Ms. Timmons meet you at reception and we can enjoy our meal in my private dining room, if that meets with your approval," said Mr. Trundle. "My direct line for your convenience and future needs is (212) 555-7142. Please call me Randle, and I'm sure I can have Charles get you back to Manhasset for any evening engagement you may have planned."

"That's sounds perfect, Mr. Trundle…I mean Randle. I look forward to lunch and furthering our discussion. I will see you tomorrow," and I hung up feeling like something big and unusual was about to go down.

Feeling lucky as shit, I figured what the hell and yelled in Bunny's general direction, "Hey, kiddo, how about a few cool ones across the street?"

Much to my surprise and good fortune, she giggled and said, "Let's go, big guy, and I hope you're feeling lucky tonight!"

You bet your ass it's end of chapter period

Chapter 8

If you've never seen a Rolls Royce limo, you have a boatload of company – including yours truly. That was until 11:00 a.m. the following morning when Charles pulled up in front of Ebil's shop, a half-dozen open-mouthed local residents looking on. I swear the fucker was purple, but a really nice shade of purple if it is possible for any car, never mind a Rolls limo, to be nice in purple. Not Paris Lilac like my idiot little brothers painted their room at home without telling my folks. You will clearly see the relevance of the purple limo later on.

The growing crowd was waiting for Ebil to emerge and head for who knows where in the purple chariot. The few mouths not open dropped for sure when low-life Shorts prances through the door, thanks Charles, who happens to be holding open the rear door, and jumps in the back seat. The kids always loved taking a limo to the airport, and even at their ages the purple-mobile would have been too cool to pass up. Oh well, a wave to the love of last night, precious Bunny, and away we went.

You can buzz downtown in 30 minutes on some days, and on others the Long Island parking lot could piss off Mother Teresa. Today would have been a bad day for God him/herself (covering all bases till I get in front of those pearly gates) as we passed Woodhaven Blvd at 11:45 a.m. Charles was cool though and mentioned the refreshments in the unit built into the side door to my immediate right. Now my favorite daughter holds up her left hand and makes an L with her thumb and pointer finger to tell her which is left and the other must be right. Me, I'm a big grown-up and can figure it out without the use of visual aides. Plus, I swear I can smell the suds from 20 feet away.

Two cool ones later we pulled up to Trundle Towers on Madison and 57th Street. For the Curious Georges in the crowd, a nifty little address to be housed in. I don't think it goes for 15 bucks a square foot.

I swear Charles was opening my door before the car came to a stop, and Ms. Timmons was just inside the front entrance ready and willing to serve. I doubt her version of "being of assistance" was the same as mine, but it was too early in the game to rush judgement. For the professional wrestling fans in the crowd, she possessed the total package for sure.

"Come with me, Mr. Shorts," Ms. Timmons smiled. I did and I'll tell you, those weren't visions of sugarplums dancing in my head.

Trump has nothing over my new idol, Mr. Trundle. The atrium seemed to rise 20 stories with more glass, marble, waterfalls and live trees bigger than Manhasset's best, and they have some big ones. Randy's office (my name for M. Randle Trundle, among us friends) was on the top floor, number 54 on the elevator floor indicator panel. By the time we got to the top floor, it was just Ms. Timmons and moi surrounded on all sides by mirrors. She looked damn good in every one of them and she knew it. It was at that very instance that I realized her exquisitely snug dress was a perfect shade of purple.

"Walk this way, Mr. Shorts," she whispered loudly, but my ass couldn't move like hers if two guys each grabbed a cheek and swung me back and forth. Smitten would be an understatement.

"I'm right behind you," I said, and thoroughly enjoyed every second of it.

Now, I'm no art expert, but the stuff on the walls in the reception area would blow away most galleries. I had a lady friend during my travels who tried to culturize me for a short time before reality finally set in and she figured out a lost cause was a lost cause. But in our brief museum period I saw some pretty good painters and artwork. Randy spared no expense as confirmed when my guiding princess pointed to the Renoir and said it was their newest addition from Mr. Trundle's trip to Paris last month. Bitch of a job, but somebody had to do it. I guess.

I followed her sweetness past the reception desk – the redhead

da bushes

manning the phones out front was no slouch either – and down a short corridor that opened to a sea of purple carpet and five hundred-year-old leather furniture arranged in small groupings. I began to wonder what Daddy Warbucks did for a living and guessed it wasn't widgets. Remind me to ask Ms. Timmons later just in case I don't find out from Randy. Perhaps she and I could discuss it as Charles drops her off at her place after work. You're probably right – fat fuckin' chance!

Plopped my ass down in one of the chairs and picked up the *Wall Street Journal*. I wouldn't have the slightest idea what half the stuff in it means, but I used it as camouflage while assessing Ms. Timmons' qualifications as she retreated to wherever she retreats to. I wonder where Charles hangs out when not squiring around private dicks and the like.

I was getting quite comfy when Mr. Trundle opened his door and waved for me to "come on down." As I stepped through the doorway I caught myself before uttering some stupid and vulgar comment along the lines of "what the fuck where you thinking?"

Randy combined a firm handshake with a grab of the elbow and pointed me toward a chair opposite his desk. He assumed the old power position behind his big old desk with me in a little old Chippendale side chair probably from the 17th century.

You the man, so shoot the works, Randy.

The intercom chirped, and Trundle picked up his antique phone with a flourish. I took in the surroundings and quickly calculated that the furniture in his office was probably valued at more than my total net worth times some factor. That factor was higher than I could imagine, so it wasn't worth trying to figure out. But the color that stood out was, you guessed it, purple. Not anything gaudy or glaringly obvious, but it pervaded the whole office nonetheless. Drapes and carpet. Is this guy a fruitcake or what?

"Sorry for the intrusion, but business is very demanding right now and requires my attention almost 24 hours a day. My Number One is in Europe and I man the helm when he is away from headquarters. I've asked my assistant to give us the rest of the day so we should be OK. She will deal with any situations that may arise. This is of equal importance to me," said Randle.

My razor sharp mind quickly processed what I just heard and wondered if his Number One was kinda like Charlie Chan's #1 son, and if the assistant in question was the lovely Ms. Timmons. Me and Charles can decipher my problems on the 10-hour ride back to Long Island later on. That is unless the all-important assistant is Ms. Timmons and she does accompany me in the limo extrordinaire.

For your information, I can't spell for shit and I make up words, so don't fuckin' bother me or my schiester editor with your "I found an error bullshit." Stick em all where the sun don't shine and pay attention to the story or you will miss the clever clues I drop here and there. Now, I've got your attention, I hope?

Endofchapterperiod

Chapter 9

We chatted about the World Series and those amazing Yankees. If you don't like the Yankees, you obviously don't know shit about the game, and I can say that 'cause I'll probably never meet you anyway. My new bud Randle wasn't a Yankee fan, but I let him slide for obvious reasons. The state of sports in general took about five more minutes, and we were ready to move to his private dining room.

"I didn't even see the door and I was staring right at it the whole time," I said as we stepped through a portal and entered a different time and place. The room could sit twenty-five in style with room to spare. Antiques galore, but the best part was the guy in white gloves there to serve us. The Ebil's gonna love this story when I tell him.

"Let's move to the other end of the room to take advantage of the view," said Randy. "I don't get to see the park that often and I just love it."

OK, what fuckin' park could he be talking about in the middle of Madison Avenue?

"Oh wow" just slipped out as I got to the end of the room and turned toward the floor-to-ceiling glass wall. The park Randy was so fond of was Central Park and we were high enough to get an unobstructed view of the whole length. I got what he was talking about and couldn't put into words how I felt.

"That's how I get every time I look out there," said Randle. "Let's sit."

The cool ones during the ride in had me primed for a coupla more during lunch. I've never been a big fan of squashed grapes, but the wines served with each course went down smooth as could be. Now follow along with this luncheon soiree for the two of us. The Crab

Louis appetizer was a perfect portion and set up the transfer to caesar salad with little tangerine slices mixed in. Leg of lamb with a rosemary and dijon mustard coating was almost as good as the one I can whip up for special occasions. I am very fond of my own cooking, so a little prejudice may have seeped into the opinion. But yes, I do digress.

I can tell you I was enjoying the hell out of this encounter. It's as if he knew what I liked and put them all in one neat little package topped off with Tartufo for desert. I would have bet the ranch that you can't get a wine to go good with Tartufo, but luckily I don't have a ranch, and would have been sleeping in the car again if I did. Did I say in the car "again"? Forget I said that, OK?

"I try not to discuss business while I eat," said Randle. "The finer things in life are meant to have our undivided attention, and I value good food as I value fine art. No need to cram things together, as everything has its own time and place."

Fort Knox borrows from him and he's a philosopher too. Where the hell does he find the time?

While I don't smoke as a steady habit, I do enjoy a cigarette after a real fine meal, or any meal for that matter. But just in case you were wondering, I've never been partial to a cigarette after a roll in the hay. Been there, done that. That macho-man bullshit is very overrated in my opinion, unless the lady cares to indulge, which makes it the thing to do, I guess.

The reason I bring up the subject is we had finished our little feast and White Gloves was clearing away the last plates, leaving the china coffee cups filled with cappuccino. I never saw the guy until the box of cigars appeared before me. "Don't mind if I do," I declared and had the feeling Fidel was finding himself a few short. Randle didn't indulge as it "clouds the taste buds," but drew his enjoyment from providing "the finer things in life to people important to him and his family." Jump back, Jack, Harry Mickey Shorts is moving into uncharted territory heretofore unseen by this ShitBum's eyes.

Maybe, just maybe, Mr. M. Randle Trundle sees something in Harry Mickey Shorts that the rest of the world, and me included, have yet to experience. Beats the shit out of me what it could possibly be, but the

da bushes

gravy train is motoring down the track and I'm on board for all its worth.

Always get out on a positive note if possible, so end of chapter period

Chapter 10

We adjourned to the private room only Randy has access to. It's where he does his serious thinking and planning. It was time to get down to business, but not his all the time business. His and my mutual business is what I meant. Oh fuck you if you can't figure out what I'm getting at. I'm having a good time here and you are tinkling on it. Go get a beer or a glass of wine, I'll wait.

There, feel better now.

Randle was passionate about his dedication to make his franchise the #1 minor league team in the United States. "I want those boys to have every opportunity to succeed, and each and every fan walking into my park to get their money's worth each and every game. There is no room for compromise, and I'll stop at nothing to ensure both points are met. If you can't share my goal than you should consider our business concluded."

Man, does this guy get his engine revved. Need to cool him down a notch or two, I reckon.

"Mr. Trundle, Randle, I'm here and I'm listening. Tell me what went wrong and how you think it happened. Who did you piss off along the way, either in your business world or in securing and building this team? Point me in a direction; I won't need a compass to keep on track, but I can't put together a game plan without all the facts. And, I mean all the facts. Even if you think it's petty or insignificant, it's important. Just talk and I'll listen."

It was dark when I got done listening with a good understanding of what happened, but little to go on in figuring out the when, and who, and how. I made it a point a long time ago to take notes when interviewing clients 'cause the amount of brain cells I've killed leaves

da bushes

the memory a tad shaky on occasion. Here's what my scribbles looked like:

Randy played for New York University back when they had a big time baseball program and was good, but not that good.

Got a degree in marketing, but it was understood he would go into the family business after college – plastics from what I could gather.

The old man died when he was 24 and tag, he was it.

At 30 he owned 16 companies grossing $450 million a year.

His charitable contributions then were well-publicized, and he now donates over $10 million a year to a slew of needy groups.

Voted CEO of the year three times and the employees throw him a party every year on his birthday.

The franchise cost him peanuts compared to his net worth; I still didn't have a clue what we were dealing with.

The $3.0 million he spent building the stadium and the team was approved by him personally – every dime.

The only person hurt by him getting the franchise was some old geezer whose name he didn't get at the time and died a short while later – no other bids involved that he knew of. That was the only competition when the final bids were opened.

The players liked playing for the team, the coaches were well paid and cared for and the town was raking in the dough from lots of sources after the Schooners got there.

He had no idea who would possibly want to do something like this, and it made him sick to even think about it.

The players who fell under this mysterious spell all got back to 100% within a month of the season's end except for the off-season ticket salesman Trundle hired due to his marketing degree from Michigan State – he still isn't feeling back to normal yet.

Money is not an issue in fixing this situation.

There was obviously much more involved in the five hours we talked. Nada to go on came from it, but I was in and maybe, if it was possible, I was as pissed as Randy. Together we were plenty pissed.

"I had the opportunity to go somewhere in this game and threw it away," I told him, "but these guys sound like solid citizens who deserve the chance to play out their dreams. Let's see if we can flush out the bastards and make 'em pay for screwing with a bunch of kids and you."

Told the big guy I'd be in touch and was pleased as punch to see Ms. Timmons waiting for me as I left Randy's office.

"Seeing as it's late, I wonder if I could persuade Charles to drop you off somewhere on our way out of town," I tried.

"That's a very nice gesture, but I have my own car to take me home. Perhaps another time if possible?" I walked to the front and left her with a handshake and a thanks for all her help.

"Don't think I'll forget the raincheck," I said, and she smiled, turned and walked that special walk just for my benefit, I'm sure.

I always wanted to say it and finally got the chance. I jumped in the back and said, "Home, Charles," and away we went to the sounds of Credence Clearwater singing the tune we all now know by heart – end of chapter period

Chapter 11

Rainy days are really weird. They can bum you out beyond belief sometimes and be as good as chicken soup on others. Just what the doctor ordered. Today was a particularly nasty one with that kind of sideways wind-driven rain that just soaks you to the bone no matter what you do. People were scurrying down Plandome Road resembling a parade of semi-drowned rats as I watched through Ebil's big front window that frames the outside world perfectly. I sat back and reflected on yesterday's activities and tried to sort out the details into some working order. Beats joining the soaked rat race, plus I had nowhere better to be.

It was almost time for me to doze off in preparation for spilling my coffee cup on Ebil's carpet. Before I got there the front door opened, and it seemed as if sunshine flooded the office even though it was still monsoon season outside. In swept Bunny, fresh as a daisy and dry as a bone.

"What did you do, dance between the raindrops?" I queried.

"Oh, it's just a little bit of rain and I only parked across the street," she whispered in that voice that makes my doodle dipsy with glee every time.

"How was your day yesterday? I was here all by myself till late and it got real lonely. I was kind of wishing you were around when it was time to close up."

That couldn't have been a fluttering of the eyelashes, could it?

"Well, well, Ms. Malone. Do I detect a slight hint of 'I missed you'? Not getting sweet on little ol' me, are we?" I teased.

"That quaint little expression you use to illustrate your name, something like 'in-your-shorts,' was more what I had in mind." Her eyes never left mine, which was good, 'cause if they drifted a bit lower I would have had some big-time explaining to do. Or maybe not if one was prone to believe lightning could strike twice in such a short period of time.

Saved by the big guy wandering in booming good mornings to everybody. Ebil does have a sense of timing that is right on the mark about once every three years.

"Hey Mel, how they hanging, babe?" He hates Mel, but life sucks and then you die. In between, his penance is to put up with me. Could be worse, I could have married one of his kids, of which he is four times blessed. All went to or will go to the same college and cost him a fuckin' fortune. The next guy you meet whose four kids went to his alma mater will be the second one you know. More power to him – they all turned out to be good kids. My mom can't necessary say the same thing about her little bundle of joy. Of course, she hasn't said anything to me at all in the last three years. I loved the Snoopy cards she would send for my birthday and Christmas. Guess I'll have to mention that to Ms. Bunny in one of my dreams.

"It's raining like a bastard and I can't even get a spot in front of my own building."

"How far did you have to go?" I asked to be polite. I really didn't give a rat's ass, but I needed some information and Mel knows his financial stuff. He spends every morning figuring out his stock position and hopes one day it will jump up and say "you got it, babe – time to pack in this real estate gig and retire." He bought the business and the building we sit in so there is no "man" to answer to. When it's time – he's gone and he ain't planning on looking back.

"I had to go back around and park in front of the Village Green," he barked. "I'm drenched to my skin and I hate when my wingtips go squish-squish. And by the way, your rent is due today."

In the worst case scenario, the guy never forgets a buck.

"Talked to a guy yesterday and wondered if the name rings a bell," I tossed out to see if he was available for conversation or going to be pissy all morning.

"Who?" he growled, which at least meant I had a 50-50 shot at some feedback.

"Guys name is Trundle and he owns a bunch of stuff in different parts of the world from what I can gather" was as vague as I could be while attempting to pique his interest at the same time. "M. Randle Trundle is his full name I think, if that helps."

"If it's the Trundle Industries guy I'm thinking of, you have a live one, and I'd sink my teeth in real quick before he gets away," he said.

Seems Mel knew quite a bit about my new benefactor. Some of the same background I got yesterday, but a nice little addition was the fact that Randy did business with a few guys in town that Mel knows pretty well. Mel baby actually liked the guy, I think, and not just because he had a few hundred shares invested.

'Scuse a second while I allow Bunny refilling her typing paper supply to distract me, for all the right reasons. She has on one of those cowgirl skirt numbers with the frills on the bottom that bounce when she walks.

Thanks, I needed that.

Mel rambled on for a few more minutes, but I wasn't catching any of it. Once distracted I can't always jump back in where I left off. I caught bits and pieces of stock market this and analyst that, but nothing that would stick in my brain or be of any use by the time tomorrow rolls around.

Anyway, Bunny was heading my way and I figured I'd throw out a line, hope for a bite.

"Pretty bad day to be driving, kiddo; you have such a long way to go when you leave here," I said in my most compassionate voice.

Nada.

"We could grab a quick bite, maybe rent a video," I tried. "My place is just up the block in case you may have forgotten, and you would save that long drive home. It is just frightful out there."

A whole lotta nada to go with the first bit of nada.

Mel looked and wanted to say, "You have to be shitting me with that frightful crap," but just shook his head instead.

She was out the back door for a smoke break. That "bing" that goes off in my brain when I realize I forgot something suddenly binged.

"Hey Mel, know anything about the Bayport Schooners?"

"The Bayport what?" came out of his mouth.

"You know, the Schooners, the baseball team that started up last year out on the end of the Island. Double A team from the Tampa organization I think."

"Where in the hell did that come from, and sorry to say, I guess I'll bite – what about them?"

Seemed odd that Mel knew so much about Trundle Industries, but very little about the man himself or his interests outside of business.

"Trundle owns the team and the park they play in. Ever hear of them?" I asked.

"Nobody knows much about what Trundle does outside of business, and you can bet I've asked," was Mel's reply, and I got the impression he was now telling me it was end of conversation time.

Puzzling turn of events. Randy opens up like a leaking water main to me and Mel says there isn't anything available on him outside of Trundle Industries. Why me? I have no clue. Connie.

With another QAS under our belts – you did realize you were just QAS'd, didn't you? – let's dim the lights for now and go with end of chapter period

Chapter 12

Connie was quite an interesting one. A real looker with legs that wouldn't quit, and bright as a 150 watt bulb to boot. Just like Bunny Malone, I couldn't make this one up either. And don't ever forget that I sometimes question myself whether I'm telling the truth or not. Connie is a linguist.

Now go ahead and ponder that one for a second. My razor sharp mind got it immediately. It is razor sharp when it comes to trivial shit like this, somewhat mushy at other times as we have discussed before.

OK – did you get it? For the ladies in the group who are still hanging in there, just close your eyes for a second and don't look if you have been embarrassed by anything so far.

Connie linguist in case you didn't make the connection first time around. I swear I didn't make it up.

OK, ladies, you can open your eyes now. My mind does go to strange places at times, but I will try to stay on track for awhile, I promise.

"Hello, may I speak to Connie Walker, please," I said in my best Mike Hammer impression.

The receptionist at the museum was quite pleasant and asked for my name.

"Mr. Harry Shorts and thank you," I replied, hoping that I would have something to be thankful for.

Van Morrison came on the line and entertained me with his classic "Moondance," which happens to be an all-time favorite of mine. When you get a real goodie from your Muzac-on-the-phone excursions, you hate for the person to come back on the line. This was one of those times, but I got to hear about half of it. I'll have to dig out the CD when I get home, get my Van fix. Wonder if Ms. Bunny even knows who

Van is?

Connie came on the line and I asked, "How have you been, kiddo? Everything remain quiet since we parted ways?"

"It is good to hear from you, Harry. I think of you on occasion, and yes, all has been quiet since you helped me with my little problem."

I can't get into all the details of Connie's case right now for obvious reasons, but I promise to give you the skinny at a later date. Let's just say somebody was paying way too much attention to Connie than she cared to receive.

"I've been meaning to give you a jingle, but time just seems to fly by. I hope you won't mind if I ask to pick your brain on a subject you know quite a bit about. Please say you will. Please, pretty please."

Sounds kind of schmucky, but it worked once before, and if at first you do succeed, try it again, dummy.

"Save it for another rainy day, Harry. You never know when it may come in handy. You know I'll be more than happy to help you with whatever it is you need. Well, almost anything," she laughed.

"I'm doing my initial background research for a new case I just picked up, and I seem to have a few holes that need filling. Believe it or not, you happen to be an expert on this missing info."

"Me?"

"Yes, you, kiddo. A Mr. M. Randle Trundle has retained me to assist him in solving a problem that is a top priority in his life. He mentioned he was your uncle, and I'm guessing he got my name from you. Any truth to the rumor?"

"Wait until I get my hands on that bastard," she fumed.

"Hold on, sweets, he just said he heard that I had helped you and it came out satisfactorily in the end."

"That's no excuse for using me to get to you. He of all people should know better than to do that."

"Calm your jets and do that breathing thing you do. I'll wait."

Connie got pissed big time once during her ordeal and used this deep breathing exercise while I was with her. Can't tell you where; I'm not the type of guy who would kiss and tell. Let's just say it was above and beyond the call of duty on my part.

da bushes

"Thanks, Harry. Sorry I went off like that for a second. Of course I'll help you."

"How about an Irish coffee at Patrick's Pub? I'll even sport for the drink."

"I've got some things to do, so I'll meet you there. Seven-thirty OK with you? We can beat the Friday crowd if we get there early," she asked.

"Seven-thirty it is, and I'm looking forward to seeing you again."

"Just don't expect to be seeing all of me again," she laughed. "I'm due at work early to finish up a project and can't be delayed like last time. That is if you remember last time, Harry?"

"Your wish is my desire, oh queenly one." That brought on a good belly laugh from both of us as she hung up the phone.

Time to hit the Manhasset library for a little research, then a little nap before the nightly activities. One can always hope, can't one!

End of chapter period

Chapter 13

My favorite table at Patrick's Pub allows me to watch the front door and scan the ladies at the same time. Got there early and settled in with one of their famous Irish coffees. Connie was right on time and looked just as I remembered – good enough to eat. She had the ability to put on a pair of jeans and sweatshirt and look like a million bucks.

"Don't get up, Harry," she said as she brushed a kiss across my cheek and grabbed the chair next to me. Good sign when they have the choice to sit next to you or across the table, and they nestle in as close as possible.

Grabbing at straws, you say? Last time we were together it was a lot more than straws I was grabbing.

"You look fabulous, kiddo. Not hanging around with me doesn't seem to have hurt you a bit."

"Bet you say that to all the girls, Harry."

"If I had the girls to say it to, I probably would," I replied with a smirk.

"Will you have an Irish coffee or something else to get you started?" I asked Connie as Dollie the aspiring actress-waitress cruised by.

"Hi, Dollie, good to see you again. It's been awhile. A Becks would be great." Connie had adopted my beer of choice when somebody else was buying. Bud was still the one for me when it was my nickel.

"I apologize for jumping on your ass when you called. I don't see my uncle that often and it surprised me when you said his name out of the blue. Forgive me, Harry?"

"Swept from the memory banks as if it never happened. I should have brought up his name in some other fashion and not surprised you like that. I'm sorry."

da bushes

Her Becks arrived and we toasted to cases solved, and hers in particular. She was a happy person again and the world was better off for it.

"So what is it Uncle Randle is into this time, and why you?"

"You know the drill, kiddo; I never discuss my cases, and most of the time I don't know what the problem is anyway. I just wander around until I bump into something interesting and the rest seems to fall into my lap."

"OK, wise guy, what do you want? I don't have all night."

"It's not the whole night I want, just most of it. I'm not as young as I used to be, you know," I teased to see what kind of reaction I could draw.

"In your dreams if you're lucky, Shorts," she laughed, but I could see that mischievous little twinkle in her eye. Being a trained investigator I can spot those subtle clues.

"Let me throw a few thoughts and observations on the table, you give me the first thing that pops into your head. Don't think, just react. Will that work?"

"You know I like to think about what I say before I say it, Harry. But for you, I'll give it a try, depending on what you toss out. Shoot."

"M. Randle Trundle owns Trundle Industries and there is plenty of available information on the company but nothing on the man outside of his business world. He obsesses with the purchase and building of the baseball team he owns and every aspect involved, until opening day, and then disappears from the scene. The people that work for him are the same and clam up when you ask any questions. What's with the purple?"

I took a deep breath and gave her a chance to reply to those questions. Answers to them would give me a start and point me in more directions I hoped.

"I dunno, I dunno, I dunno, NYU!"

I took a quick look around to make sure somebody else hadn't said those words, and when convinced they had emanated from the direction of fair Connie's mouth, I said, "Excuse me, but what the fuck was that?"

"Eloquent as usual, Harry."

"Sorry, but a bit more verbiage would be helpful, if you might."

"Uncle Randle guards his private world like his life depends on it. He will sit and talk about Trundle Industries with the media and anyone else who will listen for hours on end. But any mention of his non-business affairs ends the conversation. We see him rarely other than big holidays, and a shield nobody dares penetrate protects his immediate family. Better?" she asked.

"Yes, that helps, but it doesn't help. At least I know it isn't just my inability to get details on him. What's with this baseball team of his?"

Connie scrunched up her face a second and then said, "He just stopped his involvement and gave the responsibility to his son. Nobody knows why and he refers all questions concerning the team to Junior, as you affectionately call him. It's almost like he accomplished what he wanted to do by building the team and then stepped back to view it from afar. I know, seems weird, but he sometimes does things that look and seem weird."

I was no further along than when I arrived, and frustration was beginning to set in. I'm not used to brick walls, and I usually either go through or over them. Since I was on a roll, I proceeded on and asked, "You want to talk weird, what's with all the purple?"

I adore Connie's laugh and she didn't disappoint me with this one. "It's not purple, you silly goose (just so you know I hate being called a silly goose), it's violet. The New York University Violets is where it comes from. He graduated from there, is on the board, and perhaps Trundle Hall rings a bell. He bleeds violet, not red."

"I'll be damned" was the best I could come up with. The ex would swear I already have been, but we won't go there right now.

"I never made the connection. Now that you mention it, Trundle Hall is in the village on 3rd or 4th Street right across from where my brother's fraternity was located, before they screwed them and moved them a bunch of times. How can a guy that big not be hounded all the time. The photo bugs should be all over him like white on rice."

"Invasion of privacy and a $10,000 fine was what the judge gave that newspaper photographer about three years ago. That was good old

da bushes

Uncle Randle protecting him and his and he's like a bulldog when you screw with him. He doesn't allow you up for a breath and never loses. Nobody dares go near him after that case was settled."

Connie was looking at her watch, indicating luck was not going to be my friend tonight. From experience I know it's two looks, a glance, and she is on her way.

"One more so we can catch up on what you've been up to and I'll send you on your way," I tried.

"How about a rain-check, Harry. I'm actually heading downtown right away to work on the project tonight and staying at a friend's so I can start up again early in the morning. This is a big very deal for the museum and I'm really anxious."

"No problem, kiddo. Hit the road and call me when this big deal is over. We can catch up properly."

I guess my smile was too big since she cracked, "You're incorrigible and virtually impossible to put up with."

Another kiss across the cheek and she was gone with a promise to call. A coupla more rain checks and I'll need a whole lotta Noah days to use them up. But if I wanted a few rain checks, Connie and Ms. Timmons were pretty good ones to have.

I sucked down a few more Irish ditties and checked where I stood in this mess. No additional knowledge on the guy who hired me and no idea what was going on with the Bayport Schooners. I did solve the purple mystery, but it still meant Randy was a little weirder than the average bazillionaire.

My brain's starting to hurt, so I better give it a rest and leave you for a bit with end of chapter period

Chapter 14

Dreams can be great, and they can really fuck you over at times. Had one of my recurring dreams during my little catnap that provided a good soaking sweat to wake up to. Bad baseball dreams are the worst.

Might as well spill the beans on how I managed to get myself from schoolboy hero to broken-down P.I. That way we can get on with the Bayport Schooner story. Here goes nothing.

Florida was a real drag. Up early for conditioning drills and baseball all day long. First coupla weeks it was great since that was what I was good at. Problem was, every guy down there was just as good, or better. Probably the first time in my life I actually had to break my balls to excel at my calling in life. But I did and nobody could accuse me of not giving 100%. And by the way, you can't give more than 100%, and it drives me crazier when some jerk talks about giving 110%. If you hear that, tell them to get a grip.

At the end of my first season in A ball I had put up some numbers that warranted a second glance. The organization talked of fast tracking me all the way to Double A based on my performance, but there was the small problem of my well know reputation for extracurricular activities. Long periods of nothing translated into bars and girls, and worse, and the world has eyes and ears within baseball organizations. Another year in A ball didn't sit too well with yours truly, Mr. Star.

That winter I didn't do myself any favors. The wife had our first munchkin and I wasn't anywhere to be found when the time came. Already pissed at the world, I didn't need crying and pissing and shitting all the time. The crying wasn't just the kid either, as me and my future ex had a tough winter. Life was just fuckin' me over, and 18 years old was a bad age to be in that spot. The bonus money was moving like

da bushes

shit through a goose and I couldn't figure out how to stop it.

Grease them skids, kiddo, 'cause I'm on my way!

End of February rolled around and my ass was in bad shape. Kissed the wife and kid bye-bye and headed to Florida to show them bozos how wrong they could be. I was quick to find out that if I were in any worse shape I would have been dead. Sucking wind halfway through the first day of drills did not bode well, and that was the high point of my first several weeks down there. Harry the baseball star was in deep doodoo!

Did I mention the wife called me sometime after I got to Florida and informed me of the future arrival of our next little munchkin? Guess a little selective memory loss caused that one. Yep, I was gonna be daddy times two pretty soon. Don't congratulate me – you'll regret it later. I was ready for the second one about as well as I handled the first little bambino.

The good side to being in Florida again was that I already knew my way around from my first visit to vacationland. Hopped right back in the saddle and hit the hot spots with every available minute and ounce of energy. Unfortunately, that left little energy to do the things the organization expected – like hit, and catch, and contribute to the team's success a wee bit. The summer came and went with a poor batting average, little power and injuries that had me on the disabled list for a month. I truly wasted the entire season, and the powers-that-be knew it.

I got down on my knees and begged them to let me play winter ball, and I don't know why, but they agreed. Probably trying to salvage something from their bonus money is my only guess. Nice try, but nope, didn't work. But I'm sure you could have figured that out without me telling you. When they found me passed out dead drunk in the dugout one morning, it was adios muchachos and home I went.

Well, not exactly straight home. I did a bit of a "walk-about" and managed to spend the next several months of my life in places I can't even remember. How I stayed alive I don't know.

Arrived home to find my son. Missed another one, and the worst part was I didn't even know he had been born.

The rest is history. I kicked around several organizations for a couple of years and found myself out in the cold at 22 years of age. The only thing I could do in this world was play ball, and it was gone. I had pissed it away but good. The one truly smart thing I ever did was give my brother-in-law $250K from the signing bonus I got and made him promise never to give it to me. When I left and started my ex-life, the ex-wife to be had that to remember me by. I'm sure it was the best thing I ever did for her. She might weigh the kids against it, but she wouldn't agree with me out of principle anyway.

Now you have it – the whole story of baseball bonus boy gone to pot, and booze, and all the rest. The "how I got to be a P.I. story" will have to wait 'cause it's end of chapter period

Chapter 15

I was in Florida for a month and Bayport for another month and a half, with essentially the same Schooner team as last year. Trundle was adamant and paid big bucks to keep "his" team together to prove they were capable of winning. Persistence was a virtue and a God-given right as far as he was concerned.

Have to agree with him on one thing – he put a pretty good bunch of guys together who could flat out play baseball. The pitching staff had two definite locks and one other potential major leaguer along with a closer who shut the door each and every time. The second baseman could go up the middle and turn in the air firing a strike to first like he was born to do it. Another nickname gem of mine - since he had real quick feet just like a cat, that was his name from the minute I laid eyes on him. Power at the corners and an outfield that could fly, both on the base paths and in the alleys. Steiner, the young catcher Randy stole from Harrisburg, is gonna be a good one and will take over when I solve this baby and hit the road. But, hot damn if I wasn't having the time of my life, and holding my own, I might add.

My entrance was a clever idea Randy and I cooked up early on. Since I was still involved in the game as player-coach of a real good semi-pro summer team called the Great Neck Yankees, I joined the Schooners in the same capacity – a player coach. My role was to lend a little age to the youngsters and help Steiner progress as everyone expected he would. Last year's slump was the entrée and the guys seemed to accept the addition of some experience. The coaching staff was told to use me as they saw fit, but when M. Randle Trundle personally says something, you better listen. Yes sir, boss, I do that right away, boss, is the proper response. They did.

Junior was another story altogether.

I watched these kids day in and day out and couldn't fathom them going into the kind of cliff dive Trundle had described, and I was able to confirm, both in print and by word of mouth. Talent just oozed everywhere and was contagious. The spirit was "we the best," and they could walk the walk, not just talk the talk. If this wasn't a championship team, I've never seen one in my life. And don't forget, been there, done that, kiddo.

I hope you don't mind if I call you kiddo. We are old friends by now, aren't we?

Warbucks Jr. was still doing his shtick and beginning to get on my nerves. But seeing Mrs. Junior in the stands behind the first base dugout was worth putting up with him and his antics. Give him credit, the dumb shit, the fans kept on coming and we played before packed houses just about every game. It definitely helps you get up for games when the fans are screaming and you are the cat's pajamas to every last one of them.

Since I was a bit older that the rest of the kiddies on the team, Mrs. Warbucks Jr. and me got to be kind of friendly. Junior was always in meetings with his marketing staff or off scouting what the competition was doing so he could one-up them with another hare-brained promotion. I was only trying to promote good will and harmony within the organization by keeping her company when she was feeling lonely. Bayport to Manhasset was a hike, and stopping off to cheer up the boss's wife on the way home was at a convenient filler-up spot, and the least I could do. I know, what a guy.

There was one particular time when Teddy baby was off to Erie and I was "visiting" on a day off. She was loose from a few margaritas I threw together and starting telling me how they met. Turns out she has an MBA and was working at New York University in Alumni Relations in the president's office when Junior met her at some school function honoring the old man.

"Maybe it was the money, maybe just a way out of the daily grind of having to work every single day of the week. But, I loved that job, and I was real good at it. The president didn't want me to leave, but I

da bushes

didn't listen to him, and Teddy and I were married four months later. I'm sure his daddy still thinks I'm nothing but a bimbo money grubber."

Here I am looking for a few drinks, some laughs and a little sack time. What do I need with *True Confessions* and tears? Please, not the tears thing. She seemed to go from anger at Junior to anger at herself for letting it happen. It was strange though, as I held her in my arms and she cried her baby blues out, I wanted to hold her and didn't want to let go.

We talked for hours about her life and career before she met Junior, and life with the asshole after they got married. Ever since this baseball thing started he was always on the road and never around, and when he was, he obsessed about baseball. Something struck me as weird when she said, "All he talks about is having his own damn baseball team." I said he had his own team, the Schooners, but she corrected me by repeating his exact words in quotes: "That's still his team, not mine!"

"We were both really happy in Arizona, and him being the boss running Daddy's pharmaceutical company made him feel important. I wish the Schooners never existed and we could go back to what we had before. At least he was home some of the time."

"Shorts" cardinal sin was committed that night – I didn't leave! Jeannie and I spent that night and had breakfast acting like the young kids we wished we could become again. If this means what I think it means, and what you think it means, I'm in deep shit. And that my friends could be a major problem, but definitely requires an end of chapter period

Chapter 16

Let me continue to run down the Schooner organization for you…

The management was also the same as last year. Scootch continued to nap at the end of the bench until he was needed. The hitting coach knew his stuff and was a lifer minor league guy. Divorced and remarried with no kids left him with baseball as his primary passion in life. He had a "leave me alone" attitude to go with it when the season was over, or so I heard. Hard to get to know much at all, and very protective of his private life for some reason. Punch is still a wild card bearing watching.

The two base coaches are check-cashers who are hanging around baseball with no thoughts of going anywhere, but both like to tip a few and keep this old baseball has-been company on the road trips. The sport is full of them, but they serve an important role and we couldn't get along without them. Knowledge is key at this level of the minor leagues and these guys forgot more about the game we love than the average guy will ever know.

Two guys left to run down and a story goes with each. Doc was the trainer and a strange one. I'm still not sure I have the right handle on him, and he's a harder guy to figure out than I imagined after our first meeting. I'll work the phones a bit more to get the skinny on this dude. He helps anybody who asks and does a good job, but I'm not sure he's really enjoying it and has his heart in it. Last year may have taken too much out of him to rebound. There's more to keeping a team together than liniment and tape, Vitamin C and salt pills.

The field general is an old friend and somebody who taught me the meaning of why we play this silly sport. Coach, as he is called and always has been by me, was my high school baseball coach and learned

da bushes

me a lot about the game and how to play it. The most important thing he taught me was the "will to want to win" and do the very best and more whenever I stepped on that field. Why to play the game and why you should play it well is much more important than the how. Slow and smooth was his way, but you didn't dare fuck with him – he was the man and we knew it. You played and learned and appreciated it later when you got smart enough to figure out what he did for you.

Couldn't let anyone know about our past, so me and Coach went about our business like we never met. But I'll always remember him letting us pour champagne over his head after we won the city championship game. Coach, Mr. Curran, was the best damn high school baseball coach God ever put on this earth. Not a bad basketball coach either, even though he missed my basketball greatness and didn't pick me for his teams. I thanked him for making me a better person.

I'm getting soft in my old age, so better split with end of chapter period

Chapter 17

Personally, I have no use at all for lawyers or their legal mumbo-jumbo. After I get the facts of a particular case, I usually take some time to gather and analyze the info, then decide whether the case interests me. Life is too short to spend a lot of time on some boring-assed wild goose chase or trying to make a whiny-face dumb-bunny happy. Fun and challenging is what turns me on and the tougher the better. If it fits the bill the monetary side takes care of itself. When I'm sold I'm ready to jump in with both feet.

It took two weeks to hammer out an agreement with the Trundle Industry legal wizards, and I'm telling you, I almost walked. Twenty pages of bullshit I didn't understand and didn't care to either. An agreement only needs a handshake as far as I'm concerned, and my reputation guarantees you will be happy with the results or you walk with only my expenses as payment in full. I don't even have a personal mouthpiece. At the last minute Randy called me after hearing from the elusive Ms. Timmons, there seemed to be a problem. Two minutes later he said thank you and the one-page document was hand-delivered to me the next day.

"What's the problem, Harry?" he asked, and I said, "Just have them say I will solve the problem we discussed and you will pay me whatever you think it is worth when it is finished to your satisfaction."

"Done" was his response, and it was. The chase was on and I'm a mean son of a bitch when I put my mind to it. This would be all I would concentrate on for a long time to come.

It was October already and there was a lot of work to do before I would be able to say I was prepared for this gig. Being "in shape" was a relative term, and for the kind of ball I was playing I could get by and perform reasonably well. Double A was light years removed from summer fun ball. I hit the gym with everything I had and starting throwing three times a week inside to work on my release, and once a week outside to stretch it out with long tossing. Weights and aerobics aren't my favorite, but I bit the bullet and punished my body beyond the limits I would have thought I could stand.

Size wise I'm bigger than average at 6 foot 1 inches and 185 pounds. That's walking around weight and has always been good enough to get the job done, even in this business. Six months of boxing lessons from an ex-middleweight world champ and years of martial arts training, just for the fun of it, allow me to handle most situations without getting too hurt. Guns aren't my weapon of choice, but I do own one and can shoot well enough if I had to. I hope I never have to.

The problem was this was something totally different from a physical standpoint. The grind of playing high level baseball against the best in the world every day is very demanding. Your body has to be able to take a lot of punishment and come back the next day asking for more. Catching is the worst position due to the wear and tear on your knees and the constant beating your hands and body take from foul balls and flying bodies as you try to block the plate. The worst part is that your mind needs to stay sharp at all times 'cause you're always at work trying to outsmart the hitters and opposing managers. If your body goes, your head follows, and you are dead meat. Stick a fork in, you're done.

Been at it for a month and the original soreness came and went. Picked up five pounds of what seems to be all muscle, and I have to admit the old body is starting to look pretty good right about now. The shoulder is holding up and tolerating the extra throwing and actually feels stronger than it has in a long time. My knees creak every once in awhile during, and after, squat drills; but that's good, as it reminds me I am a thirty-something-year-old washed-up ex-catcher. Perspective is a good thing.

Gotta finish my research on last year's swan dive, so library, here I come. The walk is good for me, and besides, the moms from town are always bringing their kids to the library, which creates excellent scenery during research time. I'm gone, so go amuse yourself for awhile, as it's end of chapter period

Chapter 18

In general, numbers suck, and looking at large amounts of numbers sucks two times. The exception to the rule is baseball numbers, and I knew a guy one time who could get a hard-on just thinking about baseball statistics. That fanatic I'm not, but I have always liked playing with and keeping baseball stats. Taught both of the kids how to keep score at games and when we go to the stadium (there is only one stadium, which happens to be Yankee Stadium for the unknowing in the crowd), they stay involved by switching back and forth each inning keeping score. I think it's pretty neat and should be part of every child's educational process. But, then again, I'm not your normal run of the mill kind of dad either.

The Manhasset Library is small in size but has most of the technology needed to go back in time and find information. I started with the beginning of the previous Schooner season and tracked every player for every game for the whole season. Let's just say that is a shitload of numbers and information. It took almost a whole week of six- to seven-hour days and nights to gather all that data and about the same amount of time to read game stories in *Long Island Newsday*, the local newspaper. The initial coverage was great with a big splash for opening day, everybody jumping on the bandwagon as they took off running to start the year and stayed in first place for a few months. That would soon change.

Jumping on the bandwagon turned into jumping ship when the team hit bad times around July. First there was the normal talk of a slump by a few key players, which turned into an overall team slump, and finally into maybe they weren't as good as was first thought. Coverage started to diminish to the point where only box scores were included in the paper with a few lines of same old, same old by a third-rate writer who just started in the business. Could have been the janitor for all I know, and wrote about as well. I copied the stories no matter how small or poorly written and hoped to draw some pattern from the info I had gathered.

Hope springs eternal, somebody once said, but I have no idea who, or when, or why.

Anyway, I had schlepped all the stuff to the Tree house over time and was ready to go to work figuring out what in the hell happened to the Schooners last season. The Tree house is what the Emil calls the garage apartment I live in down the block from Mel's office. Give yourself a gold star and jump to the head of the class if you got ex-mother-in-law as the Emil referred to in the last sentence. The place is at the top of the driveway behind the main house a friend of Mel had converted into three apartments. There is a four-room apartment over the two-car garage, and Mel did me a solid and got me in when I returned to town about two and a half or three years ago. I still haven't figured out why he did it, and one might even begin to think he likes me when he does shit like that. It's few and far between, so don't get too excited.

The place isn't all that bad, with a deck off the living room and a small weightlifting area in the extra room. It allows me to eat, sleep, shit and lift. Is there anything else to life? It would be a tad nicer if the bedroom window didn't overlook a cemetery, but it is quiet back there at night. I'd give you the old one about "people dying to get in there," but even my mind isn't that warped.

The best feature is the single mom and daughter who moved into the main house middle of one summer and took to sunbathing in the back yard. Moms must be pushing forty, with the daughter having graduated from high school this past June. But she sure knows how to keep it together, and isn't afraid to show it off, either. My deck looks down on the main house backyard and turned into my favorite place to pass the hours last summer. Mrs. Taylor, or Sandy as she has asked me to call her, has my vote for mom of the year; and before I forget, the daughter wasn't too bad either. Like mother, like daughter, comes in real handy when you're a poor lonely P.I. strategically located just above

da bushes

their outdoor tanning salon.

Well, I've got to attempt to put some meaning to this large mess of info, and it seems I continue to digress. You guys are definitely a bad influence on me. I'll get back to you when I have something to go on. Till then, end of chapter period

Chapter 19

My kids are growing up before my very eyes, with my favorite daughter Brianne turning thirteen recently, and the little guy Max (a nickname – surprise, surprise) not too far behind. That's what happens when they come popping into the world so close together when you are nothing but a kid yourself.

When I moved back to Manhasset the ex decided we didn't need visitation rights since they would be living in the same town as me. It's easier that way for everybody, and we kind of coexist better that way. I see them when I do and make an effort to be around at least once a week, preferably when the ex isn't. She and I also coexist, and if I hadn't fucked up her life, we might even like each other.

The two munchkins are real good kids and I'm proud of who they are growing up to be. Having a bunch of relatives in town helped along the way, and the ex's brother, big Mel, has been great to them. He punishes me enough; he should be good to my kids. Hard for me to say the words, but the ex is actually looking pretty good these days. Must be the long hours I've been spending working out combined with the tedious number crunching affecting my brain in funny ways. Forget I even said it….

The kids always get to choose what we will do on our once-a-month all-day Saturday extravaganza. They plan the day all month and spring it on me as a surprise. That's easy when they have my credit card number and can get reservations or anything they want in advance, within reason. The "within reason" is I'll tickle them to death if they go outside of our agreed-upon dollar limit. Unfortunately for me and my bank account, they both have died several horrible laughing-fit tickle deaths already. My accountant, he doesn't laugh. But as I have always said,

da bushes

fuck him if he can't take a joke.

Instructions were to arrive promptly at 9:00 am and just honk. Saves me from having to go to the door and run the risk of an ex-attack. The kids have witnessed the verbal thrashings I got when I first ventured back into their lives upon my reincarnation in Manhasset. Honking is their way of protecting my privates in case I have been a bad boy of late. Things keep going as smooth as they have and I may get brave enough to go to the door again.

Better go slow, big guy, danger lurks when least expected, especially when the "ex-factor" is involved.

The day starts with breakfast at International House of Pancakes (IHOP), requiring large quantities of almost everything they have on the menu utilizing the "sharesee" mode of consumption. Just like Chinese food, plates of eggs, waffles and pancakes, bacon and sausages, with toast and English muffins a plenty are dropped in the middle of the table and a free-for-all begins. Watch out for any misdirected fork and eat fast or you're shit out of luck. We do this often so the waitresses all know us and eagerly await our monthly visit. This one was one of our better shows and drew applause from the whole IHOP crew as we left. I did discover early on that a "night before" one of these Saturday mornings isn't a good idea. I may not be getting any smarter, but I am getting wiser in my old age.

"Head down Northern Boulevard and hit the bridge," directed Brianne, our travel guide for today.

"I assume the Throggs Neck bridge is the one you are referring to, and I also assume you don't actually want me to hit it," I tossed in their direction with my most serious game face in place.

"That would be correct, and be careful, since you know what happens when you ASSUME something," she tossed back, dragging out A S S U M E in her best "let's mimic Mommy" voice.

"Very funny, young lady, and what do you think you're laughing at, pip-squeak?"

"Well, you of course!" said Max. "You just make it too easy even for little – but getting bigger all the time – pip-squeaks like me."

"Don't ever forget, oh wee small one, I know where you live and I know what you did last summer!"

"Don't ever forget, oh wee big one, you were with me when I did the deed in question last summer and moms wouldn't be to pleased too hear that, now would she?"

The little guy knows where the sun don't never shine, and if I wasn't his father and an upstanding human being, I'd tell him to stick it there. The pain of being so good has never been worse. And I am totally full of shit sometimes, this being one of them.

Lots of traffic on the bridge, so let's idle awhile with end of chapter period

Chapter 20

Late fall is the perfect time for a trip to the munchkins' destination of choice for today – the Bronx Zoo. No crowds to contend with and the sun isn't beating down on the top of your head threatening to bore a hole right into your brain. The animals are still moving around pretty freely, just a tad slower, with hibernation for the winter still a ways off. The kids love the zoo, and it gives me a chance to see them both happy and content. It also gives me a chance to spend the time with them I never had while I was off gallivanting around the country being one of those ever-popular absent-father assholes.

The lions and tigers and bears were all out as we passed their way. We arrived in time to see the mama gorilla showcase her newborn to the world for the first time ever. Papa gorilla was hanging out in the background, but I'm sure you wouldn't want to screw with him about now, or any other time for that matter. The little ones are cute and do the funniest stuff.

The penguins are my favorite, and we always save them for last. Fat little waddlers in tuxedo monkey suits who swim like a bastard when they hit the water. It seems we always spend at least a half-hour watching them as it starts to get dark. Funny how some things never seem to get old.

I had a feeling I knew where we were headed, but I let them give me directions to this joint on Fordham Road in the Bronx that has as its specialty "The Kitchen Sink." Picture this if you can, but if you don't love ice cream you may not want to picture this for your own good. They take an aluminum bowl and put fifteen hefty scoops of every flavor of ice cream in there and cover it with whipped cream, chocolate syrup and nuts. Lots of whipped cream and one big cherry on top which we save for later. We each get a long spoon and dive in with all the gusto we can manage. Neatness does not count in this little endeavor. Tummies have been known to come within a fraction of an inch of exploding from the "Kitchen Sink" experience.

The cherry trick still thrills them every time I do it. But remember, I am a trained Private Investigator, so please don't try this at home. I can't be held responsible. I can tie the cherry stem in a knot in my mouth without the use of my hands. Of course, I have been accused of being able to make extraordinarily good use of my tongue during other activities on more than one occasion. This is just one of those occasions, and the only one the kiddies will ever see. I am proud to say, it does get 'em every time. The things I do for my children.

It was about 10:00 p.m. when we got home, which is still within the "you're late," but not "your ass is in deep shit late" time frame. The kids reminded me they were embarrassed to be seen in my 1975 Datsun B210 Honeybee which is gold and actually has a Honeybee painted on the side of the car. It's my everyday, get me where I need to go car and happens to run like a charm. Plus, my customized vintage Mustang Mach 1 only has room for two. That's what I use when I need to impress the ladies or get where I need to go in a hurry. I'll show it to you some time, especially if you happen to be of the female persuasion and like it fast and hard. Ladies, you can take that one any way you wish.

Kissy-face all around and they were gone. A softy would gush over how great the day was, but being a supposed tough guy, I better split before I ruin my image.

End
Of
Chapter
Period

Chapter 21

The Schooners played 142 games last season and that translates into more fuckin' statistics than even God in his/her infinite wisdom would care to look at. And you can bet the ranch trying to analyze that many numbers to find the answer to a question you don't even know is ludicrous. The QAS would probably be – Why did the team take a nosedive? I don't know. Check the stats for any pattern. So, I did, and here's what I found.

On June 24th the Schooners had played 72 games and their record stood at an impressive 50 wins and 22 losses, also shown as 50-22. They had an eleven game lead on the Harrisburg Senators, the second place team. Life was like a bowl of cherries – the pits were still to come.

Now, I've seen statistics displayed in a thousand different ways, and each one can be confusing. I'd charted the primary players who contributed the most during the year. Let's try this one and see if I can illustrate the pattern I think I found and when it started:

Name	*First Half of Season* Ave. / HR / RBI / SB	*Second Half of Season* Ave. / HR / RBI / SB
Cat Hoffman (2B)	.327 / 2 / 24 / 26	.274 / 0 / 13 / 12
Howdy McDuff (SS)	.289 / 17 / 51 / 2	.245 / 9 / 36 / 0
Pete Sanchez (OF)	.301 / 11 / 37 / 17	.287 / 10 / 31 / 15
Dee Smith (3B)	.265 / 21 / 49 / 3	.222 / 11 / 29 / 0
Scoot Munoz (OF)	.311 / 3 / 21 / 21	.261 / 1 / 15 / 9
Bugs Bradford (1B)	.272 / 24 / 62 / 0	.243 / 16 / 36 / 0
Tom Westbrook (C)	.245 / 9 / 24 / 3	.189 / 1 / 10 / 0
D.J. Smalley (DH)	.277 / 22 / 51 / 1	.236 / 9 / 30 / 0

Summary: Leading the league in doubles and home runs and blowing away everyone in stolen bases by a wide margin during the first half of the season. And here's where statistics can be very misleading. A few year end numbers:

Cat still hit .300 for the year and stole 38 bases, missing the league title by only one, and he got thrown out twice in the last game. He made the All-Star team.

Howdy hit 26 homers and drove in 87 runs as a short stop, which is big time numbers, and was voted the best fielding SS in the league with only five (5) errors – all in the second half of the season. Also an All-Star.

Bugs (another nickname of mine) led the league in home runs and was second in RBI's.

The team led the league in HR's and stolen bases.

All in all, the year's statistics and accomplishments make it look like a very successful season. But when you analyze the numbers like I did, you see the definite drop off in the second half of the season by almost every player. Most of the second string subs had similar first halves and bombed out after the All Star break. The team just plain went into the shitter big time, and I'm gonna have to find out why.

Pete Sanchez, the health nut, hung in and had a real good year overall with no obvious fade in the second half. The write-ups make it sound like he can really go get it in the outfield. He may be a key if I can isolate his performance and routine from the rest of the regulars. What I need to know is, what was it about him that was so different?

The catcher Westbrook went into a fuckin' free-fall. I'm told he barely made it to September, finishing the year on the bench in utter exhaustion. He actually packed it in, and I heard he's selling insurance at his old man's agency in Connecticut. Another important part of the equation would be learning what he did or didn't do that was different from the rest of the guys. Scoot Munoz (no, not mine, sorry to say) lives close by, so I'll probably start with him when I get around to the interview process.

da bushes

Rusty Jask and Smokes Randolph made the All Star team after going a combined nineteen wins and three losses in the first half, with an ERA of 2.23, which is mighty good. Second half numbers of a combined nine wins and twenty-two losses tell a different story. Slam Wilson was the team's closer – the pitcher who comes in at the end of the games for an inning to finish it off. He went from 15 saves and three wins with no blown saves in the first half to six saves, seven losses and nine blown saves in the last half of the year. The pitchers just ran out of gas and got their collective brains beat in for a few months. I'll have to take a closer look at Bill Wong, who I understand goes by the handle of Dong for a very specific reason. He was steady all year going eleven and eight with a consistent ERA both halves.

The team went 30-42 in the second half, losing their last nine in a row. Best minor league team ever to a piece of dog turd in a few short months. I'm sure they weren't very short to the Schooners, and from what I hear, Randy was beside himself. The only one not going off the deep end, as you would have expected, was Junior – go figure that one out.

But you will have to figure it out by yourself for now, 'cause you guessed it again – end of chapter period

Chapter 22

The winter months suck, as far as I'm concerned. Anything below 65 degrees is cold, and it gets well below 65 in New York for most of the winter. I was working as hard as I had ever worked to get my body prepared for playing a kids game at age 31. The information I had accumulated continued to stare me in the face, and I was no further along in figuring it out. Time to start talking to people instead of paper, numbers and mostly myself.

Charles got me at the ridiculous time of 6:00 am on a Sunday morning the week after New Year's. Trundle agreed to see me when I called, but he was going out of town for a few weeks leaving that Sunday afternoon.

"Do you play tennis by any chance, Harry?" caught me totally by surprise.

"Well, I have a racket and can get it back over the net on occasion, but good I'm not by any stretch," I replied, hoping this was just idle chit-chat if I was lucky.

"Sunday morning?"

Sunday morning comes after Saturday night; I don't get a chance to see it very often. Sunday afternoon is much more to my liking, with the papers in bed and football on the telly. Alone isn't that bad, but company never hurts. I guessed I needed to inquire, so I did.

"Sunday morning, Mr. Trundle?"

That's when he informed me we would be playing tennis at 7:30 a.m. Sunday morning at the Trundle Building. A few quick sets and I could ride with him to Teterboro Airport in New Jersey before he left for Europe. We could talk on the way.

I gathered I wasn't invited to Europe.

Now, you must be thinking a few things. First, there is no way Harry gets going in time to be ready for Charles at 6:00 a.m. on a Sunday morning. Second, even if he does, can his stomach handle the violet – not purple limo in the condition it will be in? Third, the Trundle Building is on Madison in the middle of a concrete jungle. Buying this book makes you pretty bright to begin with, but if you got those three you are approaching Merlin status.

Let me enlighten you if I may. Harry the "good twin" was in bed at 10:00 p.m. and up at five to loosen up and stretch. Charles and I had a good chat on Randle, Junior and the Mrs. of each along with the violet chariot he actually hated with a passion. The Egg McMuffin he brought for me went down just fine and we stopped for more on the way downtown. I sprang for the refills. Now, about that tennis court thing.

We entered the building through the underground parking garage I didn't know existed. Charles used his key to the elevator and there was only one button to push. I don't know what James Bond would have done, but Harry Mickey Shorts, I pushed it. Instead of going up, it headed south of street level. The elevator stopped and the doors opened to what my eyes saw but my brain wasn't having much luck processing. How the fuck do you get a full-size clay tennis court below the streets of Manhattan, not to mention the gym and sauna, etc. etc. etc.? The place was lit up like the Vegas strip on a Friday night. Randle was just finishing his warm-ups with the company tennis pro and waiting to devour me for breakfast.

I managed to get my jaw closed and moved to the bench area to prepare for battle. I got the upper hand immediately when I removed my sweat-suit, showing off my newly purchased Andre Agassi Violet Tennis Togs. Randy broke out in this monster grin and we proceeded to smack it around for an hour. He took it easy on me, and I did better than expected. A pair of 6-2 sets later, we were ready to hit the showers after a 15-minute sauna. If you've never had somebody serve you orange juice over crushed ice in a sauna, you haven't lived yet.

Charles rolled up the glass divider, and Randy and I got down to business.

"I appreciate you taking the time from your schedule to see me Mr. Trundle, especially on such short notice." I figured a little brown-nosing to start couldn't hurt.

"I've been thinking about you recently and wondered how your investigation was going," Randy replied. "Busy doesn't mean I neglect the things I enjoy, or did enjoy for awhile."

Time to take two steps back, grovel and attempt to rebound. "I didn't mean to imply you neglected the team or non-business issues, Mr. Trundle." Nice try – bad result, and I'm digging myself a bigger hole as I go.

"First of all, and for the last time, please call me Randle and not Mr. Trundle. Why don't people listen and believe me when I tell them that? You can show someone the respect they are due without having to address them as Mr. all the time, especially in private. Secondly, I apologize for sounding a tad testy. This return trip to Europe is tedious and unnecessary, and it comes at a very bad time. I trust your discretion enough Harry to tell you my Number One has botched things miserably and I detest fixing something that shouldn't be askew."

I had no idea what the hell he was talking about and wondered what his definition of "askew" was, but figured he wasn't done yet, so mums the word for me. Brilliant P.I.'s sense these things, and I was correct as usual.

"The family is at the chalet in Aspen and I'm going to miss our annual charity skiing event. I have never missed this event and Teddy will make a mess of it, I'm sure."

OK, I'll bite. "Sorry, Randle, but I'm unfamiliar with the charity event you're talking about, and not sure who Teddy is." As I was sounding both uninformed and stupid for not knowing who this guy Teddy was, I looked out the window and wondered where the fuck we were at the time. Nothing looked familiar, although I've only been to Tetterboro once before, and probably couldn't remember much anyway considering the shape I was in at the time.

"Trundle Industries is the behind-the-scenes financier for the week-long Feed the World event that draws every phony celebrity in the world to Aspen each January. Luckily, corporate donations fill the

da bushes

coffers each year, because the celebrity donations come to about 10% of the total dollars collected. I have very generous friends in the business world, Harry. And Teddy, it so happens, is Theodore Trundle, my son and the general manager of the Bayport Schooners."

Instant and severe case of "Foot-In-Mouth-Disease" getting more severe every time I open it.

"I've been concentrating my research so far on the 'on-field' portion of the organization, Randle. That doesn't excuse my ignorance with regard to your family and it's relationship to the franchise." Another dumb attempt to cover another dumb fuck-up.

"Relax, Harry, and stop apologizing for everything. Why don't you tell me what you have so far and what if anything I can do to help."

Employing the shortened version technique, I hastily relayed the information I had gathered so far. The revised statistics, even though common knowledge, still surprised Randy. He wasn't aware of the severity of downward motion the team experienced in the second half. The buzz in the baseball sports community was one of confusion and a complete lack of understanding. There had to be something else causing a collapse of this magnitude in so talented a ball club. This doesn't happen without somebody saying something to someone else. Scuttlebutt normally abounds in these situations. In this case, nada all around.

Randy listened intently and thought long and hard when I said, "And I'd like to talk to as many of the players and coaches as possible before we go down to Florida. Any thread I can grasp might make a difference."

We were pulling up to the terminal when he finally responded. If I didn't know him I might have thought he was asleep with his eyes open.

"Talk to absolutely anyone you need, Harry. Charles is at your disposal locally and the company plane will take you anywhere you need to go. The only request I would like you to honor is to leave Teddy and his wife alone for the time being. Can you do that for me, Harry?"

"Yes sir, Mr. Trundle. But some day you will have to tell me why, if you don't mind. It seems to me it took you a long time to come to that exclusion, and if it were pertinent, I'd kind of like to know why. Deal?"

"Harry, I don't make deals – I make money. But for you, as you say – deal."

Charles and I were getting to be bosom buddies, and if this kept up, I might even get to see Ms. Timmons again one of these days.

I'm gonna nod off awhile on the ride home, so end of a too-long chapter period

Chapter 23

"Where you been, putz?" was Mel's version of a friendly greeting upon my arrival Monday mid-morning. "I was beginning to think my luck had changed and you were history."

"And a fine cheerio of a morning to you too, big guy. And your luck won't change till the morning the *New York Times* has the magic stock combination that allows you to adios this place. By the way, where is the Bunnster this fine morning?"

It wasn't really a fine morning unless three inches of new snow, with the promise of more on the way, tickles your fancy. For me, snow means it isn't 65 degrees, and as I have said before, that's too cold. Maybe a trip up north for a little skiing and R&R is in order. All work and no play, and all that.

"If you mean Bunny, she had to go home to see her mother, who apparently fell and broke her leg. Her dad was scheduled to be overseas for a few weeks and can't get back till the weekend."

"I gotta split town for a few days," I told the ever-pleasant Ebil. "If I get any calls I'll pick them up at night off the answering service. If Bunny calls in, tell her I'm sorry to hear about her moms."

"Yeah, sure" was what I think he replied.

The game plan called for me to hit the road and see as many of the Schooners as I could. First hand information beats he said, she said any day. But not in the snow, especially since the catcher Westbrook was my first target and is up in Greenwich, Connecticut. You don't just up and quit a promising career unless it's serious business. He was as good a place to start as any.

Scoots Munoz turned out to be playing winter ball when I called and will have to wait for now.

Ms. Timmons had forwarded the entire team's winter residence listing with home phone numbers and work numbers if they had one. The Westbrook Insurance Agency was high brow and very successful from what I was able to find out.

"May I speak to Tom Westbrook, please? This is Harry Shorts."

"Would that be Junior or Senior?" came the inquiry from a very sexy sounding voice.

"I guess it would be Junior, and you are?"

"I'll get Mr. Westbrook for you, Mr. Shorts, and for future reference I am the office manager, Nancy Westbrook."

"And for future reference, it's Harry, Ms. Westbrook."

No correction, so I guess another potential candidate just hit the Harry "could be" list.

"Tom Westbrook, how can I help you?" caught me by surprise, mostly because I wasn't paying any attention to the phone. The street corner right outside Ebil's office is in the shape of a T and can be a bitch on good days, down right hazardous on days like today. The current three-car pile-up could definitely be classified as hazardous, I would think.

"Tom, this is Harry Shorts. I'm looking into some matters for Mr. Trundle and would like the opportunity to speak with you at your convenience."

"What does that son-of-a-bitch Teddy Trundle want now? He already got my career, and that's more than enough as far as I'm concerned."

"Hey, Tom, I'm not working for Teddy Trundle. I'm working for his father, Mr. M. Randle Trundle," seemed to calm him down a little bit.

"Sorry, Mr. Shorts, for my outbreak. This is a very trying time for me, and I'm not quite settled with my decision to stop playing a game I've loved since I started walking. My dad is happy to have me, but I'm not myself yet. Please forgive me, and anything I can do for Mr. Trundle is yours. Just name it."

I pondered that for a second and would have thought Randy was his long-lost dad if I didn't know better. Well, strike while the iron is hot, I always say. Actually I don't think I've ever said that before, so forget

da bushes

I even uttered those words. Must be the alcohol deprivation reacting again. Maybe I need a St. Bernard to follow me around.

"Tom, Mr. Trundle has asked me to look into the circumstances surrounding last season's decline of the Schooners after the All-Star break. If I could come up there and speak to you for awhile, perhaps I could begin to understand it a little better. You could be a big help to me if you can handle it."

"How's this sound, Harry? I have to be in the city on Wednesday for the majority of the day. I was thinking of catching the Knicks game that night, who just happen to be hosting Shaq and his friends. Why don't we get some dinner and then go to the game? That would give us plenty of time to talk."

Dinner in the city and a Knicks game against the Lakers would be tough to put up with, but that's the life of a private investigator.

"That would be dynamite. If you're going to be downtown, how about Harry's at Hanover Square? Happens to be one of my favorite restaurants," which was the absolute truth. Oh no, there's that Absolut word sneaking around again. I may have to fix that problem real soon.

"Harry's it is; I'll meet you there about 5:30," Tom replied.

I can't remember what day Beef Wellington is the special of the day at Harry's, but the prime rib will do if it's not Wednesday. Either would be enough to kill somebody for if there was only one meal left. Trust me, I almost did once.

"I'll be there, and thanks, Tom, for giving me the time."

"Mr. Trundle has been very good to me, and I'll do anything to find out what happened to me and the rest of the guys. And I mean anything!"

Tom needs a "calm-your-ass-down" pill and I need to make some more calls, so beat it – end of chapter period

Chapter 24

It snowed like a mother all day and through most of the night, with a total accumulation of 16 inches. School was closed the next day, which prompted a call from the kids to come on over and help them build "the best snowman anyone has ever seen."

Nothing has changed; I still don't like the snow, unless I'm on skis. And that's mostly so I can get to the aprés ski time in the lodge with all the ski bunnies. And by the way, what the fuck is "aprés ski" supposed to mean? Can't we just say after you're done skiing? Why make everything so damned complicated? That was a good digression, so be quiet.

Imus was finishing up for the day, so I figured it was a sign to get my ass moving and do the dutiful father thing. Actually, I look forward to our snowman building day every year since I've been back. The kids love it and it gives me another excuse to spend time with them. I also get the opportunity to pummel their little bodies with snowballs and get even for the abuse I endure from them the rest of the year.

The assigned meeting time was 11:00 am in front of their house on Linden Street. The front yard was just big enough to construct a man-sized snowperson with all the trimmings. Last year's was female, so this year we go back to a male snowman. Nice tits on Ms. Snowlady last year and the whole town got to see them. The local newspaper *The Manhasset Press* dropped by while we were in full construction mode and stayed to take pictures after we were done. They ran it in the following week's issue for all to see. The ex is a tad short in that category, so I think the kids were having a bit of fun by being overly generous in their endowment.

Emil wasn't pleased at all, but Mel thought it was hilarious and sent copies to all the relatives. The kids were the hit of the whole school over that one. Me, I got my ass chewed out but good by the ex, but in the end we laughed so hard I almost pissed myself. If I didn't know better I'd think Sherry might have been a little jealous of Ms. Snowlady.

Snowballs were flying everywhere and fallen angels were evident throughout the yard. Inspite of all of our shenanigans we got Mr. Snowman built by 12:45. Not bad if I do say so myself, and I do. The piece of black hose strategically placed by Max was removed before a repeat of last year's pictorial could occur. Somehow, I would venture a guess, it might get replaced later after I'm gone.

Off we went to Villa Milano, the pizza joint, to stuff ourselves silly. Pepperoni and sausage for Max and me, green pepper for the little princess. The required two pieces of takeout were boxed up and lugged home in the snow so Her Queeness won't bitch and moan over missed pizza. The pieces of crust I saved for the Airedales were included in the treasure box. Never forget the fuckin' mutts, even though they can be a royal pain in the ass. But so can I, that's why I put up with them when visiting the kids.

A few last-minute snowballs and I was headed home for much-needed rest. All in all, it was a pretty good day. Go ahead and try it when the snow arrives if you haven't done it before – I gotta go anyway, with end of chapter period

Chapter 25

Wednesday morning and Bunny was still home tending to her mom, who did indeed break her left leg. It was quiet and boring in the office, so I decided to hit the gym and do my workout early. The soonest I could get an appointment to see anybody else from the Schooners of last year was next Monday. Westbrook would have to do for now, and I was looking forward to the promise of some new information tonight.

Workouts can be a bother when your mind is preoccupied. This was one of those instances, and I finally decided after a half-hour that I was wasting my time and probably would hurt myself if I continued. No chickameritas to ogle over, so I cut my losses and headed home. Some of you ladies need to quit working and hit the gym in the middle of the day to keep us lonely P.I.'s company. It's good for you, it's good for me, and if the gods are with us, it might even be good for both of us in tandem. One never know, do one!

Got lucky and caught a ride with this guy who owns a limo company in town who was headed downtown to pick up a couple and drive them around the city for the evening. He brings me along for company if he has a one-wayer into the city and I happen to be headed there myself. Luck was a lady tonight and we get along pretty good anyway. Mark's got a passel of kids just like Mel, so that's how I met him – they are buds.

Harry's is a neat place and you have to walk down a flight of stairs to get in. When you enter you see an old wooden bar a million years old that has held up the best of all walks of life in its time. And me, too. I bellied up and had a Becks while I waited for Westbrook. I don't come in here that often, and I wanted to savor the coupla minutes of atmosphere by myself. Stock market and bond traders, executives of

da bushes

all kinds frequent Harry's. If you've never been there, you owe it to yourself to do it just one time. You won't regret it. Have an Absolut Gimlet – best in the world – and just enjoy.

Tom Westbrook came in about 5:40 p.m. and was a lot bigger than I imagined. A stocky 5 foot 11 inches but built like a brick shithouse. Power just exuded from his frame, and his handshake was firm but gentle with a voice like one of those smooth-talking ad hawkers. He was gonna make it big in the insurance world, you could just tell, and he definitely wasn't your run of the mill wussy-boy quitter.

"Let's get a table, Harry, before the crowd hits and we get stuck in that back room in the basement. We can get the how's life bullshit out of the way and you can ask me whatever you want. OK with you?"

I have had the displeasure of being last in at Harry's and like to eat in one of the better rooms if at all possible. There are about a thousand rooms in the place and they should issue road maps when you sit down.

"I'm right behind you, Tom; let's eat," I said.

He walked over to the guy who seemed to be in charge of doling out the tables and addressed him like an old friend. "How are you, Paul? It's been awhile. Can you squeeze my friend and me in someplace?"

"Mr. Westbrook, it's good to see you again. There is always room for you here, you know that. How's your dad?"

"He's great, Paul, just doesn't get downtown as much as he would like to."

"Freddie will see you to your table in the upstairs room if that suits. And say hello to your father for me. Tell him it's been too long without his favorite Beef Wellington. Maybe I'll have to send him some. Enjoy your meal, Tom."

All at once it was beginning to get big time busy.

A few lefts, a coupla rights and up some stairs, we finally arrived at our table. I told you it was big. We settled in and I ordered another Becks, Tom having a Coors light. The get-to-know-ya chitchat was over by the time we were ready to order and we both decided to have the same thing. Two prime ribs, medium, hold the potato, whatever it is. The ex loves her baked potatoes, but I have no use for them. Tom agreed with my point of view on the subject and we both chose not to crowd the plate with French fries. The prime rib (end cut if you are really lucky) takes up the whole plate already and needs your total concentration. That's how good it is, trust me on this one.

That task accomplished, I asked the obvious question, "So what happened?"

Tom had been having a good time up to that very moment. His facial expression changed and he said very slowly, "Someone decided to ruin a good thing for a lot of people and hurt us, and me in particular, very deeply. This was no accident, and whoever did it knew a great deal about the human body and how to manipulate its chemistry. You can take that to the bank, Harry."

"That's a pretty powerful statement to make, Tom."

"Harry, I'm a well-educated man, having graduated in the top 10% of my class at Stanford. Business administration may have been my major, but the sciences are my true love. My dad's business is mine when I want it, and can handle it, and that's what I'm trained for. The whole family has known it would go down that way since I graduated from high school. Baseball was never going to be my life, I knew that. But I wanted to be the one to say I had enough and it was time to go. Not this way."

That blew me away and I must have shown it.

"This was well-orchestrated and had to have been done by more than one person. The brains behind the scheme knew his chemistry or hired somebody who did. Even when I knew I was fading, I couldn't figure out why. It wasn't until after the season was over and I began to feel normal again that I started to think clearly. If you're smart, you know Pete's a key since he didn't fall apart like the rest of us. And Harry, I get the feeling you're no dummy."

Bad timing as the food showed up at that very moment. At least we got end cuts. Tom and I are gonna chow down, so end of chapter period

Chapter 26

Never one to look a gift horse in the mouth, I had arranged to have Charles pick us up at Harry's and take us to the Garden. Again, for the poor misguided souls in attendance who don't follow New York sports, or who happen to live in a bubble, that would be Madison Square Garden.

Tom had a tough time relaying the details of the season for obvious reasons. I had the feeling he knew more than he was saying but couldn't put my finger on it.

"The guys just melted with each day we played. You struggled to get up in the morning and your muscles didn't want to cooperate. The power hitters couldn't get any lift on the ball and starting spraying the ball around the field. In the end, even that didn't work. Our speed got slow and the pitchers were throwing batting practice during games. Man, I cried myself to sleep one night I was so frustrated for myself and for all the guys."

"Any clue how or who could be behind it?" I asked to get his mind on a different track for a second or two.

"Nothing I can prove, and I don't make accusations I can't substantiate" was his reply, but I could sense he wanted to point me in some direction.

We had arrived at the Garden and it was time for our surprise.

"Hey Charles," I said, "head into the parking lot over there and lose this purple buggy. We have an extra ticket, and you are joining us for the game. There is no room for debate, and you better hurry; we don't want to miss the tip off."

"Only doing as ordered, Mr. Shorts. I'll try not to spoil your evening by cheering for my man Shaq too loud in front of the Knick fans."

"Tom, I'm beginning to think we may have made a tactical error dragging one of the Laker Girls along with us. If he says hello to Spike Lee, I'm outta there!"

We laughed our way into the Garden and watched Shaq demoralize the Knicks to the tune of 42 points and 21 rebounds. Charles managed not to embarrass us too much, and we got out in one piece. I'm enjoying him more and more every time I see him.

Dropped Tom off at Grand Central Station for his train ride back to Connecticut, and Charles and I motored on to Manhasset. After about fifteen minutes Charles just blurted out from nowhere, "Tom's a nice guy, but a very troubled man. Someone has done him a terrible wrong, and he strikes me as the type of guy who isn't going to forget it that easy."

"Charles, I think you hit that nail square on the head. I believe Tom and I will be speaking again before very long."

Man, I couldn't have been more wrong.

I'm gonna doze on the ride, so end of chapter period

Chapter 27

When the phone rings at 7:30 in the morning, it is never good news. Knocked the phone on the floor and finally found the mouthpiece to mumble hello. What happened next shocked me awake, pronto fast.

"Mr. Shorts, this is Tom Westbrook, Senior. I'm sorry to call you this early, but we are a little worried about my son, Tom Junior. He never arrived home last night and we believe you may have been the last person he was with before boarding the train at Grand Central."

Talk about your confused guy. My mind started running through the sequence of events, and everything seemed cool.

"Mr. Westbrook, we dropped Tom off at the train station at about 10:30 and he hustled in to catch a 10:47 to Greenwich. That's all I know at this time. You haven't heard from him?"

"He called just before he got on the train and said he would get a cab from the Greenwich station. A ten-second conversation was all we had and he was gone."

"I'm sorry, Mr. Westbrook, but I just don't have a clue what could have happened to Tom. We had a good talk and a great time at the game. We parted planning to speak again in the near future. What can I do to help?"

"Mr. Shorts, Tom means the world to his mother and me. If anything has happened to him I don't know what we'd do. There was all that trouble last summer and Tom mentioned you were working on an investigation and that he was going to meet with you to see if he could help. If you can help find my son, I'll pay anything; anything I have is yours. Will you help?"

"Slow down, Mr. Westbrook. We don't know for certain that Tom is missing. He could be having breakfast right now, getting ready to call you and explain where he is. Let's give it a few hours before we jump to any serious conclusions. But I will make a few calls just in case. And call me Harry, please."

"Thank you, Harry. If you hear anything, anything at all, please call me immediately."

As I hung up the phone, a bad feeling came over me with a shiver. Maybe I need to talk to Randy and let him know the price of poker seems to have gone up. Better sort this out in my mind and come up with a new accelerated game plan, and that's going to require my total concentration. That being said, end of chapter period

Chapter 28

The three S's taken care of (shit, shower and shave), I sat down to try and find Tom Westbrook. The good part about being a private investigator is you know how to do things like this. The bad side is you have to do things like this.

Calls to the New York police, Grand Central security, and railroad cops all came up empty. No report of any injured passengers in Grand Central or along the route to any stop in Connecticut. The call to an old friend on the New York police force was really just a heads up to let him know what was going on. If Tom's name hit the wire, he promised to call me, but I wasn't holding my breath.

Several hours of contacting every cab and hack company in or around Greenwich produced diddley squat for my efforts. Right about then I was starting to get worried to the point of "this ain't good," and for me, that's bad. The old light bulb went on and I realized I had neglected to call the Greenwich police. No need to panic, but maybe it was time to speed up a bit.

"Hello, my name is Harry Shorts, and I'm calling to see if you have anything on your 8:00 a.m. reports on a Mr. Tom Westbrook from either last night or this morning. I'm a private investigator and checking into it for the family."

"Sir, this is Officer Sampson. Are you wishing to file a missing person report at this time?" came the standard reply you get every time you ask a question like the one I just asked.

"No, I'm not. But a little help would be appreciated. If you could just check the overnights it will save me a call to every hospital within fifty miles of you. It would be most helpful, Officer."

"Hold please."

The clock slows to an unbelievable speed when you are waiting for information like this. That second hand seems to be going backward.

"No Westbrook on the overnight, sir, but there was an unidentified male with no means of identification found at the Greenwich train station at 12:15 a.m. He was unconscious and transported to Greenwich Hospital with no further information available at this time. Best I can do."

I thanked him and made the dreaded call to the hospital. Twenty minutes of unnecessary fuckin' bullshit and I finally had the hospital administrator on the horn.

"He is about 5 foot 11 inches with a big frame. Blond hair cut short and he was wearing a gray pinstripe suit and black wing tip shoes. Stanford College ring if it was still on his finger." I didn't think anything else would help at that time.

"Mr. Shorts, you have to understand it is highly irregular to discuss admitted patients over the phone, and particularly with someone outside of the immediate family."

"I do understand that, but if it isn't him, there is no need to alarm the family at this time. They are already worried beyond where they should have to go. Please help me with this."

"Against my better judgement, Mr. Shorts, the description you have given me seems as though it could fit the John Doe we have in intensive care who was admitted last night. He was brought in with no identification and is presently resting comfortably, but he is in a coma. I'm not sure how we should proceed at this time."

"I'm gonna be in my car in one minute and there in less than an hour. Please do not call anyone until I get there, and I mean anyone at all. There could be criminal implications involved, and I'll handle it if it actually is Tom Westbrook. The name may ring a bell if you are from town," I threw in to give him some perspective.

"All right, Mr. Shorts. But please hurry."

Mach speed in progress as we approach end of chapter period

Chapter 29

Shepherd was a thin beanpole of a man and waiting nervously for me at the front door when I pulled up. The look on his face scared the shit out of me, and the first thought that popped into my head was that Tom had died. Turns out he always looks like that and is in serious need of a lifestyle change.

"If you are Mr. Shorts, I'm grateful you are here. Mr. Westbrook is a well-respected member of this community, a generous benefactor of this hospital as well as other charities in the area. I pray it isn't his son."

"Well, let's go see if it is or isn't," I urged.

I'm not big on hospitals, having been through far too many in my time, for all the wrong reasons. Other than having babies, not much good happens in hospitals. Of course, since I missed both of my kids being born, I'm no expert on that front either. I know, no time to beat myself up now.

Shepherd moved into the ICU with me right behind him. Gowned up and prepared for the worst, I ventured forth. Yep, sorry to say it was Tom. His head was bandaged quite a bit, but in general, he didn't look that bad. No damage to his face, but a broken wrist probably from the fall after getting conked on the back of the head with the usual blunt instrument, whatever the fuck that is. The problem was he presently resided in la-la land and comas are tricky. One day or a lifetime – no way to tell. His brain wave activity was good, so they were very optimistic at this time. Just no way to tell for sure.

I identified John Doe as Tom Westbrook, Junior and went to make the dreaded phone call to his parents. A cop's job must really suck when this time comes.

"Mr. Westbrook, this is Harry Shorts. I have found Tom and he is alive." You have to get that out immediately so they don't panic and think the person is dead.

"I'm with Tom right now and he is resting comfortably in the Intensive Care Unit at Greenwich Hospital." Another key is to get them calm. "Unfortunately, I'm told by the specialist he is in a coma, but he is in no immediate danger. Perhaps it would be best if you came down right away."

No shit, Sherlock. Could I have said anything dumber than that?

"I'm on my way right now; I'll see you in ten minutes. Thanks, Harry," and he was off. I hate waiting, but there wasn't anything to do now but hurry up and wait. The question was for how long.

Tom Westbrook, Senior was Tom Westbrook, Junior, just older. They could have been twins. I recognized him immediately and we shook hands and hugged like we had known each other forever. Tragedy can do that.

"There's no change. Let's talk before you go in and see him. He is in a coma and the doctor wants to speak with you about his condition. If you need, I can stay with you till you get things sorted out. Just tell me what I can do to help."

At that moment the doctor came up and introduced himself to Mr. Westbrook.

"Sir, I am Doctor Fuller, the resident neurological specialist attached to the hospital. Can we talk for a minute?"

"Yes, but I want to see my son. May I see him, please?" The signs of a hurting parent were beginning to appear all over his face, and he also showed signs of slipping over the edge to tears at any second.

"Please sit, Mr. Westbrook. Mr. Shorts has been most helpful and we have your son admitted with the absolute best care available being given to him. He is in the first level of coma, and that is very good. His brain activity shows all signs of a complete recovery, but as you know, we don't have all the answers when it comes to comas. Cautiously optimistic are perhaps the best words I can use at this time."

Tom looked right through Doctor Fuller like he never said a word. Strange how a strong man can turn to mush in these situations.

da bushes

"Tom," I said to him, "let's get a drink of water and then we can go in and see Tom Junior. I'm right here all the way."

What I needed was a real drink and to be a million miles from this place. This is the guy I was enjoying the Knick game with not eighteen hours ago. Life can really be a shit sandwich sometimes.

While Tom spent time with his boy, I went back to the phone to put in a call to Ms. Timmons. I needed to talk to M. Randle Trundle, and fast.

Shit happens, and so does end of chapter period

Chapter 30

M. Randle Trundle of Trundle Industries was in deep conference in Paris for most of that day and caught me just as I was getting home from the hospital. I hustled in and grabbed the phone, somewhat out of breath.

"Harry, it's Randle. Ms. Timmons said it was urgent, so I'm calling between very tricky negotiation sessions, and I only have a few minutes. What is the emergency?"

"The long and short of it is it looks as if somebody tried to kill Tom Westbrook last night and he is in a coma in Greenwich Hospital. I happen to have spent last night with him discussing the problem I am currently looking into for you. It could be a coincidence, but I'm not big on coincidences."

There was a long silence, during which I thought we could have been disconnected. Finally, Randy said, "I can leave immediately if you need me, Harry. This is just business. I have known Tom Westbrook for thirty years and watched his son, young Tom, grow up. I know what he means to Tom and his wife, and that is what is important in life, not business. Just say the word, I'll leave right now."

"Mr. Trundle, there isn't anything either of us can do that isn't already being taken care of. Finish your negotiations and I'll dig like a tiger to get some answers to this whole mess. If there is any development with his medical condition, I'll get news to Ms. Timmons. Trust me to watch things for you on this front."

"When I get back we will sit together, you can tell me where we are. I better call Tom right now. Thanks, Harry, and you can rest assured you have my trust. Anything you need, just tell Ms. Timmons, and it is yours."

da bushes

Messages from Charles on what time we were leaving to get to the airport on Monday, and confirmation of the remainder of the arrangements from Ms. Timmons were on my answering machine. First Florida to see the two players at their Instructional League complex, then on to Arizona to chat with Doc, the trainer, and Punch, the hitting coach. Any other time and I'd enjoy the hell out of limo rides and private jets. Unfortunately, Harry Shorts on a mission is mind-numbing with no rest until I get what I want. I'm really fuckin' pissed now; somebody is going to have to pay for it in triplicate.

Called the kids, which made me smile and forget the rat bastards for a minute. On that good note, I better signal for end of chapter period

Chapter 31

Up at 6:30 a.m. the following Monday and well into the three S's when a funny story just popped into my head for no reason. Charles is due at 7:30, so I'll have to keep moving while I relay this little ditty.

My ex-darling of a wife used to have this endearing name for me when things were at their ear-splitting best. If I remember properly it went something like "You Fucking Bastard" and on from there. Considering my general behavior back then, it was a regular occurrence, and for awhile I had the feeling she forgot my real name and thought that was it. I guess she hung onto it after I vacated the premises, because it came back to bite her in the ass a few years later.

Middle of July, and hot as a mother. She was driving down Plandome Road, the windows open, and stopped for a light at Andrew Street. The car next to hers was honking its horn something fierce and pissing off Sherry when a voice from the back seat yelled out loud and clear "You Fucking Bastard." The guy in the car next to her gave her a look that could kill and the ex gunned it, taking off like a bat out of hell. The little munchkin, Brianne, in the back seat, was doing the "like mother, like daughter" routine, repeating what you normally said when you got pissed off.

I laughed like crazy when I heard that story and thought you might find it amusing.

Charles was waiting for me when I got downstairs. Mrs. Taylor was heading off to work and gave me a big smile to brighten up my day. Store it into my memory bank; I'll have to look into that one of these days.

"Kind of friendly lady isn't she, Harry?" was my good morning

da bushes

from Charles as I jumped into the limo. "Last time I got a smile like that it was on the back end of a most enjoyably midnight tango for two."

"Very funny, Charles, and don't ever forget you're driving around in a purple limo, my man." I believe that's a gotcha.

"How's the Westbrook kid?" Charles inquired.

"No change this morning. I gave them this car phone to call if there is any change. I'll call from the plane when we get on board. Hey, can we swing by the house and drive the kids up to school?"

"You the boss, Harry, so point the way."

We beeped the horn, and the kids couldn't get out of the house fast enough. A slow crawl to the front of Manhasset High School had half the student body wondering what star was about to grace their grounds. Charles played it up big, donned his hat and went around to open the door for them. Cat calls and "nice wheels" rang out as the munchkins marched up the front steps in front of all their friends, king and queen for a day. What are dads for anyway, I ask?

I was in the mood for some company, so I jumped in the front seat and off we went. Charles was unusually quiet, which wasn't like him at all. A fuckin' chatterbox you normally can't shut up is his typical M.O. Something was up.

"What's up with you, cat got your tongue?"

"Sometimes I don't understand how people can do the things they do. Little Tom and his dad have been in my charge more times than I can remember, Harry. Mr. Westbrook and the boss go way back. Mr. Trundle has treated Tom Jr. like he was his own son, to the point where I sometimes think he wishes he was his son instead of that S.O.B. Teddy."

"S.O.B. is a bit strong, isn't it, Charles? And by the way, is it Charles, or would you like to be called something else?"

"Between you and me, that boy will come to no good sooner or later and hurt his father bad. I personally will be very upset by that, and it's Charlie to my friends. You can call me Charlie if you would like, Harry."

"I'd like that very much, Charlie. Now get this rig to the airport, I gotta catch some rat fuckin' bastards!"

"You do that, Harry, and if you don't mind, I'd like to say end of chapter period"

Chapter 32

Bobby "Cat" Hoffman and Howdy McDuff were down in Florida working on their defense, especially turning the double play. When things were going good they were considered the best 2nd base / shortstop combination in the Eastern League. But practice makes perfect, and they were sacrificing part of their off-season to get even better, individually and as a pair.

January in Florida is a crapshoot with this year coming up sevens all over. Man, did it feel good to get into some shorts and a tee shirt and walk around in the warm sun. Even 70 degrees was a Godsend. Harry Mickey Shorts was gonna milk it for all it was worth.

I spent about thirty minutes just admiring their footwork and the skill they exhibited around the infield. Cat could go into the hole between first and second, spin and throw to the second base bag like he was born to do it. Howdy would go behind third and be just as graceful. It was a joy to watch two gifted professionals excel at their trade. Hands as soft as butter and arms like cannons on both of them. Man, it was beautiful to behold. They seemed as strong as any pair of infielders I had ever seen.

In the batting cage, Cat sprayed the ball everywhere. Like a machine it went – two line drives to left, two to center, two more to right. Fifteen minutes and he never veered off that pattern once. Howdy was banging balls off the batting tee into a net while he waited. When he got in the cage he could pound it. It was clear he had a bright future as a good fielding, power hitting shortstop. They happen to be few and far between.

I was psyched to get on the field with these two guys on a daily basis and watch them perform their magic.

It was getting late when they finished up, so we agreed to meet for burgers and brews at a local sports bar. When they heard I was buying, their enthusiasm picked up quite a bit. They acted like poor bush leaguers and not the semi-bonus babies they were. I guess old habits are hard to break.

The hotel was the best in the area, and I would have to thank the lovely Ms. Timmons for taking good care of me. Caught a 30-minute nap and spruced it up a bit before going back out. The place was typical sports bar, with TV screens everywhere and a variety of events to choose from. I chose the waitresses in short skirts and halter tops as my viewing pleasure. Ordered up a cool one and enjoying the passing scenery while waiting for the boys to get there.

At 7:00 p.m. they strolled in, checking out the action for later on. We grabbed a table and ordered a round of refreshments. What somebody drinks tells you a lot about them. Cat ordered a Rolling Rock and Howdy a screwdriver to jump start the evening. I got another Becks on Randy's tab. I told them the story of this place down at the South Street Seaport, in Manhattan, where you can order a "Bucket of Rocks," which is several bottles of Rolling Rock in an actual aluminum bucket. I've had more than a few myself; they thought it was cool.

Time to get down to the nitty-gritty and do what I do quite well, and often – lie like I was born to.

"I know you guys are wondering what I'm doing here and why I asked to meet with you. The name's Harry Mickey Shorts, and I'm going to join the team next year as a player coach. I like to get to know the players before we start, and it won't be long before we will be coming on down to get started. There you have it."

Short and sweet – the best way to lie.

"Funny we didn't hear anything about it before now," said Bobby, as Howdy shook his head in agreement. "Whose idea?"

"Who came up with the brainstorm, I don't know and don't care. One of the organization people called me and made the offer, saying they wanted a little experience on the team for next season. That a problem?"

When two young kids look at each other saying nothing, you wonder

da bushes

what gem will come from it. I doubted they were dummies, but at the moment it didn't look like Einstein had anything to worry about.

"All we know right now is you're a catcher, and I guess we could use some help behind the plate. Westy ain't coming back, and the new guy doesn't know the system yet. You any good?" was as good a question as any.

"Let's say I used to be real good and can still play enough to get by."

Mexican standoff time interrupted by the cutest little blond thing bringing a fresh round. I would have won.

"Hello there, sweetheart, and what might your name be?" I ventured, showing off my years of experience to the two kids. Imparting one's wisdom as an educational tool to the younger generation is the least I can do.

"Listen, asshole, I'm not your sweetheart, and the name's on the stupid button hanging off my left tit for all to see. And in case you need a diagram, I'm not having a good night so far, so don't add your bullshit line to make it worse. Comprende, partner?"

She dropped the drinks and left without waiting for an answer. Mutt and Jeff were laughing their collective asses off while I went to take a leak and splash a little water on my tongue-lashed face. It's gonna take a minute, so end of chapter period

Chapter 33

The boys had calmed down when I returned, only to start up again as soon as they saw me.

"Alright, that will do," I said. "I stand before you with my ego slightly dented, but we have not seen the last of that little spitfire. I'm not done yet."

Guy bullshit went back and forth, and they could hold their own with yours truly, the master of bullshit. Having exhausted every angle they could think of to attack me, we gave it up and went to work.

"I'm interested in hearing from each of you what you think happened last year. Your year's stats don't look bad, but I've researched the first half vs. the second and can see the substantial drop-off. What happened?"

"It was a very strange year," started Cat, who was clearly the more confident of the two. "We were steam-rolling everything in sight, then all of a sudden the wheels came off full tilt. The best way I can explain it is a combined feeling of overall tiredness and muscle fatigue. Rest didn't help, and daily rubdowns didn't help either. Nothing at all seemed to help, no matter what we tried."

"Pete was the only guy who seemed immune to the disease that was eating its way through the whole team," interjected McDuff, whose first name turned out to be Jerry.

A feeling of sadness was visible on both of them. I couldn't blame them as they thought of what might have been, and who knows if it will ever be again.

"What was different about your daily routine from the All-Star break on? Any change to the food before or after games, or the drink provided in the dugout during games? Too much work, or not enough; game day

da bushes

routine or road trip itinerary changes? Anything at all either of you can think of?" I was truly fishing by now.

"We just kept busting our butts during the games, religiously getting worked on by Doc. Dehydration was ruled out with all the water we were drinking and salt pills we were taking. The food was the same and the sport drink/water combination didn't change as far as we know. The water was tested and came out clean as a whistle. Scheduling on game days got more lax, if anything, and we had more days off as we went along. We all just flat wore down."

"When did your strength come back and you begin to feel better?" I asked, trying to move to a more positive subject. Maybe back end I could come up with something useful.

"Bobby and I came right down here to Florida after the season and hit the beach. It took about a month before I felt any better, the first of the year till we both were back to normal."

Another hour of going around in circles provided nothing. There was something there, but I couldn't get a grip on it, and it was beginning to frustrate me beyond where I like to be frustrated.

"Fuck it. Let's throw back some suds and forget that nightmare for now. Maybe Ms. Congeniality can get us some menus and we can enjoy the rest of the night."

She was hustling her buns off and stomped over to the table in a huff. "Sorry, guys, for forgetting about you, but those jerks in the corner are going way beyond what I can tolerate. Look at the menus; I'll be back in two shakes to get your order."

Those "jerks" turned out to four jamokes from some local softball team celebrating a victory at the waitress' expense. I was hungry, pissed at the world, and that's a bad combination for me. When they continued hassling blondie, I had had enough.

"Excuse me, guys, but I think it's time to put a stop to those idiots." As I got up, they did the same, and we wandered over to see if we could persuade them to behave in a more hospitable fashion.

I looked right at the biggest jerk in the group and said, "If you wouldn't mind, fellas, we would like to eat tonight, and you seem to be holding up the works with your childlike antics. If you promise to be nice to the lady, we can go back to our table, get our food, and everyone can enjoy the rest of the evening."

Big man in town decided to make a mistake and shouted, "Who the fuck do you think you are, asshole?" loud enough for a good number of people to hear. Big boy, local yokel putting on a show for his fans.

"I'm the guy who's gonna give you two, and only two choices. Choice #1 is we all go outside and I personally beat the living piss out of you just for the fun of it. Then my two friends will kick the shit out of your three buds 'cause they feel like it, and because you have been rude to a nice lady trying to earn a living. And trust me, that will all happen. Choice #2 is you shut the fuck up and let the lady do her job. Now pick one, and fast."

Three blinks in a row usually means big guy with no balls.

"We were just having some fun and perhaps we got a little carried away. Why don't we all relax, enjoy our meal, and everyone can have some fun."

"Wise choice, big guy. Thanks for your understanding, and maybe an apology would be in order, if you should see fit to do so," I urged.

It turns out blondie's name was Dana, an aspiring actress who was working during the day in one of the shows over at Disney World. I knew her name since I cheated and peeked at her left tit. Maybe I lingered a second or two longer than necessary, but it is bad form to get the waitress' name wrong, as you all know. Fortunately for me, she was too pissed to realize it.

"I appreciate what you did, but I have already had more than enough of this shit long before they started in tonight. I'm 30 years old, and it looks like acting just isn't going to be a reality for me. Being good just isn't enough, I guess. Tomorrow I planned on getting on the bus and going up to New York to see my sister for awhile, try and figure out what to do."

You know that light bulb we have talked about before. Well, it just went on again in case you weren't looking directly over my head.

While the boys were off following Mother Nature's orders, I volunteered my services. "Dana, I'm heading back to New York after a stop in Arizona for a day or two. Can't explain why, but I have a private

da bushes

jet at my disposal, and you are welcome to hitch a ride if you want. Count it as payback for the sweetheart crack."

She must be a New Yorker. It took her exactly two seconds to say "You're on, and for your information, sweetheart is the nicest thing anyone has said to me in a long time."

We finished making arrangements to meet tomorrow just as the boys were getting back. "And I'll have French fries with that, too. What do you guys want? Since we finally seem to be able to eat, we better order fast."

The food was normal sports bar grub, but the suds were Becks' best, and the rest of the evening was spent getting to know both Bobby and Jerry a bit more. Tomorrow would prove to be interesting, and to get there, let's go with end of chapter period

Chapter 34

You would think that after the long season ends, the winter months would be a time of rest and relaxation for minor/major league ballplayers. These days they start preparing almost immediately for the next year, working out virtually twelve months of the year. I stopped on my way to the airport to say goodbye to the boys who were already hard at work by 8:30 a.m. I like these two, and unless something bad happens, they both have a damn good chance of making it to the big show.

They took a break and came over to where I was standing, sweat dripping from every part of their bodies. "Wondered if you were gonna stop by before you left," said Cat.

"Just have a minute, but I wanted to thank you guys again for last night. I'm heading out, but I'll be back before you know it, and we can get down to some serious working out. Hang tough till then."

A "you got it, man" from both of them and I was history.

Small private airports are great. I walk out of the gate, directly onto the plane that was fueled and waiting for me. Or us, I should say. Dana was waiting at the gate, bags in hand, and ready for a new start.

"Well, good morning there. Let me help you with those bags."

"Good morning to you, too, and thanks, they are a bit heavy. The taxi driver dumped them on the curb and was gone before I blinked with my $5 dollar tip. I can't tell you how much this means to me. Thanks again for last night."

"Hey, no problem. If we didn't do something, we might have starved to death and you would have had three bodies to worry about."

An actual smile crossed her face for the first time, and the morning was beginning to look better all the time. She was even cuter when she

da bushes

smiled, if that was possible. It must be the animal magnetism that draws them to me, or maybe it's just plain dumb luck. We can vote when our journey ends, if that's OK with you.

"Good morning, guys. This is Dana; she will be joining us for the remainder of the trip to Arizona and on to New York."

"Welcome aboard, Dana, and per regulations, we will need her last name for the flight manifest, Mr. Shorts."

"It's Dana Sherwood, like the forest," she replied, saving me the embarrassment, since I had neglected to find out what it was before then.

"Great. Anything else, Mr. Shorts, before we take off? The morning papers are on the couch and there's danish and donuts on the table. Coffee's brewed – regular or decaf, Ms. Sherwood?"

"Regular with cream and one sugar would be great, thank you," she whispered rather sheepishly, almost like she was afraid it was all going to disappear any minute.

"Settle in and we will be in the air in two shakes. Get something to eat and Greg will bring the coffee back as soon as he's done stowing your bags. There's quite a bit of weather between here and Arizona, so we will be taking the scenic route this morning. Should be about four and a half hours if all goes as planned."

"Greg is the copilot, and that was the pilot, George, who heads up this team," I explained to Dana. "I heard they refer to them as the G Men, and it took me a few minutes to figure it out."

The plane had four captains' chairs up front, a couch on one side, and a table that sits six comfortably in the back. The rear of the plane had a cabin with a double bed and shower. Not a bad way to travel at all, if you ask me.

After our continental breakfast, I told Dana it had been a long night with the boys and I was gonna catch a nap in the back. Seems she was also up late packing for the trip and was also a few hours short of a good night's sleep.

"A little cat nap would do me good. And Harry, unless I'm mistaken, I'm sure you're like any other guy who wonders right away if the girl really is a blond. Perhaps, if you are curious, Harry, we can find some way to mutually solve that riddle for you?"

"Dana, I just love riddles, and solving them is the best part!"

I told you it was gonna be an interesting day, but even I didn't know it would start out this interesting. Since it seems I'm gonna be busy for a coupla hours, amuse yourself with end of chapter period

Chapter 35

We landed in Phoenix right about four and half hours later, just as Captain George had said. The weather was pretty bad, so we didn't miss anything being otherwise occupied as we were. Luckily, we emerged in time for a bit of lunch and a few light jabs from our crew.

As expected, Ms. Timmons had made all the arrangements at the Hilton, including a room for Dana adjoining mine. Have to remember to thank George for taking care of that for me. Good news is I'm enjoying this attention and special care immensely; bad news is it will go away before I want it to.

Dana went for a swim while I called Eddie "Doc" Snyder to set up our meet. Nice compact package in a bikini made a swim look like a much better idea. But duty called, and Doc picked up on the second ring.

"Hi, this is Harry Shorts. I believe you were expecting me to give you a call. How are you today?" Always try to be nice, at least in the beginning.

"Yes, I did expect you to call, but unfortunately I was hoping it would be earlier. I'm on my way out and won't be back till late tonight, if at all."

"That's OK. Perhaps tomorrow morning for breakfast would be better. I'm at the Hilton, if that is convenient for you. I could come there if you prefer."

"The Hilton's fine. Breakfast at eight, if that is convenient for you."

I hate when people parrot back something I said, especially when I think he is breaking my balls by doing it. And I was sure that was the case with Doc. Perhaps I was right, and I'm really not gonna like him as I had hoped.

"Eight's fine. I'll meet you in the lobby," and I hung up the phone. Not off to a good start with this one, but you can't win them all.

My next call went a whole lot better than the first. Punch, whose real name was Paul Tennly, was in the garden tending to his off-season passion. His wife chatted me up for a minute, then got Punch, who actually sounded a lot older than I expected.

"This is Harry Shorts, and I believe someone from the Schooners let you know I would be calling. I'm here in Phoenix and hoped we could get together to talk about the team, maybe rehash what happened last year. I like to go into a season as prepared as possible, and I'm trying to get with as many people as I can that were there last year."

"Good to hear from you, Harry, and I have been looking forward to your call. The wife and I have guests till Thursday and I don't see them all that often. Would it be an inconvenience if we met on Friday for lunch? You can enjoy our city for awhile and I'll have the wife whip up some goodies for us here at the house."

Whip up some fuckin goodies? Not the kind of expression I would expect from a hitting coach at this level, or any level for that matter. But the thought of a day and a half of free time on Trundle Industries' dime with my new heartthrob was something to consider. I considered it.

"That's fine, Punch. I wouldn't think of intruding on you or your company. Friday for lunch is great and don't give it another thought."

That wasn't the conversation I was expecting, which was starting to become a habit. My initial research and first impressions from both calls didn't meld at all. I thought I was making some headway; now I had to jump back and reassess.

I called down and made a dinner reservation for 7:30 p.m. and couldn't get the trunks I rented from the hotel on fast enough. Perhaps if my dick wasn't standing at attention and getting in the way of putting on the swimming gear, I could have gotten down to the pool faster. Get a grip, Harry, you're not in high school, you know.

Dana was surprised to see me. Luckily for me, my little friend had calmed down by the time I got to the pool. It was a bit cool outside so we were in the inside pool area. I jumped in the hot tub with the

da bushes

refreshments I had dragged along. Hot tubs and beer are God's way of saying life can be pretty damn good at times.

A quick swim and we were back in "our rooms" by 5:30. The door adjoining the two rooms opened, and Dana pranced in wearing one of the more attractive birthday suits I had seen in a long while. And if you must know, she was a true blond. We barely made it to dinner by 7:45.

End of chapter period

Chapter 36

I woke up at 7:00 a.m. feeling and looking like a tornado whipped in, tossed me in the air and dropped me on my head from way too high up. Large doses of Dana, Absolut and Becks, and more Dana had left my head spinning and my body limp. Some parts more limp than others from definite overuse. I hadn't felt this bad and good at the same time in a long while.

At ten minutes to eight I was waiting in the lobby for Doc. Dana, thank my lucky stars, was still in sleepy-by land. I wanted to size up Doc before we met to get a mental and visual picture in my head. He wasn't at all what I expected.

He told me he would have on a blue windbreaker and gray slacks. I spotted him right away and took a double take. Doc was 5 foot four and weighed about 120 pounds soaking wet.

"Harry Shorts," I introduced myself to him as I held out my hand.

"Glad to meet you, Harry" sounded sincere, and I was beginning to think I misjudged Doc by a lot. Reassess wasn't the right word – start from scratch was beginning to look like a possibility.

"Let's go on into the restaurant and get some breakfast. We can talk while we eat," I said. Of course my body was adverse to the idea of food right about now, but I was just gonna have to suck it up.

Orders done and our initial "eye-up the other guy" routine out of the way, we settled in for the business at hand. I figured I'd get the ball rolling and stir things up a bit at the same time.

"The team wants a little more experience for the next season and has hired me to come aboard as a player coach. They are hoping it wasn't anything sinister that ruined this past year and perhaps I can help set things straight in the coming season."

da bushes

"Interesting initial statement, Harry. I assume you are qualified and I will know before the season starts if that's a fact. Some experience wouldn't hurt, but it wouldn't have made a whole lot of difference in the second half. It wasn't conditioning and it wasn't physical breakdown either."

Lately it seems food always comes at the wrong time. It did give me a second or two to assess Doc's comments that were heading in a direction I hadn't anticipated. No, I'll admit I don't always guess right.

"I'm good at what I do, Harry, and I take a great deal of pride in my work. So we both are on the same page here, I inherited a great deal of money from my parents when they died while abroad five years ago. I do this because I love the game of baseball and helping the kids I don't have myself is gratifying. If you have any thoughts that I was in any way responsible for what happened last year, forget them. It wasn't me."

Wishy-washy Doc wasn't. But it didn't fit either. All signs pointed to him having at least some responsibility in this due to the fact he controlled their bodies more than anybody else involved. Harry, the master sleuth, was beginning to look like Harry, the major dunce. Man, I was confused beyond belief now.

"Doc, I wasn't pointing fingers at anybody. I'm confused on how something like the total collapse of the Schooners could occur, and anyone that looks at it would have to assume the possibility of foul play could be involved. You don't agree?"

"I didn't say I did, I didn't say I didn't. Actually, Teddy or anybody else in control never asked my opinion and didn't seem to think it was my fault either. Very confusing would be a good way to classify what happened and how it was handled internally within the organization."

Doc sipped his decaf and then floored me with "And who are you really looking into this for, Harry?"

Not spitting out my coffee was a trick, since I couldn't have been caught more off guard by his question. What the fuck do I say to that?

"What are you talking about?" I tried, knowing it had about as much chance for success as me making it back to the majors.

"Harry, as I just said, I have more money than I could ever spend.

When the office called, I put out a few feelers and came up with a P.I. license issued to one Harry Mickey Shorts. Relation of yours, or pure coincidence?"

"Doc, or do you prefer Eddie? We might as well put all the cards on the table. How's that sound?"

"Eddie or Doc is good, and I'm sure playing it straight would be beneficial to both of us. Tell me your story so I'll have a better idea of how to help out."

Your gut tells you when to put your trust in someone, and Eddie was gonna have to be a good guy for me to get the results I needed. The money angle never came up in my initial look at him, and that disturbed me. How much is a lot and where was it if I didn't find it.

"OK, Eddie, I'll play for now. But for your information, if I find out you're bullshitting me, you can bet your ass I will personally nail your butt to a wall."

It was close to 11:00 a.m. when Doc went off to do a little research he had been putting off. Our mutual indications of where the problems might lie pointed him in the direction he was already heading, with a small detour after getting my input. We were on the same wavelength now and promised to talk next week when I got back to New York.

You trust your mother, but you cut the cards. That I don't ever forget, and Doc seemed to fit the profile perfectly.

Dana was out when I got back to the room, which was good, 'cause this old body needed a rest. You may take your leave along with end of chapter period

Chapter 37

Every kid plays trampoline on his or her bed at some time or another. If you didn't, you led a deprived childhood and missed a solid biggie. I was in dreamland and thought I was back in my kiddie days making like a champion gymnast when I woke up to find Dana doing her best Cathy Rigby imitation on the bed I was currently laying in.

"Yo, what the hell has gotten into you?" I screamed, while trying to protect the Shorts crown jewels at the same time.

Like a little kid, she just kept repeating, "I got an acting job, I got an acting job," over and over again.

Sweeping her legs out from under her brought her crashing down to the mattress, and she starting laughing out of control. The clock read 4:12 and it took a few minutes for Dana to gain control. Me too, since I awoke from a dead sleep thanks to the laughing hyena next to me.

"If you would be so kind as to tell me what the hell is going on, I would appreciate it, Dana dear."

She gave me the biggest kiss I had gotten in a long time and said, "I got an acting job here in Phoenix. The national tour of a production headed to Broadway is here in town and they just lost their leading lady to pneumonia. I did the role in Orlando this spring in local theater and can step in tonight. I'm an ACTRESS!"

I couldn't have been happier for her, but wondered how she got hooked up with them. So I asked "How did they find you, or you find them?"

"I was eating lunch downstairs and the director was at the next table moaning to the producer that he was sunk without a lead or understudy, who, it just so happens, left last week to start a leading role of her own. An 'excuse me' later and I was auditioning in a back conference room for the two of them. It's a role just made for me, or I'm just made for it. I'd don't know which, but they were blown away by the ten minutes I did for them from memory. No music and I still hit every note in the big finale song, which I just adore and sing great. Harry, I was damn good and they were floored.I got the part right there. Oh Harry, you made this all possible, I can't thank you enough. Or can I?"

    She had that look in her eye, and I knew I was in for another long night, but I wasn't complaining one single bit. Turned out to be another brilliant deduction by Harry the P.I. The only bad part was Dana would be staying on in Arizona and not coming back to New York with me. Better make the best of these two days starting right now, so you best scoot and take end of chapter with you

Chapter 38

Arrangements were completed and I would be leaving first thing Saturday morning, all by my lonesome. Lunch with Punch on Friday, plus Dana's debut that night, which would be followed by a celebration party for two. The G Men were happy to be heading back to New York after their detour to Canada on company business, while I frolicked in sunny desert land. Ms. Timmons, her most efficient self, told me Mr. Trundle would be back from Europe on Monday evening and was looking forward to seeing me the following day, if it fit with my plans. His nickel, I'd be there.

Mrs. Tennly answered the door wearing a housecoat and pussycat apron. Late fifties was my guess. The gray hair made her look older, without any attempt on her part to change that impression. Nothing is making sense in this case at all, and I for one am getting rather annoyed.

Paul Tennly came to the door and shook my hand with a vise grip that could cripple Superman. He was in his late fifties, too, if I had to guess, and I wouldn't want to fuck with him if he was pissed. This guy was put together and knew how to keep it together – playing in the garden didn't fit at all. I may have to change my name again to Harry Confused Shorts, 'cause it would fit me a lot better right about now.

"Come on in and make yourself comfortable, Harry. Roberta will get us some lemonade and we can talk in the sunroom. How's Doc?"

"Did I mention I was going to meet Doc?" which was both a question and a planned attention-getter at the same time.

"No, you didn't, Harry, but Doc and I belong to the same health club here in Phoenix. I ran into him yesterday on my way in for my workout. You look like you keep yourself in pretty good shape; what do you do?" Very deft transference of direction by the Punch man.

"Little bit of everything, from free weights to a boxing routine and some martial arts. Never was one for running much, and I do just enough to keep the wind under control. What's your pleasure?"

"I use the weight room quite a bit, plus all the other machines from rowing to climber, or stepper, as it's now called. And of course, I do all the work in my garden myself, by hand. I have no use for the new tools that take all the fun out of working with your hands and the earth beneath us."

A good bit of shadow boxing so far, and I was starting to get inpatient. Time to move up the pace a bit I think. "Doc and I had a very nice conversation and most interesting" was all I said.

Punch was hoping I would continue, but he had a long wait coming. He got lucky and his wife brought in the drinks at that moment and poured us each a big glass of pink lemonade. I hate fuckin' lemonade.

Ignoring my jab, he plowed right ahead with, "So, what are your plans for next season, Harry?"

Having blocked his right cross, I parried with, "I'd like to get a handle on last season before moving to next year. Any thoughts?" leaving it as open ended as possible.

Absorbing that straight right hand, he launched into a diatribe on poor eating habits, late night carousing, and not taking proper care of their bodies as having a detrimental effect on today's athlete, in general, but nothing particular to the Schooners or the players in specific. Back peddling gave me an opening I never fail to take advantage of.

"Odd you should say that Punch, since you were the coach responsible for the daily pre-game meals, distributing daily doses of vitamin C, and making sure they took their salt pills religiously. And weren't you in charge of scheduling rub downs, especially with the outside physical therapist the team brought in later in the year?"

Side step and return with "You can only do so much, Harry, you can only do so much."

How true, Punch, how true.

My conversation with Doc was a straightforward give and take that culminated with action plans for both of us. Punch and I danced the "I ain't telling and you can't make me" dance, and I was sure he was

da bushes

enjoying it. Play with the peckerwood washed-up bush leaguer and send him on his way was his game. Little did he know two were playing the same game, and I do it for a living, and for keeps.

I never got my answer to the ten-year gap in Punch's baseball career. Ms. Timmons will have to save the day on that one.

Lunch was pleasant, and a walk through Punch's garden with Paul and Roberta Tennly brought the day to an end. Seemed strange his greenhouse was off limits and not even open for discussion. As I was leaving, I noticed a photo of Paul arm and arm with an older man who could have been Mrs. Tennly's twin.

"That's my father," said Roberta. "He and Paul got to be very close until he passed away unexpectedly recently."

With that I departed, and it was even more evident much had to be done before I left for spring training in Florida.

The car ride back to the hotel was a good time to collect my thoughts and plan my strategy going forward. Breakfast with Doc and today's lunch provided valuable information and cleared up a few loose ends that could prove to be key. Some degree of confusion eliminated, other areas of confusion added, and no solid answers as of yet. There was something about that photo that was screaming "see me," but I couldn't put my finger on it. I wished I had it right now. Oh well, sweetheart Dana awaits, so I'll see you on the other side of end of chapter period

Chapter 39

I've never been around actors or actresses before, and naturally assumed they would be walking basket cases before their first performance. Either that isn't the case or Dana is a show business abnormality.

She was due at the theater at six for an 8:00 p.m. performance. But forty-five minutes before she was due to leave, she was still engaged in some rather energetic extracurricular activities that totally pleased her participating audience of one – me. If I had any energy left I would have applauded her performance as being superior in my eyes. To my amazement, she hopped in the shower, jumped into some clothes and was gone before I even caught my breath. Well, she is younger than me, you know. Yeah right, who am I trying to kid.

Almost time to head on out when the phone rang and the pleasant voice of Ms. Timmons came on the line. Today had been a halfway decent day, and I was hoping she wasn't going to put a dent in my good mood.

"Harry, I just got a call and thought you would want to know. Tom came out of his coma about thirty minutes ago and is resting comfortably. It's still too early to tell, but the preliminary prognosis is he will make a full and total recovery with no lasting side affects. His dad wanted you to be one of the first to know."

When you're on a roll, sometimes it just seems to keep coming up sevens. I called the hospital as soon as we hung up, thanking Ms. Timmons for calling me right away. Time to get her first name I think – that is, if she has one. Could be Ms. for all I know.

"This is Harry Shorts, and I'm a friend of the Westbrook family. I understand there has been a recent development in Tom Westbrook's condition and I was wondering if Mr. Westbrook, Sr. was anywhere in the area." After I said it, I realized I was talking to the reception area, and Tom wasn't likely to be hanging around the front desk waiting for me to call.

"I.C.U., can I help you?" put me where I needed to be, and I repeated my message of a minute ago.

"Yes, he is right here. Can you hold a second?" I assured the nurse I could do that.

"Tom Westbrook here," and he sounded like a million pounds of bricks had been lifted off his shoulders.

"Mr. Westbrook, it's Harry Shorts. I'm out in Arizona, but I just heard the news and wanted to call right away. How is he doing?"

"He's doing just great, Harry, better than we could have ever imagined at this point in time. He came to, started talking immediately and he's moving all his limbs. His memory of that night is a little shaky, but that's understandable. He asked for you, Harry, and as soon as he can take calls, he wants to talk to you immediately."

A little involuntary shudder crept into his voice, and I almost lost it myself. Incidents like what happened to Tom don't always turn into good news in this business, and when they do, you hang on for dear life. I had both arms around this one, and you can bet I was squeezing with all I had.

"Harry, thanks for being there, and I mean that more than you can imagine" was real nice to hear.

We ended the call with my promise to see both Tom's as soon as I got back to New York. Didn't sound like we would be getting any information on who did this to Tom, but I hadn't been counting on any coming my way that easy.

I didn't want to be late for Dana's debut, so I hustled over to the theater double time. With the way things were turning around, Dana had to be good. I wasn't disappointed, and she got a standing ovation as she took her curtain call at the end of the show. Having experienced her passion first hand, I knew she would be a natural up on the stage. Good guys or gals do finish first some of the time.

We went to a cast party and then slipped away to celebrate on our own. I told Dana how proud I was of her, and she actually started to cry. The damn tears thing again. I do have a way with the ladies, don't I?

When we got back to the room the message light was blinking, and I just knew it would be good news. When I get rolling I can ride a hot streak for days and days. Don't know how they do it, but Ms. Timmons had made arrangements to extend the room for another week to allow Dana to stay there while the show would be in Phoenix. Trundle was getting scary if you ask me. And let's just say Dana was most appreciative in her own imaginative way, far surpassing her performance at the theater earlier in the evening. You don't really want to know and I wouldn't tell you anyway, so end of chapter period

Chapter 40

As we jetted our way back to the East Coast, I had plenty of time to assess my trip in terms of accomplishing what I had set out to do. My mind kept floating back to Dana and seeing her succeed on the stage fulfilling her childhood dream, which was a good memory to have. We should all be able to do the things we dream about as long as they don't fuck up other people at the same time. As wonderful a story Dana the actress was, the Schooner tragedy was equally as horrible.

Hearing from Dana again was a long shot, but I gave her my number in Manhasset and told her to give me a call when, and if, she ever got to her sister's. She had the part until the real lead got back from pneumonia, with realistic hopes of sticking as the understudy. Stars are born every day, luck playing a big part. Maybe Dana finally got lucky big time. I know I'm lucky to have been along for the ride, even if it was only for a short time.

With my daily dose of sentiment tucked away for now, the phone brought me back to reality. Ms. Timmons wanting to know if everything was satisfactory at the moment was beginning to become a habit. A good habit, but a habit nonetheless.

"Life is grand," I told her, and proceeded to give her my anticipated arrival time and my desire to go directly to Greenwich to see both Tom Westbrook, Jr. and Sr. A few loose ends were dragging around in my mind. I hoped to clean them up if I could.

"Charles will meet you at the airport and take you to Greenwich Hospital directly. If you wish, I can get you a room in Greenwich for the night and have you picked up in the morning to go back to Long Island."

"No, that won't be necessary," I said, but I thanked her anyway.

"I'll stay for awhile and then head home if that is OK?"

"Whatever you want is yours, Harry," Ms. Timmons stated, and gave me the information I had asked her to gather for me when I spoke to her yesterday. It was thorough and comprehensive and answered a big question that was clouding up the works. Just as she was finishing, that damned light bulb went on and the nagging blurry impression of the photo at the Tennlys' almost came into focus. If I could clear up that vision things might become crystal clear in my mind. I was getting closer and was now ready to begin the season.

"Thanks for your help, Ms. Timmons, and I'm going to hold you to that some day soon." Let her figure that one out if she's as good as she seems, and boy am I hoping she is!

The rest of the trip was spent organizing the information I had and the things I needed to follow up on over the next month. I couldn't wait to finally talk to Pete Sanchez, who was crucial to my theory and hopefully would fill in a gap or two. Scoots might be helpful, but I don't know what he will add that the boys from Florida hadn't already given me. The rest of the team will have to wait till we get to spring training in Florida unless I can hook up with a pitcher or two like Jask or Randolph. They aren't local, and time is starting to be a problem. I'll have to call as soon as I get back and set it up. Let's see what Sanchez lends to the equation and go from there, Harry old boy.

I was tired and decided to take a nap before we landed. The G Men were at their best and hammered me unmercifully over my last nap on the way to Arizona. "Just because the two of you were playing private hand games up front while I entertained our guest is no reason to be snippy," I laughed. The vivid picture in my mind made it hard to fall asleep, but Shorts can sleep anywhere, any time, and this was no exception. I do like those two guys though.

We're about to land and I'll meet you in the car. End of chapter period

Chapter 41

It was 5:30 p.m. and pitch dark when we landed. Charlie was waiting at the gate to help me with my bags. It had snowed about six inches and it was still looking angelic white and clean all around. Even when you wished it was warm and breezy, pristine snow like this has a way of warming your heart. Mother Nature knows we need a "beauty boost" every once in awhile and gives it to us with snow. Give it a day or so, it'll look like gray mushy shit.

I wondered if the kids had built another snowperson out front. One a year is all I would allow myself, or they might get the idea I was part of their life on a permanent basis. Worse than that, I might try and fool myself into thinking it was a possibility.

Charlie offered me a refreshment when we got in the purplemobile, and my taste buds were set for a cool one after the long plane ride. "Don't mind if I do, Charlie. It was a long coupla days and I could use a little rest and replenishment. How you been?"

"No major complaints to speak of, Mr. Shorts. It's nice of you to ask, which you don't get a lot of from that side of the glass. The kids are home for a week or so, and we are enjoying their visit quite a bit. Love the grandkids to death, I do."

Charlie was right, and I felt bad about it. We take people who do a service job for granted and don't think of them as husband or wife, grandfather, or anything else for that matter. Do this and do that is all we ever care about. I'm gonna try to be cognizant and considerate more often.

"I'm probably gonna be about an hour or so, Charlie, so you can either wait here or get something to eat if you haven't already. Unless you wanna wait for me and I'll spring for dinner?"

"Haven't eaten as of yet, Mr. Shorts, and if you would like, I'd be pleased to have a meal with you," said Charlie, which was a pretty big stretch for him.

"Done deal – I'll ask Tom Sr. for a suggestion for someplace local."

The hospital business was slow in Greenwich, which is always a good sign. The place was almost deserted when we got there going on 7:30 p.m. The ICU unit is not a festive part of the hospital, and I found Tom Sr. and his wife talking to the doctor out by the nurse's station, both smiling broadly. I hung back for a few minutes, giving them a chance to finish their discussions.

"Harry, come over here and meet my wife. Dear, this is Harry Shorts, who we have so much to be thankful for. Harry, this is Tom's mom, Donna."

"It's a pleasure, Mrs. Westbrook. I was so glad to get the news on Tom Junior and came up as soon as I got back to the East Coast. How is he doing?"

"He is getting better every day, and we thank God for that. The doctor wants to keep him for a few more days and said that if all goes well he can be home by the end of the week. Tom's wrist is going to be OK, but his main concern is Tom's inability to remember the last few hours of that night from when he got on the train till it happened. But he said that can happen, and it shouldn't be a long-term problem."

Not what I wanted to hear, and it would prohibit him from being able to reconstruct the ride up to Greenwich. Anyone traveling on the train with him or in the station when he got there is buried deep in his memory, and I was hoping to review the last coupla hours for any clue at all. Not now, I guess.

"That sounds great, and getting home will due him wonders. Any chance I can see him for a quick second?"

"He is pretty tired by this time of night, but I'm sure he would be thrilled to see you, Harry," came from Tom Sr. with a big smile.

"I'll be damned if it isn't Harry Mickey Shorts in the flesh. You have a way of being in the right place, at the right time, I'm beginning to see. Good to see you, Harry."

da bushes

He sounded pretty good, but still had the LLS profile – Looks Like Shit!

"I'll only stay a minute. I know you're beat. Just figured if I got you into this mess, the least I can do is stop by and say howdy. You hanging in there?"

"I'm pretty good considering the alternative. I never saw him at all until it was too late and I was heading for the pavement at a rapid pace. We had such a good time I was just rolling along, content with being able to be of some help figuring out what happened last year. I know I saw him though, Harry. I just can't get it to the surface."

That surprised me, and I didn't know what to make of it. "What do you mean you saw him, Tom? I thought your memory is gone for several hours before it happened, right up to the time of the attack."

"It is in general, but I think a picture of his reflection in the station window is tucked in my brain somewhere. I can't tell you why I feel that way, but I do. Maybe it will come back to me, Harry, and we can nail the SOB to the wall."

"Tom, get better and get home with your mom and dad. I'll get him sooner or later, and he will have to pay a little extra for this stunt, that I promise you. You pick the wall and I'll provide the hammer and nails. Before you know it we'll be dining on Beef Wellington and laughing our asses off over the whole thing." And I believed every word of it, too.

Charlie was reading the newest Patterson book when I got back to the car. James Patterson, not Richard North Patterson. They are both great, and as it turns out, Charlie is a big fan of each, just like me. When you sit around waiting as much as Charlie probably does, reading is a perfect way to pass the time.

"How's ribs sound, Charlie? Tom tells me there is the best rib joint in the world next town over. Me, I love ribs. We can talk about Tom Jr. while we eat."

"Than ribs it will be," Charlie agreed, and we were off to try and make believe the world is great and indulge ourselves with food and drink, so you do the same. We can all indulge in end of chapter period

Chapter 42

Monday morning, I'm back in the office in Manhasset planning my next series of moves, feeling like I had been away for weeks. Getting out on the road is a necessity for me – revs up the engines and removes the same old, same old from my life. It has always worked and returns me to a hungry state.

If my thoughts were going in the right direction, Jask and Randolph may be important pieces to the puzzle. I still had plenty of time for another road trip before I needed to head down to Florida, and with Randolph being in Vermont, a day of skiing might be in order.

My body was telling me I needed to hit the gym and hit it hard. Throwing sessions this week would preclude me from leaving town, and that was good, since I needed to stay put and get organized. I had accumulated a good deal of facts and information that needed to be added to the case file documentation.

"Look what the wind blew in" informed me Ebil had entered the premises. Middle of the winter and the son-of-a-bitch was wearing his typical windbreaker over button-down oxford shirt. My ass is frozen solid and he's prancing around like its spring already. Drives me nuts, but what is a private investigator to do.

"You show the old broad you're squiring around today that shack on Westgate you've been trying to pawn off on somebody since the summer?"

"That shack, as you call it, has five bedrooms and is on the market for $890,000 for your information. And the answer to your question is yes, I did, but she thought it was a bit confining for her tastes while being 'annoyingly overpriced.' I've dragged her ass all over town with nothing to show for it, and it's really starting to piss me off."

da bushes

He wasn't pleased that Bunny and I couldn't stop laughing and proceeded to throw his beloved business section from today's *Times* in my general direction, which caused us to laugh even harder.

Two hours on the PC, the Schooner file was updated, a tentative schedule in place for the next month. Now all I had to do was convince all parties involved that my timetable fit theirs. Convincing Bunny that the first item on my immediate schedule – lunch with me at Publicans was in her best interest – proved to be an easy one. If you're buying, she's flying, and on occasion dessert is the best part, if you catch my drift. Since I was buying, we flew the coop with two large pointed mounds of whipped cream flashing through my brain.

Unfortunately, my brain was the only place I would see them today.

The phone rang about ten times and I was about to hang up when a voice shouted, "Yeah, hold on a sec." Any person is better than no person, so I held on a sec, which turned into more like 25 secs. I can be most patient when the need arises, which is part of my private investigator training.

"Rusty here. Sorry."

"Rusty, this is Harry Shorts, and I'm going to be a player coach with the Bayport Schooners next season. If at all possible, I like to get to know the other guys on the team before the season starts. Wondered if we could get together some time soon to meet and get the ball rolling. I can come up to your neck of the woods to make things easy."

"Howdy called me and gave me a heads up, so I've been expecting a call. Sounds like a great idea, and for my way of thinking, the idea of a little more experience on the team is very welcome. Do you know where I'm at?"

"Just outside of Boston is the address I have, and I've been in and around the area some. I'm pretty sure I can find it."

"When did you have in mind?"

"Next week, something like Tuesday or Wednesday would fit my schedule pretty well," I said. "I'm gonna try and shoot from your place up to Vermont and see Smokes Randolph if I can."

"Let's do Tuesday, and I may bum a ride with you and do some skiing with Smokes if you don't mind. Haven't seen him in awhile, and I wanted to get together before we headed south. How's that sound?"

"Got an even better idea if you're game. I'll pick you up, we can shoot right up to Vermont, spend a few days together on the slopes and find some way to pass the nights. Let me talk with Smokes and we can firm up plans later today. Stratton OK with you?"

"Stratton's fine and I'll wait for your call. Glad to hear from you, Harry, and I wanted you to know I'm real excited about next season. I pride myself in being able to finish what I start, and I've never experienced anything like what happened last year. I'm a winner, Harry, and I plan on being a winner again this year!"

One down, one more to go. I dialed Smokes' number and got an answer on the second ring.

"Hello," was all she said.

"Hello to you, too. Is Smokes Randolph there, please? This is Harry Shorts calling."

The muffled conversation sounded like "Hey babe, there's a guy on the phone looking for some smokes and shorts, I think. You wanna try and figure out what the asshole's talking about, or should I tell him to fuck off?"

"I'll take it. Joe here, who's this?"

"This is Harry Shorts, and I hope I'm not catching you at a bad time. I can call back later if you want. This is Smokes Randolph, isn't it?"

"Good a time as any right now. This is Smokes; what are you selling?"

"Fast balls up and in and curves down and away, if you're in a buying mood. The Schooners hired me to be a player-coach next season, and I'm contacting some of the guys to get a jump on the year. Talked to Rusty and we're heading up to Stratton for some skiing and bummin' around next week. Interested?"

"Been meaning to call Rusty for awhile, so it would get me out of that hole. When you planning on going, man, and how you getting there?"

"Picking up Rusty on Tuesday and heading straight to your place.

da bushes

My ride and I'll make the arrangements with a guy I know at Stratton who owes me a solid. Shouldn't cost us much. You down?"

"Snow bunnies, here I come" was all I needed to hear, and all you need to hear is end of chapter period

Chapter 43

Declined a purple chariot ride downtown on Tuesday 'cause I wanted to stop at the Garden and pick up some Jethro Tull tickets. That accomplished, I cabbed it up to Trundle Industries and planned my arrival to get there fifteen minutes early, hoping against hope I'd run into Ms. Timmons. 'Twas not to be, though, at least not on this day. The *National Geographic* I read while waiting had some pictures, but they didn't compare to the real thing.

If I had to take a wild stab, I'd say Randy wasn't in the best of moods when I finally got to see him. He was in the midst of an animated phone conversation with someone who wasn't seeing things in the same light as Randy.

"You didn't take that posture when I was there, and now that I'm back here in the states, you turn 180 degrees on me. We have terms and conditions on paper that we both agreed to in Paris, a deal that will benefit both companies. Why revert to a prior position after the fact that you already know I can't, and absolutely won't, agree to?"

He listened and didn't like what he heard, or he usually gets red in the face when he talks on the phone. I'd bet on the first option. And I'd also bet he wasn't going to back down either.

"I'll be there in the morning, and you better get your lawyers ready, because I'm not going to back down on this. You need this deal and I'll be getting my product elsewhere if you don't change your mind overnight. And if you bring up that cocksucker's name once more I'll personally guarantee your company will be out of business before he finds another job, if he ever does."

Didn't know that word was in Randy's vocabulary, and if it was, I didn't expect him to run it up the flagpole at that time. If I weren't

da bushes

wary of him before, I surely would be now.

Not to worry, I already was.

"Harry, I'm sorry you had to be subjected to such unpleasantness, but I don't like that man, and his use of one of my employees against me is intolerable. Let's put that nasty business aside and catch up. Tell me where you are, and most importantly, tell me about Tom Jr."

"Before we begin, I want to thank you for everything you have been doing to make it as easy as possible for me to work this case. Ms. Timmons has been a doll, and the available transportation allows me to do things that would have been much more difficult otherwise."

"We are in this together, Harry," Randy interrupted, and I could see he meant every word of it.

"Tom is doing much better and will be going home either tomorrow or Thursday. The docs believe he will make a full recovery with no qualifiers. I spoke to him yesterday; he sounded 100% improved from Saturday when I saw him, and he looked better then. He still doesn't remember what happened, but I haven't given up hope on that reflection possibility I told Ms. Timmons about. It's a long shot, but I've cashed more than one ticket betting on nags with less chance than this one has."

Randy's face lit up with the news of young Tom's recovery as if he was getting the news on his own son. I could see what Charlie meant.

"The boys in Florida didn't provide any new information, but I have a better feel for their mental state, as well as their physical breakdown. I'm seeing Rusty Jask and Smokes Randolph next week and hope to solidify my impressions of the players' downward spiral if I get the answers from them that I expect. Westy is a smart kid, and I'd grab hold of him if you could, Mr. Trundle. I'd want him on my team, no matter what we were doing."

Trundle reflected for a minute, then he said, "Very perceptive, Harry. Tom Sr. and I have already worked that out, and when golf starts to get in the way of his business, Trundle Industries will buy his agency and Tom Junior will run it for me. Thank you for the suggestion and recommendation."

Again, Randy seemed to be contemplating something while he said that.

"How was your visit with the two coaches in Arizona? And for your information, Ms. Sherwood got the understudy position and is very happy," as a big smile crossed his face. Why do I think Mr. M. Randle Trundle had something to do with that development?

"My view of the situation changed dramatically after meeting with Doc and Punch Tenny. I would have bet the ranch on Doc being a part of the problem, mainly due to his position with the club. He was too involved with the physical end of the team and the individual players not to be involved in some way. Maybe not the brains behind it, but involved somehow. After our talk, I came away with a different impression based on the segregation of responsibility he laid out, and just a bottom line gut feeling he's not the guy. And my gut has been pretty reliable in the past."

Mind you, I don't ever rule anybody out until the fat lady sings, and she isn't even warming up in the wings yet.

Trundle had that look he gets and jumped in with, "I'm glad you think that, Harry. Eddie was a personal hire of mine when we built the franchise and management team. I trust him and would have been most disappointed if I was wrong about him."

All at once I got the funny feeling I wasn't in this to solve a mystery, but to verify what the bossman already knew, or at least expected. Subtle remarks and innuendo pointing toward certain things made me believe the yellow brick road was somewhere down the road I was presently on. I realized a classic Shorts QAS had occurred – How best to correct this problem? Proof. Get Harry Shorts to expose the culprits. If that was the case, I was on solid ground so far, and figured no reason not to shoot the works.

"The Tennlys proved to be another ballgame altogether," I plowed on. "Punch, the man, was not who I expected to meet when I got there, and I guess I just assumed he was younger. Bad assumption on my part, but no harm done on that one. The extra job responsibilities he was doing somehow seemed wrong and out of the ordinary for a hitting coach. But the thing that bothered me was he didn't complain about them, and indicated it was his choice to take those away from Doc,

da bushes

who would normally control them. Maybe I'm reading more into it, but I don't think so."

I still didn't know how far to go without real proof and decided to hold onto the picture idea as a trump card for later. If I was correct, Randy already knew about the relationship, and it would come out later. If I was wrong altogether, somehow I'd find that out. And anyway, it's good to hold onto something in case you get in a bind and need to bluff your way out.

"There's more to Punch than meets the eye, Mr. Trundle, and Ms. Timmons gave me some information that needs verifying. That trail should lead me to the answer, I'm certain, and at that time we can bring all this out in the open. I think the basics are there, and we are very close already."

"That's good to hear, Harry. Go down to Florida and confirm what you believe to be true, and have some fun playing baseball again. Justification will come when it is time."

Heavy words from the judge and jury all rolled into one – Mr. M. Randle Trundle. I didn't doubt him one bit and I was going to enjoy the shit out of being there for the execution. A little b-ball in the meantime was fine by me.

"Charles is waiting for you downstairs to drive you back to Long Island. If you don't mind, Ms. Timmons will see you out. As you witnessed, I have a rather difficult problem to resolve. Thanks for coming in to see me, and tell Tom Jr. I'm thinking of him."

The "Total Package," looking as good as ever in that purple dress I admired so much, was waiting for me as I left the big guy's office.

"Been awhile, hasn't it? You're looking particularly good today," I said.

"Why thank you, Harry, and you look as if your trip did you some good. You wear that tan very well. That is, at least the parts I can see. I trust your meeting with Mr. Trundle went well?" she fished.

"Went very well, in fact, after a curious beginning. I understand he if off to Europe again right away."

"The negotiations seem to have hit a snag this morning that was totally unexpected. Without his Number One, he is handling this 100%

himself, which is most unusual for this organization. I've never seen him this perturbed."

"Well, I'm sure he will get what he wants. He doesn't strike me as the type to lose too often, if at all."

"You are totally correct in that assumption, Harry – he never loses at anything when all is said and done. And I do mean anything!"

As we approached the front, her beeper went off, and she excused herself in a big hurry. She took off in a flash for the elevators. When the big man calls, I guess you run – literally.

"How are you, Charlie? The kids gone or are they still brightening up your days?"

"Left yesterday for South Carolina and the wife went with them for a visit to the old home town. Really went just to spend some more time with the kids and grandkids, I think. Loves her family, she does. And how are you, Harry?"

"Good, Charlie. Can't complain much. Can't complain at all, in fact," as I settled in for a nap on the way home, dreaming about end of chapter period

Chapter 44

Neglecting your body for a week while in training mode is a big mistake, and I was paying for it double time. My muscles couldn't seem to remember where they were a week ago, and they were protesting in unison – loud and clear. Top that off with the bitter cold prohibiting long throwing outside and I was falling apart at the seams. Oh well, a few beers will make me feel much better, and a few is exactly what I had.

The week proved to be a real challenge to my fortitude and my desire to follow through with the resumption of my baseball career. I had hit a wall in my ability to push my body and mold it into playing shape. It wasn't like I was really gonna have a shot at playing professional baseball again – it was only gonna be make believe for a little while. If I got to hang around for the whole season, even as a coach, that would be asking a lot. Probably too much.

On Thursday, it was do or die time. I couldn't lift any more weights, and my legs where as strong as they would get from gym time and roadwork. The punishment your knees and body absorb while catching couldn't be duplicated in the gym or on the road, and if it could, I wasn't able to figure out how. Time to don the tools of ignorance again.

Since I knew the high school coach had his kids throwing inside, I thought I'd give my friend a try. "Hey, it's Harry Shorts. Can you use a practice catcher for your kids in the gym?"

"Didn't know you touched the stuff when it wasn't beach weather. If you can handle it, come on up. We work from six to eight after the basketball teams are done."

"Thanks, coach, I'll see ya tonight."

Catching the kids at the high school, coupled with gym workouts, dominated my life through the following weekend. I was itching for some fun.

On Monday, I rented a minivan and loaded up my skiing gear and provisions for the trip north. The provisions consisted mostly of Absolut, Bud and munchies. You can go without real food for days in an emergency, but munchies are a necessity. I speak from experience here, and if you don't believe me, go ahead and try it. You'll kill for a Funny Bone or Yankee Doodle before long.

The Ebil was getting ready to close up shop when I rolled in late that afternoon for a few hours of paper and PC work. He must have had the old bag out again because he looked pissed at the world.

"What's up, Mel?" didn't improve his demeanor one bit.

"My ass is dragging lower than snail snot, and the old bitch just called to tell me she bought a place in Sands Point yesterday for $1.3 million. I told her how nice for her, but what I wanted to say was 'fuck you, the horse you rode in on, and your $1.3 million.' "

"Sorry to hear that, big guy. A few cold ones across the street to drown your sorrows might help you feel a lot better."

"On top of that shit, I'm getting dragged to some black tie benefit fiasco that's costing me $250 a pop. Do I look like I need to piss away five hundred big ones for rubber chicken and worthless shithead speeches?"

"You're on a roll, and it seems the carousel ain't stopping any time soon," I tried, with the hope of wallowing in pity with him for a sec. It didn't work and he stormed out with a "Lock the door when you leave, or don't lock it for all I care." That was all that needed to be said.

After I updated my file with the recent events, I printed a copy for my records and one to send to Randy to show him he was getting something for his buck. I neglected to include Dana in my report, as it was immaterial to the facts at hand. Randy probably already knew more than I would want him to know right about now on that subject. How I might explain a few of the Arizona expenses would be tricky, but creative accounting has always been one of my strong points. Results are what count, and the road I take to get them sometimes has a few bends and dips you have to be able to bear.

da bushes

Locked up and couldn't decide between bellying up across the street for a few hours or heading home to get ready for tomorrow's trip. The good Harry twin won again, and I hoofed it up the block to the tree house, planning on hitting the sack early. As I walked up the driveway, Mrs. Taylor was pulling in at the same time.

"Hi, Harry," she said as she reached into the back seat of her car for what looked like the results of a rations trip to the local grocery store. "If you're not busy, Harry, it's freezing out here, and I can't carry all of this in one shot. Be a doll, grab my box and come inside."

She turned, took two steps toward her door before stopping dead in her tracks. She was as red as a beet as she turned around and said, "I can't believe that came out the way it sounded. You did get what I intended, didn't you, Harry?"

"That depends on what you actually intended, I guess," I managed to get out while trying to play the cool one.

"Very clever, Harry. Very clever indeed. Now pick up the box of groceries from the back of the car and bring them inside, please and thank you" was her reply as she again turned and headed for her front door without waiting for an answer from me. I did as instructed and wondered what the hell was gonna happen next.

"Put it on the counter over there, Harry. Did you manage to get the car door closed?"

She was removing her coat and looked just as good up close with all her clothes on. I never figured using binoculars for a closer view during her summer sunbathing days was a cool idea at the time. I was regretting that decision right about now.

"Yes I did, Mrs. Taylor," and got scolded again for not calling her Sandy. "Right after I grabbed the box and was getting ready to come inside," I said with a mischievous smile I have perfected for just such a time and place.

"You will have to do a lot more than just grab the box if you expect to come inside, Harry" was her reply. With that she threw a lip-lock on me that nearly sucked the breath right out of my body. The "Down the Hall two-step" was a tough dance to master while trying to get our clothes off without letting go of each other. She must have taken the same lessons I did, since we hit the bed, sans clothing, still in full hot-blooded embrace.

You learn at the oddest times that older can indeed be better for some things in life. Sandy was equal parts voracious tiger and playful kitten for the next two hours of our lives. Having been around a lady or two myself, we meshed beautifully. Large firm breasts with nipples the size of silver dollars. I could have sucked on them forever, which would have been fine with Sandy 'cause they seemed to be a rather hot erogenous zone for her. We took turns enjoying each other, pleasing one another, never seeming to go wrong in anything we tried or did. Thoroughly satisfied beyond our wildest dreams, we climaxed with me entering her from behind, finishing the way we began as I "came inside the box," as previously instructed by my elder. When Sandy repeated that comment, we laughed about it hysterically as we lay there exhausted and content. Some time later we fell asleep by necessity.

It was 10:30 p.m. when we finally drifted back to the world of the living, awakened by the sound of that damned fire station alarm blaring in the distance. Sandy's nipples looked a little dry, so I dutifully moistened them for her, for which she was most grateful. I assume there were parts of me that were dry also, as Sandy went about moistening them as well, which led to what you might expect it would. She finished on top this time, rode me till she had no strength left.

Later, we showered, and I left with the feeling that a meaningful friendship based on mutual need had been formed. There is no way to explain it, but I just knew it was right and would be good for both of us. I felt better than I had in a long time and slept like a baby that night.

After reading that you are probably off to see your significant other or somebody, so I'll let the two of you do end of chapter period

Chapter 45

To beat the Long Island bridge traffic, you need to get up with the roosters, and dilly-dallying won't do at all. By six the next morning, I was over the bridge and through EZ-Pass on my way to snow country. The headlights probably weren't necessary with my face's residual glow from last night's activities enough to light up the entire road. Man, I was still feeling great. Not even big Mel could have shit on my parade right about now.

I've done my share of long distance driving, and it's funny what occupies your mind during these hours. There was no rhyme or reason for it, but this past Christmas just popped into my head. I missed a whole bunch of them, so I try to make up for it by spoiling the shit out of the kids as much as possible. Sherry gets her share too since I kind of messed up her life a little bit as well. When I feel real bad, I remember the $250K she got and don't feel quite as bad.

We used the same routine as the past coupla years which seems to work pretty well. Sherry insists on going to the kids Mass at St. Mary's ever since Max was Joseph in the Christmas pageant. They do it at the local parish church every Christmas Eve. I swear she will be late for her own funeral and for everything right up to it. We arrived just in the nick of time, and naturally there was bupkiss for seats left. Standing for the entire Mass is my annual punishment I think, and if she didn't hate standing as much as me, I'd swear she does it on purpose.

I managed to make it through another year, and the kids are really cute. It amazes me they use a real live baby and nothing has ever happened. Somebody upstairs must be paying attention and watching over that particular stunt every year.

The annual Christmas list is a trip. If the kids got everything on their two collective lists, Sherry and I would be paupers for eternity. It hurts enough as is, and we only hit about 75% of the big stuff. When they get to this age, it's CD boomboxes and video games that can break the bank. I get much too much for each of them, the rest is Sherry's problem.

After church we go out to dinner, kiddies' choice. This year we went to a new place in town where Max and I pigged out on ribs, the ladies doing their own thing, just slightly neater than the guys, thank God. Ribs and beer is manna from heaven, and I figured that on the day before such a high holy day, it was appropriate. The little guy is acquiring quite a taste for ribs, just like his not-so-old man. It's nice to eat with the kids and they like it, too. Sherry, she tolerates on the outside, but secretly loves seeing her kids happy and content. As long as it is only temporary – she does remember who and what I am, and what roads we have been down. Contrary to popular belief, time does not heal all wounds.

Christmas morning is for them; we all open one present on Christmas Eve so I can enjoy a little touch of the fun. The big people get to pick what they open, so I chose the new baseball computer game that I bought Max; Brianne got her boombox. If they didn't like them, war would have ensued, but peace reigned as they jumped for joy. They chipped in and got me a baseball tie with the Mick's picture on it; I was thrilled and touched. Through it all, the kids don't mind me too much and really love our Christmas tradition.

Sherry was busying herself with eggnog and munchies, so I moseyed on into the kitchen and gave her the Christmas present I got for her. She is into that Riverdance shit, so I got her two tickets to Radio City – fifth row center. That took some doing, not to mention many extra hard-earned greenbacks. I knew it was something she was dying to do and never would have gone out and bought the tickets herself.

"Harry, you never cease to amaze me," as she gave me a sweet kiss on the cheek.

At that very moment, I remembered the first time she gave me one of those sweet kisses on the cheek a long time ago. For the sake of my mean P.I. reputation, I beat it out of there, headed over to Publicans to

da bushes

spend Christmas Eve with the rest of the don't-haves like me. Luckily, after Midnight Mass, the place fills up and the crowd stays to celebrate with their friends. I know enough people to manage to blow through the night and leave before I'm one of the last cowboys there. Could be worse, I guess.

I really don't mind too much, and maybe some day it will be different. For now, you play the cards you're dealt and try and make the best of them. When I was away, it didn't bother me as much, but seeing the kids this time of year is great and sucks. Unless you been there, you can't appreciate how it is.

My cell phone chirped and jolted me back to reality. Better get it and keep on motoring, so end of chapter period

Chapter 46

The ride up to New England is beautiful when the weather is nice and the trees are in bloom. In the dead of winter, it's a chore to push yourself to continue on with nothing to look at but bare trees and gray mush left over from our last snow. I've done it enough to know.

My folks and sisters moved to upstate New York, leaving Queens for good some time ago. I realized I never gave you a rundown on my family, the whos and wheres of the clan. You got bits and pieces, but a complete inventory might be in order. If you don't care, I don't really give a shit – you'll have to put up with it for the good of the whole. I always loved that line – the good of the whole. What unadulterated bullshit!

Anyway, we grew up in Queens, New York in a place called Woodside, which is famous for nothing that I know of. We later move to Flushing when I was in high school, which is famous for the World's Fair that was held in Flushing Meadows Park in '64 or so. We weren't poor and we weren't rich, but we did survive and everybody got by. Most of Woodside and Flushing are like that, and if you don't know anything else, you're happy, I guess.

Two younger brothers, Todd and Mike, who also played ball and got partial scholarships, one to NYU and the other to some hick college in the South. They both worked their asses off to pay for the rest of school and actually did pretty well for themselves. The younger hick's still down south in one of the Carolinas working as an assistant baseball coach, teaching something. The older one got the acting bug and majored in drama, of all things. Stared in a few productions so far off-Broadway you would have needed a map to find Broadway. But he keeps working, lives in Soho with his girlfriend of the month, which is

da bushes

a neat place to live. Last time I talked to him he was auditioning for a big part and I wished him luck. We don't exactly talk every week, but I have some friends who keep me informed on a regular basis.

He's my cool-assed brother; everyone should have one.

My parents moved to a small burg in upstate New York, a one-light town north of Hunter Mountain, about twenty-five miles south of Albany. I used to go up and visit for a few days, which was all I could take. When you've been around, small towns get even smaller. They bought a big old Victorian with tons of rooms for when all the kids would come to visit. They did Thanksgiving every year, and if I were in that part of the country, I'd always make an effort to get there. When Mom stopped talking to me altogether, I kind of shied away from the family gatherings. I sneak in to see my sisters and their kids when I head up that way.

My older sister Sally has a pair of rugrats and married a gym teacher, which is cool, since she teaches kindergarten in the same school district. Pretty sure that's where they met, and it makes total sense if you think about it. Sally's thinking of doing some childcare and home schooling in their house, which is pretty big. They are in idon'tknowheresville, New York, don't forget.

The baby of the family lives in the next town over and has her own pair of munchkins running around. Brother-in-law #3 drives a rig, and Meg baby-sits to help make ends meet. She is dynamite with kids and has a waiting list to get in. I always tell her she should be the one doing the childcare gig. Little sisters don't ever listen to their much smarter older brother.

Anyway, no time to stop by this trip. Maybe on the flip side, if all goes well, and I can swing it heading back home. That's the long and short of it, and I'm sure you'll get to meet them some day soon.

I'm rolling through Hartford, and for me this particular road switch is always tricky, so I'm gonna concentrate on it; you can concentrate on end of chapter period

Chapter 47

Rusty must have been waiting for me to arrive. He was out the door and in the van before I could confirm the address and that it was his house. It wasn't actually his house, since he lives at home with his parents, but close enough for P.I. work.

Typical twenty-year-old, only bigger than most. He wore jeans and a ski parka hung on a six foot three inch frame that carried about 220 pounds. The longish dirty-blond hair surprised me, but I later found out it was only his winter rebellion from his in-season buzz cut. The duffel he threw in the back wasn't very big, so I guessed we wouldn't be going anywhere formal while at Stratton.

Oh yeah, snowboard, not skis, a typical twenties kind of thing.

"You must have left pretty early to be here by now," he said as he began to adjust the radio station for tunes better suited to his age bracket. This rap shit just doesn't cut it for me one bit.

"If you don't get motoring before rush hour, the traffic in New York can choke you to death. I must have been on the road by 6:00 a.m., brought my mondo-mug of coffee so I wouldn't have to stop."

"Great! I can't wait to see Smokes and hit the trails. Smokes is gonna blow you away at first, but after you get to know him, he's cool. If he couldn't throw the way he does, he'd probably be growing his own and selling, living in some hippie commune haven. He can be a bit far-out at times."

We hit the road and Rusty took me his way, which was probably shorter than the route I had mapped out. Unless we got held up somewhere, we would be at Smokes by early afternoon and rolling into Stratton just in time for happy hour. Tomorrow the slopes, and with any luck at all, I will solidify my assumptions some time after

da bushes

that.

"Bobby and Howdy called to tell me you were cool. They said to say thanks again for the food and brews. They are tight and have a big say in the clubhouse when the season's on. Lot of guys just play ball and hope to move on to the next level without causing any ruckus. They stand up and definitely get counted. If you're cool with them, it's a solid you'll do fine with the rest of the guys on the Schooners. Thought you might want to know that."

"Good guys, both of them, and anybody who jumps up to watch my back before I even know them are good people in my book. I appreciate the heads up though," which was the truth. Always good to know who runs the show before you join the circus.

Grabbed some gas and grub at a service stop and kept on truckin'. No good way to introduce last year's failure, so I didn't try and make it good. I just jumped in with "So, give me the Rusty Jask version of last year's Schooners."

Rusty must have known it was coming sooner or later, and had obviously spent some time organizing his thoughts. Articulate might be pushing it a bit, but he could express himself without any problem at all.

"Me and Smokes were just eating up the comp in the first half. Danny and Billy Wong were right behind us, and Slam was banging the door shut every chance he got. The guys were taking batting practice during games, and the coaches were pushing every button like they had already read the script. It was beautiful to watch, man, and even better to be a part of it. Harry, we were something to behold, and the press ate it up."

He stopped to take a drink of his Big Gulp, and you could see he was struggling to hold on to his temper and his cool.

"The All-Star break didn't slow us down, and we kept rolling along like a well-oiled machine. I've tried to pinpoint something, or some time, that started the unraveling, but I can't, and I don't know why. A couple of long fly balls stayed in the park late in games that we lost, or a bad pitch was hit out to kill us. I couldn't seem to get the same zip on the ball; my brain was telling my muscles what to do, but it's as if they had gone deaf. When it went bad, everybody tanked together, and we couldn't fight our way out. The snowball headed down hill, getting bigger and bigger, picking up everything in it's sights as it went. Harry, man, it was weird, and kept getting weirder."

Trying to get him off himself for a breather, I pointed him in a different direction that we would have covered eventually. I didn't need him getting all bent out of shape before the trip even got started.

"What were the coaches doing and what about the routine?"

"Interesting question, Harry. Do me a solid and pull off to the side, will ya. I gotta take a leak." So did I, so we did just that, and you can do the same instead of waiting for us while I signal for end of chapter period

Chapter 48

Back on the road and you could tell Rusty was giving my question some deep thought. He was revved on the team situation and needed to shift gears to answer this one. I guess he figured out how to go forward since he started up again without me having to urge him to jump back in.

"The coaching staff was on automatic pilot the first half. That's not meant to put down the coaches, we were just that flat-out good. Scootch kept the pitchers on their schedules, both throwing and running. We had our daily ration of vitamin C and salt pills that Punch doled out. The salt pills seemed to double when the weather started to get really hot. Both Doc and Punch handled pre-game and between start rubdowns. We just followed the chart, did what we were told."

"Let me interrupt a sec," I said at that moment. "Who had the responsibility for the chart you just mentioned, and what was it for?"

"The chart was the 'gospel according to Punch,' as we used to call it. It seemed to most of the guys that he had more authority than the other coaches. We couldn't figure out why he did stuff that you would have expected Doc to handle. Rumor had it he had Teddy's ear and let the other coaches know it. But still, nobody fucked with Coach Curran, period, and he kept a little sanity when it turned into a nuthouse."

"What stuff?"

"The daily ration of pills, for one thing. Doc ordered them and separated each player's weekly allotment, but Punch put them in your locker every day, yelled your ass raw if you didn't take them. What were we, little kids, for Christ's sake? Those pills go back to somebody's college days, I think. And the rubdowns were scheduled for Doc to do some, the team massage guru had a piece, and that freak from the outside did too many as far as the pitchers were concerned. It seemed he did most of the pitchers in the second half, especially the players with injuries. Nobody had a handle on it, but you didn't dare question Punch."

"What about Doc? Didn't he bitch about it to anybody?"

"Yeah, one time. Teddy told him never to question his directions in front of the whole team. Dressed him down good and we all felt bad for Doc – he's all right in our book."

The arrows kept smacking all over the target, but nothing hit the bull's-eye to give me that one undeniable fact that would put me over the edge. I knew I had it, but couldn't prove anything yet. Hard work pays off, and I wasn't done yet.

"Fuck it," I said. "Let's forget this shit for awhile. We can pick it up later when we have Smokes along for the ride. Plenty of time to rehash old shit later." There was no reason to get him totally bummed out this early in the trip.

We were about thirty miles from getting Smokes in Brattleboro, with a clear shot from there to Stratton. Before you know it we would be unloading at the condo that was perfectly located halfway up the entrance road to the mountain slopes, getting ready for a few days of doggin' the trails in the light and the ladies after dark. Can't rule out the daylight hours for that activity either, 'cause as I've stated before, "one never know, do one!" The condo sleeps ten and there are only three of us so far, but the potential is limitless.

Me and Rusty are gonna tone it down a notch and bullshit about sports for awhile, so find something else to do, and take end of chapter period with you

Chapter 49

"Look what the cat dragged in" would have been an appropriate expression for the likes of Smokes when he fell out the front door of his mobile home and stumbled his way to the van. Tee shirt and shorts, no jacket, carrying a plastic garbage bag that I could only guess had his ski duds and other threads. The chick that followed him out was dragging his board and bomber jacket in one hand, boots in the other. She was further gone than him and a true sight to behold. The cold was doing its thing naturally, her rock hard nipples clearly visible through the skin-tight tank top that was fighting to restrain her ample breasts.

"Typical Smokes and better than usual fuck-of-the-month" was all Rusty could think of as he took in the show and shook his head.

Loaded his crap in the back, gave sweets a squeeze and pat on the ass, and said, "I'll see ya when I do." Have to remember that classic line for when I get my own FOTM. It sounds like a killer.

Smokes greeted Rusty with a "Looking good, dude," and eyed me up and down, lids at half-mast. "I'll check you later" seemed to be addressed in my direction, and he was fast asleep before I could even get the car in gear. Sweets was headed for the warmth of the indoors, the rear view we were treated to just as impressive as the front. With Rusty's permission we lingered a minute, admiring what nature had wrought, and then headed for Stratton.

"This the usual show, or was I subjected to a command performance? Could be a long coupla days based on that start."

"Nah, he's not bad in public" was Rusty's assessment, and I had to take him at his word. I also realized it was me who was asking and figured I had been there, done that much more than once. Maybe not quite up to Smokes' standards, but in the ballpark at least.

Quiet time seemed to intervene, and we mellowed to James Taylor mixed with Smokes' snoring for the rest of the trip. Baby James is another of my faves, and they tend to get plenty of wear and tear when they hit the list. Rusty even seemed to dig this one. You'll catch the rest of them as we progress, I'm sure.

It was dark by the time we landed, and we were all bushed. I had been on the road all day and Rusty was mentally zonked from our discussion tacked on to the trip. Smokes had other reasons I'm sure I would see in living color before we were through. We each grabbed a room, the master suite mine since I hooked us up in the first place. Nice digs that would make us very comfortable for a few days. Hell, it was better than most houses I had been in.

Here's the tour: A-frame, but a big one, that had a wrap-around deck fixed to three-quarters of the first floor. A two-car garage under the deck led to the mudroom where we kept the skis and snowboards on neat racks built into the walls. Even had little cubbyholes for gloves and hats, boots, and that kind of shit right next to the racks. The whole room was heated so your boots would be nice and warm before you started the day. Nothing worse than having cold boots – they stay cold all day; your feet follow their lead.

Up the stairs you enter the main room, which doubles as living/dining room big enough for half-court basketball games. The kitchen is full service with a ten-foot long counter separating it from the dining area. Three bedrooms including the master down a long hall, stairs leading up to the loft that had bunks for four more. It was all homey and comfortable, built for families, or nutjobs like us.

The shower on the back end of the three S's felt good and I was now ready to kick-start this adventure. I decided to shit-can the name Smokes for awhile and would use Rusty and Joe. At least trying to was my plan for the time being.

The provisions I brought were enough to prime us for the evening's revelry. Bud and munchies for dinner after a round of Gimlets to start the juices flowing. The Schooners were a distant memory for now, which was fine with everyone present. I will get what I need over the next coupla days letting these two spit it out when they were ready.

da bushes

We hit Stratton Village looking to party hardy for all we were worth, and a tad more. Joe had rallied and could be a ton-a-fun when he got rolling, and man was he rolling. He took the pool table downstairs and owned it all night, mixing equal amounts of beer and babes between shots. Rusty had on this clown hat the snowboarders favor while entertaining the crowd with dynamite imitations, a verifiable blond bombshell hanging all over him. Me, I was quietly enjoying an intimate conversation with an overly friendly Julia Roberts wannabe, periodically interrupted by fits of crazy gyrations on the dance floor. You could say the boys were enjoying their first night at Stratton.

Before we knew it the house was full of bodies, all of them heading for bedrooms and unscheduled flights of ecstasy. My flight plan was properly filed and definitely came to rest at the right destination, while yours is headed for end of chapter period

Chapter 50

"Woke up this morning and got myself a beer." That happens to be a classic line from one of Jim Morrison's Doors hits, and every once in awhile seems like the thing to do. In fact, it was beers all around as the three musketeers of A-Frame troop were soaking in the hot tub that resides on the deck off the living room sliding glass doors.

It was early and the ladies were still sacked out, which gave us a chance to clear our heads, and they definitely needed clearing. At least mine did, and I was the most coherent of the three when last we parted ways. While I am a trained P.I., this is one you can definitely try without following in my footsteps. We were out in the cold fresh air at a temperature of, oh, say 25 degrees, the snow fluttering down, while we sat in the hot tub like it was summer time. It is the greatest feeling to be leaning back, buffeted by jets of hot water firmly massaging your body while snow gently comes to rest on your face. If you haven't tried it, try it, you'll like it. Private investigator license not required.

Rusty and Joe were nursing medium brain blasters, but rallying fine. I figured now was as good a time as any; who knows when we might be together alone again. Like my last approach to Rusty on the subject, head-on seemed the way to go.

"Rusty gave me a feel for last season on the way up, Joe. What's your story? Don't try and put it into the right words, just let 'em flow."

Smokes wasn't as prepared as Rusty had been when I asked the question in the car on the ride up. He stared at me as a look of disgust came over his face. It was like a mask had magically appeared, changing the person. Joe was gone, and somebody else was with us in the hot tub. It didn't seem to bother Rusty if he noticed it, but it caught my attention and spooked me a bit.

da bushes

I didn't know what to do when Smokes drained his Bud and got out of the tub. Going after him was an option, but not one I wanted to make use of right about now. I gotta tell ya, kiddos, the transformation was eerie.

"Cool it, Harry, he'll be back. When Smokes gets flustered, he trips out, walks a circle or two, and when he's ready, he plops down right where he came from. Relax and enjoy."

So I relaxed and enjoyed to the best of my ability, which was minimal at this juncture. If Rusty was right, Joe would return and be back to normal, or at least normal for him. Who was gonna return was a question, and I had to trust Rusty knew what he was talking about from past experience.

And he did. Smokes was gone probably ten minutes returning with more liquid breakfast and his old face. Like nothing happened, he jumped in the tub, handed us our beers, and started right in.

"Ya freaked me, man. I was in a cool place and ya brought me back too fast. Sorry to bolt on ya like that. Just gimme a second and I'll spill."

Rusty gave me a look that said he was back and just let him get to it in his own time. I wasn't going anywhere, so I did just that. It didn't take long.

"Harry, you probably remember Ron Guidry from the old Yanks. Same size as me and nobody could figure how he brought it so hard. I go five ten, maybe 165 soaking wet on a good day. Boggles even me some days when I get it up into the high 90's with no effort at all. Guys like me and Guidry shouldn't be able to throw that hard, but it is what it is. I never gave it a thought, I just did it, and it was always there for me."

Odd, but this semi-hippie freaky kid had a brain on his shoulders and knew where he was coming from. Judging the book by its cover almost fucked me over on this one. I try not to make rash judgements on people normally, but Smokes must have been an exception.

"I had been feeling gooed-up, and then one day it didn't come at all. Stiff was my first thought, but not stiff like the day after you throw a game stiffness. I was doing my day three throwing big workout and couldn't get the extension, or something. Man, my arm felt short and my muscles just felt cramped. Science ain't my bag, man, but I knew it wasn't right. Coach told me to stretch it out, but it didn't help, and I went in for a rub. It got worse and never came back. I need my body to work to do my thing, man. It quit on me and bummed me bad. It just went to shit and no rubs or anything else that we did could help. I coulda been the Dead Sea between drinking water like a camel and the salt pills. And the herbal tea tasted like shit. "

"What's gooed-up, Smokes? And what tea?" I asked.

"Your muscles feel kinda gunked up and your body slows down a notch. You wanna get it going but your body just doesn't cooperate, like it never did it before, or didn't know how, man. The tea was supposed to have extra minerals or something. Coach Tennly swore it was gonna help, and we needed something to jump-jive our system."

Rusty hadn't said a word to this point, but what Joe said seemed to hit a nerve. "That's a good way to describe it. It was like you needed your oil changed, like something was gumming up the works."

The tea needed following up. I had what I needed and that was good, 'cause at that moment the ladies appeared like floating apparitions from around the corner of the deck with a pitcher of Gimlets and a box of Twinkies – breakfast of champions. And they weren't dressed for the slopes, not by a long shot.

End of morning skiing and end of chapter period

Chapter 51

We finally hit the slopes that afternoon and got in about five runs. Rusty proved to be the same level as me – middle of the road intermediate and somewhat conservative. We were out to enjoy the mountain and get in some hard runs, sticking to our limitations. Smokes, on the other hand, was an out-and-out hot dog, but a damn good one. He hit all the jumps he could find and mogeled his brains out, leaving Rusty and me to only watch in amazement. He took a few tumbles that would have made the Wide World of Sports highlight films, but just got up and went at it even harder. Oh, to be young and foolish again – well, maybe young at least. I do foolish just fine already.

The second night the phone rang around midnight and we looked at it like, "Who the fuck could that be?" My guy's place, so I picked it up and said, "Yeah." It was pretty noisy and I could barely hear the person on the other end of the line. When I realized who it was, I felt bad I hadn't called him in awhile.

"Tom, how are you, and how did you track me down up here? Rusty and Joe are here with me."

"I know, Harry, that's one of the reasons I called. Haven't spoken to them since the season ended and I kinda miss the two assholes. I tried earlier but I guess you guys must have been out for pizza and a soda. Why don't you let me bullshit with them a minute and then we can talk."

They were in the kitchen watching the gals make popcorn, all of them whooping up a storm.

"Hey, quiet down a notch, will ya. You're never gonna guess who's on the horn."

Rusty came over and grabbed the receiver and said, "So who's got the balls to intrude on my good times?"

"It's Westy, you no good rag-armed poor excuse for a pitcher. Long time no talk."

"Westy, you son of a bitch. I heard you tripped on a sidewalk crack and dented your head a bit. Can't play ball, so you go the sympathy route for attention. Nice trick. How the fuck are ya, bud?"

"Good to know you still love me, Rusty. I've been better and I'm not sure if I can say I've been worse. My hard head saved me and the wrist is gonna be in a cast for a month. All things considered, I'm not too bad, I guess. Next time I'll try another method of getting attention as you so aptly put it. How you feeling?"

"Ego's still fairly bruised, but the body's back to normal. It took all I could to forget what happened and push myself to work it back into shape. Not quite there, but close enough."

"In case you haven't figured it out yet, Rusty, Harry is good people. Stick with him and you guys will be right back on top next season. I'll come out and catch a few games – well, I'll come and see ya play a few at least. How's Smokes?"

"Crazy as ever, but still alive and kicking. But after seeing him on the slopes today, you would think the boy has a death wish. Something not quite right upstairs with that guy. He's entertaining the guests at the moment – I'll tell him you asked about him. He's not a phone kinda guy, as you know. Be good, Westy, and I'll see ya soon I hope." With that Rusty was off; I think it hurt him a bit to talk to Tom.

"I'm back, Tom. What's up?"

"Ms. Timmons told me where you were, and I debated about bothering you while you're on R&R, or is it business as well?"

"Bit of both. Kind of killing two birds with one stone. I needed to get away before heading for Florida and wanted to see these two guys, too. You OK?"

"I'm fine, Harry. It's good to be at home and the headaches are almost gone. The wrist is gonna piss me off till I get the cast off, but I'll cope. Didn't realize how tough it is to do everything with your left hand when you aren't used to it. Try shaving or wiping your ass with only your left hand sometime. It sucks."

da bushes

"I'll take your word for it, Tom. Now, you didn't call to ask about Smokes, or just to tell me your left hand smells like shit. What's up for real?"

"With nothing but time on my hands, I've been doing more of the research I started after the season ended. I've come up with some interesting stuff and I think you would be interested too, Harry. When you get back, give me a call, let's get together so I can show you what I've got."

"You're on, Tom. I should be home Friday, and maybe I'll take a ride up Saturday afternoon if you feel up to it? And by the way, give that herbal tea you guys were drinking a thought or two."

"Will do. Saturday would be great. And Harry, Ms. Timmons said to say hi."

I went back to partying, my mind somewhere else. Ms. Timmons for one thing, and what Tom found for another were occupying my brain – that is until Julia the 2nd hopped in my lap and jump-started my dipstick. Unless I'm mistaken, morning skiing doesn't have a shot in hell.

See ya for lunch and end of chapter period

Chapter 52

The drive home, which consisted mostly of me driving and the boys sleeping, was a long haul. We split on Friday morning, as planned, after Thursday's hard afternoon of slope work and even harder evening of partying. Late in the afternoon we took the gondola to the top of the mountain. It was snowing, and the whole world was white and beautiful from where I stood. Rusty hung with me on the way down the intermediate path, and Smokes took his posse on a kamikaze mission down the double diamond trails. Somehow we all made it in one piece.

Don't know what these two guys do during the season, but the off-season has no bounds. For an old guy, I'd say I hung in pretty well. A few bumps and a black and blue or two, but no permanent damage to report. Maybe I am actually mellowing as I get older.

Smokes departed at Brattleboro with no sign of a welcoming party. Perhaps the FOTM had moved on, or maybe she was out doing the weekly grocery shopping. You can judge that one for yourself. Reminds me of my grocery shopping and Sandy escapade, but I digress as usual. Not a bad digression though, if I do say so myself.

"Hang in, man. See ya in Florida" was all we got from Smokes. Remind me to find out who his speechwriter is.

We started up again, and Rusty sacked it almost immediately. Left me to my thoughts and where I was going from here. These guys gave me the same impressions I got in Florida with a small tidbit thrown in here and there. Tom's research will be a welcome addition to my own and that of Ms. Timmons, I expected. Unless I was mistaken, talking to Scoot Munoz wouldn't be beneficial for anything more than further confirmation of what I already knew. Any additional information would have to come from an unlikely source, or by surprise. Who, or what,

da bushes

would do that, I wondered.

I was back to having lots of information from research and "field investigation" work to process with more to come in the next coupla days. Maybe the whole picture will crystallize a bit more after I digest this chunk. The only other piece to the puzzle left to look at was Richie Collins, the reserve infielder from Michigan State who stayed on to work in the marketing department after the season ended. Why didn't he get better like everyone else after the year was over? He could be that unlikely source you always hope to uncover, or he could be a wild goose chase. Why not, what have I got to lose? He's still in Bayport, and I'll call and set up something as soon as I get back.

Dumped Rusty at his place and kept on motoring. The more I tossed this puppy around in my head, the more I came up with the same answer. Who, and some version of how, seemed to be there. The exact method would be confirmed soon, I hoped, if all things worked out as I thought they would. The why was still a little fuzzy, but I was confident that would straighten itself out when all the pieces fell into place.

A trip to Florida and a summer of baseball in Bayport loomed on the horizon. What if I solved this baby before that transpired? Probably won't happen, kiddo.

Ms. Timmons said to say hi, did she? Have to hope for rain soon to make use of one of my rainchecks, while the best you can hope for is end of chapter period

Chapter 53

"Hello Mrs. Westbrook, it's Harry Shorts. I'm on my way back from Vermont and thought I'd try Tom, check if he was up to seeing me tomorrow. I know he's probably tired, but is there any chance he's available?"

As long as I was going to be stuck in the car for several more hours, I might as well make use of my time, set up a few things if I could. Tom was one, the marketing kid the second target for now.

"Hi, Harry. It's good of you to call. I know Tom is anxious to see you, and I'm sure it would do him well to talk to you. If you can hold a minute, I'll see if he's up."

"Where are you, Harry?"

"I'm in the car on the way back. Just dropped off Rusty an hour ago, and figured I'd take a shot, see if you were around."

"Where the fuck am I gonna be, Harry?"

"Not what I meant, you dumb shit, and you know it. Don't break my balls, will ya. I just spent a few days with Smokes and need sympathy."

"Sympathy my ass, Harry. What you probably need is a splint for your dick if I know those two guys. Am I right?"

"Maybe not a splint, but a soft cast wouldn't hurt!"

"You're a stitch, Harry. When you coming up?"

"If tomorrow's good, I planned on driving up after breakfast. You able to get around, or are you being waited on hand and foot by the family servants?"

"Shove the servant bullshit, Harry. I hear the doorbell every once in awhile when it doesn't actually ring, but all in all, I'm not getting around too bad. The wrist is a pain, though."

da bushes

"How's lunch sound? I'll get you out for a few hours and we can shoot the shit. Bring the results of your research with you and we can put our heads together a bit. You game?"

"Count me in, Harry. I hear you're a ribs guy, and so am I. We can do the same place Dad suggested if you liked it."

"The ribs were out of this world and the slaw was great. Beer didn't hurt the meal either; that joint will do just fine. Noon OK with you?"

"Harry, I may even get out of my PJ's for you. Noon it is and I'm really looking forward to it. See ya then."

That took care of the first item, and it was gonna be good to see Westy. I'm sure he was dying to get out of the house anyway. The inactivity must be a bitch for a guy used to running all the time.

The other appointment was a little trickier. Didn't have a clue where to call Collins, and it was hit or miss to call the Schooners offices on a Friday afternoon. Worth a shot, I figured. The major problem was I didn't have access to my Schooner team player info right now.

"Information for Bayport, N.Y. please," I said to the operator. "Business listing for the Bayport Schooners."

"Hold the line, please."

The operator came back and gave me the number, but as it was kind of hard to drive and write it down at the same time, I opted for letting her connect me. Trundle's dime.

"Bayport Schooners, may I help you?"

Caught off guard again, I stammered something unintelligible.

"I'm sorry, I didn't understand. Could you repeat that please?"

"I'm looking for Richie Collins, who works in the marketing department, I believe. Is he available by any chance?"

"Mr. Collins is out of the office at the moment, but you may be able to reach him on his cell phone."

She gave me the number, and I managed to write it down and dial the number without causing a major accident. Had to keep this number since I may need it again if I don't get him right away.

"Richie Collins – can I help you?"

I was on a major roll and had that lucky feeling again.

"This is Harry Shorts. I got your number from the Bayport Schooners office. I'm going to be a player coach for the Schooners next season, and I was wondering if I could talk to you for a few minutes about last year, and the coming season as well. How you feeling by the way?"

"Heard about you from some of the guys. I was beginning to think only stars rated a call from the new coach. I'm still feeling lousy, but not as bad as during the season."

"Everybody's a star at one time or another, Richie. Just takes time to get around to calling everybody with this many guys spread out all over the place. There are not just players, but coaches, too. Think we can get together?"

"You bet, Harry. Where do you hang your hat these days?"

"I'm in Manhasset, but I can meet you wherever you want to make it easier for you."

"How's breakfast Sunday at the IHOP on Northern Boulevard sound? You know the place, don't you?"

"Know it well. Meet you at nine Sunday. OK?"

"Sounds good."

Two for two, both of them easy as pie. Any more good luck and this case may solve itself without my help. But not before the season gets going, and certainly not before Florida. Two things were still bugging me big time – why did they do it, and Randy's instruction to let Teddy be.

From our earlier conversations, you are aware that I know IHOP as well as you know end of chapter period

Chapter 54

Saturday morning turned out to be for shit. It was one of those winter days that couldn't decide what it wanted to do, so it did it all. There was an inch of snow on the ground when I got up, and that was the good news. Freezing rain was now falling, with the temperature ideal for a tree-snapping ice storm. Ms. Weatherlady missed this one by a mile. Later on the temp was gonna drop like a rock, and snow was supposed to lay a blanket on top of the ice.

"Hey Tom, no way I can get up there today with the shit that's happening outside. Sorry, man."

"Hey, Harry, I was just about to call you. The streets up here are all covered with a sheet of ice and the whole town's shut down. Don't even think about coming this way."

"Why don't we cover a few things and I'll swing up your way next week some day? You have time now, or would later be better?"

"Well, I was just about to bang the entire harem, but I guess they can wait a little bit. Cartoons will keep them busy for the time being."

"Very funny, Mr. Wise Ass. You must have gotten conked pretty good to dream that one up, you low-life invalid. What cartoons by the way?"

"Never mind, Harry. Let me give you what I have and you can unscramble it since you're the famous private investigator. We both agree on the suspected items that could have something to do with the entry into the body. Pills and liquid were there in large quantities, but we don't have anything to test. The team tested the water and a lab tested the vitamin C/salt tablets/vitamin booster pills during the season – everything came up clean. The team used methyl of wintergreen for rubdowns and that tested clean, too. So how was it introduced?"

"Excuse me, Tom, but that doesn't tell me shit. Questions I have, a few answers would help."

"If I may continue, Harry. We agree on what it could be, but you are right – what was it that did the deed? I've isolated a substance that is medicinal at times, a poison at others. It would take some doing but it could be introduced in multiple forms, some of which fit our suppositions. I need some additional time to confirm a few things and then I'll be ready to clue you in. Harry, if I'm right, we have a couple of devious people who need to be punished."

"Tom, that's great work if you are right. If we are lucky, maybe I can come up with some evidence that will enable us to confirm your research for certain. What's the substance?"

"No, Harry, I'll keep that to myself for now. Give me a little longer and I'll have it sewed up in a neat little package for you. OK?"

"OK, my man. And before I forget, what's with the herbal tea?"

"Part of the package, Harry. Just be patient."

"I'll see ya soon, Tom, and thanks."

Westy was working hard and I needed answers. Hopefully he will be able to provide a few, which will go along with the lovely Ms. Timmons' information from her people's research. I can feel it and taste it, but all for naught if I can't prove it. As Tom indicated, a little patience is needed, which is not Harry Mickey Shorts' strong point.

Tomorrow is another day and this is another end of chapter period

Chapter 55

Saturday was spent punishing my sorry ass on the weight equipment in the extra room in my apartment that saves me when the weather interferes with my life. Yesterday was one of those times, so I pumped iron till I couldn't lift my arms or move my legs. Felt great!

When you're sweating your ass off and pushing your muscles way past where they want to be, décor doesn't really come into play. Plus, it's my room, and nobody else ventures forth into the inner sanctum. The walls are lined with full-size Pamela Anderson and the like posters on one side, my collection of sports memorabilia on the other wall. I've been collecting "stuff" for about five years, dominated by baseball, with basketball and football about twenty-five percent of the total. Occupy your mind with chicks some of the time and admire the greats of the sports world at other times. If you can't dig it, tough turdies on you. It's my life, kiddo.

When I awoke on Sunday, the ice gremlins had done their thing overnight. The branches glistened and the whole world looked like a giant ice sculpture. Man, I have to tell ya, it was beautiful to look at, but it was gonna be a bitch to travel in. I called a guy I know with a big four-wheel drive machine and begged a ride to IHOP. Richie Collins called and confirmed our nine o'clock and told me he had transportation to get there. Maybe he has a tank for special occasions like this.

My bud got me over right around 9:00 a.m. and we had a great time slipping and sliding our way down Northern Boulevard. Why do I do this shit anyway? I could have been tucked away safe and sound in my bed waiting for noon to arrive. But no, I have to be a brave private dick venturing forth into the wilds. Just plain dick is more like it.

"Thanks, but I think the guy over there in the corner booth is waiting for me," I told the cutie of a waitress who recognized me from my Saturday excursions with the kids.

"Coffee?"

"You bet. Where is everybody?" I asked since the place was nearly empty.

"The streets are keeping everyone away for now. When it melts the place will be a madhouse for sure. Coffee's coming right up, dollface." The kids like her, and she likes the kids too. She calls me dollface 'cause she just doesn't know any better. I talk to her very nicely ever since her hubby showed up one Saturday, took up the whole doorway when he came in. Does the term "built like a brick shithouse" mean anything to you?

"Richie, takes balls to come out on a day like this. That your truck in the parking lot sitting on the bank?"

"Yeah, figured I'd stay out of the way and let the other cars have the cleared space. My wheels can go where most vehicles can't." It wasn't a tank, but definitely fell within the tank family.

"So, how you doing?" was about as good as anything to start to ball rolling.

"I'm hanging in considering where I was. Mr. Trundle was a lifesaver offering me this job after the season. I didn't have anything lined up, and I'm not sure what my future is with the team. I guess I'm going down to Florida, but what happens after that is kind of shaky."

"What d'ya mean?" I asked.

"The general manager, Mr. Trundle's son, came in one day and told me the back office staff was being evaluated and my ability to generate ticket sales over the winter was crucial to my future."

"Excuse me, but which Trundle gave you the job?"

"It was Mr. Randle Trundle, Teddy's father, who offered it to me. He said he reviewed the bios for all the guys, saw my marketing degree from college, and asked what I wanted to do after baseball. When I told him I wanted to stay in the game somehow, he offered me the job on the spot. I heard back door the G.M. was steamed, but I can't figure out why. I didn't want to go back to Michigan, especially the way I was feeling."

da bushes

"How's the job going so far?"

"It was real difficult at first. If I was from this area it would have been different, but I was almost starting from scratch. During the season you play ball and travel to away games with not much time for anything else. Rest is important when you are home and a little fun creeps in now and again. I didn't have a clue about businesses in the immediate area, or Long Island as a whole. Plus, I felt like shit on top of that. It was a struggle, man."

"What got you started?"

"It wasn't what, but who. Mr. Trundle, Teddy's father, pointed me toward one of the big insurance companies out on the Island, which led me to insurance agencies, and a bunch of other contacts. Without that boost I might have packed it in and gone home. Cold calls and rejection were killing me up to that point in time."

"He is something, the old man," I said. "So you will be staying on with the Schooners if the baseball side doesn't work out?"

"I'm gonna give it a shot in the spring, and if I don't see anything long range, I'll go the business end, if the G.M. lets me."

"What do you mean if he lets you? It sounds like you hit it big in ticket sales. That's what he said you would be evaluated on, didn't he? You should be in like flint."

"You never know with him, and what the hell is 'in like Flint' anyway?"

"Old expression I guy I knew used to use a lot. Don't worry about Teddy. If the old man wants you in, and I think you have a foot in that door, you're in. Trust me on that one, Richie."

"I hope you know what you're talking about Harry, because I like the organizational people I have been working with, and Mr. Trundle Sr. seems to be a fair man. After that slow start I really got on a roll, even got to work on some promo stuff for the ballclub. I feel right at home here."

"I do, and he is, from what I know of him. Now tell me about last season."

As usual, the food showed up just as I got to the meat of the meeting. Never fails of late. We took a few minutes to get everything we needed and started to chow down. I had my usual bunch of everything and offered some of it to Richie. He had a couple of eggs over with bacon and white toast that looked like nothing compared to my truckload of eats. We agreed to tackle the whole mess together. The only thing missing was a pitcher of Bloody Marys, but you can't always have everything.

Richie didn't eat like a minor league baseball player, but like a polite kid from the Midwest, which is exactly what he was. In between bites he told me his tale of woe, and it was a sad one.

"The season was moving along, I was getting into almost every game as a defensive replacement, and starting at least once a week somewhere in the infield. You couldn't exactly say I was setting the world on fire, but I was definitely contributing. Coach Curran told me to keep on doing just what I had done and more time was gonna come my way. In June, I had a few multi-hit games and still hadn't made an error. Fun couldn't describe what we were doing out there – it was a dream run. Unfortunately, we woke up to a freaking disaster."

Richie needed more orange juice and a minute to get his mind squared away. The fuckers screwed with these kids' bodies and heads, and you can just see the pain when you talk to them. As much psychological as physical, I would bet, but it's visible no matter which way you slice it. I don't like this shit one bit, and liking it less and less as I go along.

"Sorry, Harry, it's tougher running it down than I thought it would be."

"Take your time, Richie. I got all day."

"It started slowly, mostly with the pitching staff, and spread to the rest of the guys over a two- to three-week period. We thought it was a mid-season slump and normal tiredness from the grind of playing and traveling. The whole thing was new to some of us who hadn't competed at this level before. But it escalated to the point where we had a tough time putting a team on the field. You don't blow away everybody and then lose to the bottom dwellers of the league. It just devastated the team's morale and we were done. We tried to keep it together, but we just couldn't do it."

da bushes

"Tell me about you in particular. How did you feel while this whole scene was going down, and what happened after the season ended?"

"The ability factor has always had me over a barrel wherever I played, all the way back to Little League. I just plain out-hustled and out-hearted everyone I played with and against my whole life. Too short to play basketball, but I was a star on my high school team, and we almost won a state championship. I've battled to be the best forever and can't afford not to be 100% physically fit to succeed. When this thing hit me, I was a step too slow, two ounces too weak, and not even my heart was able to keep up. That was the worst part, I couldn't fight my way through it like I've done my whole life. I didn't quit, but I was as close as you could imagine."

The kid was a gamer, you could just tell. When the time came to put the guys on the field that you knew would run through a brick wall for you, Richie would have been one of them. Life sure can suck sometimes.

"After the season was over, I thought I'd rest up and get my strength back. The guys I talked to seem to have bounced back, but I couldn't shake it at all. I was busting my butt trying to sell the Schooners and season tickets, but I couldn't generate enough energy to get through each day. It was funny how I started to come out of it and feel better after the supply of pills ran out. I thought they were supposed to be helping me."

"What did you just say?" I asked to make sure I heard him correctly.

"When the team dispersed after the last home stand, I found a batch of vitamins and salt pills in the coaches' room. Since I was gonna be hanging in here for the winter and I didn't think it would do any harm, I took the leftovers to try and help me get back on my feet. Maybe with rest and the pills I could drive it out of my system."

"Whose office were they in?" I asked, hoping to hit the jackpot all in one fell swoop.

That, by the way, is another dumb-fuck saying – what the hell is a "fell swoop" anyway?

"The coaches all used the same room off the players' lounge. The pills were in one of the lockers, and the coaches had all split for home by then. They were on the bottom of the locker behind some old rags.

I guess they fell there and weren't noticed. You're not gonna rat on me, are you, Harry?"

"What the fuck are you talking about, rat on you? Get a grip, Richie, and just listen for a minute. Did you finish all the pills or do you have any left?"

"Well, I'm not sure. The vitamins are gone for sure, but I stopped working out for awhile and didn't take the salt pills. After I started to feel better I just never went back to them. There might be a few left. Why?"

"Just curious, Richie. Do me a favor and check if you have any of them. Where would they be?"

"In my apartment, I guess, if I even have any."

"When you get home, check it out and call me. Here's my home number and an answering service I use. Call me at either one. I'll get back to you. And don't worry, you dumb schmuck – you're cool with me."

Richie smiled for the first time that morning.

We finished up our eats, and he dropped me off at the office. Things had melted some, and I figured I could hoof it up the street to my place later. I needed to get the shit from Tom and Richie down before I forgot any of it. Bits and pieces kept surfacing, with the hope for one biggie always there. That's what cracks a case wide open, and I was gonna get one soon. I could feel it in my bones.

Listen, I'm gonna be busy for a bit, so you take the rest of the morning off and take end of chapter with you

Chapter 56

When you're gonna be gone for a coupla months, there's a ton of stuff you need to set up in advance. Finished with the file update, I contemplated all the shit ahead of me. Instant headache, the ex would say, and it was starting to form a banger in my cranium. Not like I haven't done it before, but then it was "I'm off" with nothing to tie me to. The case was the big thing, but the life and times of Harry Mickey Shorts was important, too. Figured I'd tell you that just incase you forgot how much I value me.

Deep in a trance pondering when the phone rang and caught me off guard. Cup number eleven or twelve, or whatever it was, hit the usual spot on the carpet as I grabbed for the phone.

"Shorts here." When I'm pondering, words tend to be at a premium.

"Harry, it's Richie Collins. I checked when I got to my place and I do have some pills left over. What do you want me to do with them?"

"That's great, Richie. Take down this name and address and send them overnight to her. I'll do you the money for the postage when we get to Florida, if that's OK. You the man, Richie! And Richie, I'd appreciate it if you didn't mention this to anyone at all. And I mean anyone – you dig?"

"No problem, Harry. It's between me and you alone. I'll see ya in a few weeks."

Repeat after me – this one is a biggie 'cause my bones are telling me so!

Put in a call to Trundle Industries and was surprised to get Ms. Timmons' voice mail. Even though it was Sunday, somehow I expected her to pick up. Maybe she does have a life after all. Or maybe she just hit the little girlie's room and missed my call.

I ran down where I was in the investigation and the package that would be coming her way, plus instructions on what to do with it when it arrived. No need to tell Ms. Timmons to keep it hush-hush. People in her position who know what's gone down this far don't need to be told – they just do as a course of action, all the time. I had the feeling you could put your trust in Ms. Timmons.

Harry the bad twin was thinking about putting something else in Ms. Timmons, but the good side was in control right now, and business came first. It will be time for the bad twin to gain the upper hand when the rain starts falling, raincheck in tow.

The Ebil came in at that instant looking like he hit the Lotto or something. It is his office, so I guess he can come and go as he pleases.

"What's up with you? The ship finally come in?" I smirked.

"No such luck, putz. But I did hit a good-sized one over in Strathmore that should keep your little sweetie Bunny here for a while longer. And where the hell have you been lately?"

"Been all over working this case. I'm going to Florida for a coupla months soon, and need a few solids if you can see your way through."

"Just to get rid of you for that long is worth it. What do you need?"

"Here's your rent and a check for the apartment rent for February and March. Can you see it gets paid for me? And the phone messages will probably stop, or at least slow down while I'm gone. If Bunny could get them and transfer them to my home voice mail, it would help out. That way I only have to check one number for all the messages. Can do?"

"Seems easy enough. When you leaving?"

"Gotta be there some time the end of the first week of February. I'll probably stay till the last week of March, or the first few days of April. I may have to fly back once in between, but that's not definite right now. I have somebody taking a peek at my place every week, so that's covered."

"I guess we can handle it," Mel said, but it took a bunch for him to get the words out. He dismissed me as he wandered out with "Didn't forget the kids' birthdays like usual, did you?"

da bushes

Now that was uncalled for. I haven't forgotten either kid's birthday since I've been back, and I remembered a few while I was away too. Geez, forget a few dates and the world comes down on your head like a ton of bricks. Like Ebil never forgot anything, that prick. Or you either, for that matter. Big Mel doesn't subscribe to the "glass house and stones" adage, I guess.

Made the last arrangements to have my normal monthly bills paid and I was set to go. Only had to check in with Randy to give him the lowdown on where I was and get any instructions for my time in Florida. That will have to wait till tomorrow when Ms. Timmons gets back to me.

Florida and baseball – hot damn is all that needs to be said. Other than end of chapter period

Chapter 57

"Who is it, what time is it, and this had better be damn good" was how I started my Monday morning. I'm not supposed to be awake at this hour – that is, unless I'm on my way in from the prior night's activities.

"Good morning, Harry. It happens to be 6:15 a.m. and this is Ms. Timmons, as you so fondly refer to me. And you called me, so I don't know how good it is, or could be, do I?"

Ain't that a slap in the face to jump-start your day? The lovely Ms. Timmons actually being funny at 6:15 in the morning, and on a Monday morning to boot. There is light at the end of the tunnel, Ollie.

"Don't you think it's a bit early in the day to be calling someone, Ms. Timmons? I'm not on call 24 hours of the day like you, ya know. And for your information, it could be quite good."

"So I've heard. What is the package that will be arriving at Trundle Industries, and how urgent is your need to speak to Mr. Trundle? He is back in Europe and not pleased to be there, I can assure you."

Don't ya just love a gal who gets right down to business and skips the idle chit-chat bullshit? To the point all the time is our little Ms. Timmons.

I forged on as business like as I can be at 6:15 in the morning.

"As I explained in my message, the package from Richie Collins will contain several pills resembling salt tablets. He played for the Schooners and is working for them in the off-season in their marketing department. They should be coming overnight to your attention, and if they don't, I'd like to know. I need them analyzed by the best people you have for every component and/or masking agent present. It's very important!"

da bushes

Never know how many beans to spill when you're dealing with evidence without dumping the whole bag. Made a guess that what I gave her was enough for now and moved on, it was Ms. Timmons and I had no choice but to trust her 100%.

"I would like to see Mr. Trundle before I leave for Florida, if possible. It's not urgent, but more of an update briefing session, I guess. I'll be there till late March or early April, and I don't want to leave without giving him some idea of where I stand up to now. Also, I need to know if he wants me to contact him periodically or fly up in between to see him."

"When are you leaving, Harry?"

"Hard to believe, but next week is the first week of February and I'm due down there right around then. I can swing a day or two if it fits his schedule, but by the end of the week I need to be gone."

"Mr. Trundle's schedule is somewhat fluid at this time, with Friday the twenty-eighth being our best guess for his return right now. There's a good possibility that a detour through London exists, which would make his probable return the middle to end of the next week. It doesn't seem like there will be an opportunity to see him before you go under those conditions."

"What do you suggest?" I answered. I didn't have to see Randy before I left, but would have felt better with a face-to-face pow-wow on where I was, or wasn't. The gloves would need to come off soon, and I didn't want to blindside the guy footing the bill.

"I'll be speaking to Mr. Trundle later this morning and will apprise him of your request. Perhaps you and I will have to meet, and I can brief Mr. Trundle when I see him. If he stops in London, I will be meeting him there for half a day. Will that work, Harry?"

"Better than nothing, and seeing you is always a pleasure, Ms. Timmons. By the way, is there a name between Ms. and Timmons?"

It was about time I made an attempt to crack that granite wall surrounding Miss prim and proper business lady.

"I'll contact you later today, Mr. Shorts, after speaking to Mr. Trundle. And yes, there is a name between Ms. and Timmons." With that, she hung up. Not even so much as a fuck-you-very-much, Harry.

RICH KISIELEWSKI

At 6:30 in the morning, there was nothing better I could think of to do than go back to sleep, so end of chapter period

Chapter 58

Missed the *Imus in the Morning* program completely by the time I awoke for the second time. I don't like the feeling of being exhausted when I rise from the depths of sleepdom and wasn't a happy camper right about then. Bad start to what was gonna be an altogether shitfuck day.

The apartment needed cleaning, and stuff from the fridge had to get packed up and over to Sherry's before it all went bad. Think about it – two months is a long time to be gone. On top of that, a thousand errands needed to get done in a week while the case was at a true crossroads. The outstanding information I was waiting for would solidify my position, or blow it to pieces.

Confidence, my boy – have some fuckin' confidence.

I stopped by to see Helen, my travel agent, to pick up the plane tickets for Florida on the way back from upgrading my baseball gear at Sports Authority. Turns out all I could get was a middle seat, and I hate sitting in the middle. Shitfuck.

You can get by with old equipment playing local semi-pro ball, but not when you have to rely on it every day of the week. The team gives you most of what you need, but you have your own personal comfort zone with certain things, and we all have our peculiar have-to-haves. Guitar players have a pick that makes better sound, and carpenters have a favorite hammer. Ballplayers do the same thing. Mine happens to be spikes – gotta have a certain pair, or else. Yeah, I'm semi-nuts for sure, I admit it. Join the crowd if you're singing the same tune. I promise I won't tell too many people.

Bunny was in the office when I drove by, so I stopped in to make sure she was still cool with watching my place while I was gone.

Einstein's daughter she isn't, but I was confident she could handle this chore.

"How you been, kiddo? Haven't seen you in a little while."

"Taking care of Mom until Dad got back; it was tiresome and he still needs help caring for her. She is up and around more now, so I don't have to do as much. How have you been, Harry?"

"I'm good. You still on for watching my place while I'm gone?"

"Of course I am. I said I would, and I'd never go back on my word. Is there anything special I need to know, or anything different from the last time I was there?"

"Nah, everything's the same, shouldn't cause a problem. Unless you think you need to come over and take a look around. I'd be glad to give you another tour of the whole place," I said with my little-boy-wants-a-cookie smile.

"Harry, that might be a good idea. You're going to be gone for so long, and I wouldn't want to miss anything. A tour of your whole apartment might be necessary," Bunny said, with extra emphasis on the word "whole" that left little doubt where it was going.

The damn phone rang, and I was positive it wasn't gonna be good. Shitfuck.

"Shorts" was my "you're bothering my ass" way to answer the phone.

"Have I caught you at a bad time, Harry?" It was Ms. Timmons from Trundle Industries returning my call as she said she would.

"No, not at all," I lied. "How'd you make out?"

"Mr. Trundle won't be able to see you, and I have to go to Arizona later today, then on to London from there. There won't be any time for us to get together in the near future, I'm afraid. Is there anything at all we can do over the phone?"

Now you know me by now, and that line was perfectly set up for a classic Harry Mickey Shorts witty retort. For some reason I just couldn't bring myself to pull the trigger. Why don't you make up one and chuckle over it by yourself. I'll just say shitfuck three times fast.

"I don't think it's the type of conversation that's best handled over the phone. I'll call you from Florida and perhaps I can come up in a few weeks and handle it then. Any luck on the research you were

da bushes

working on; and also, did the package we discussed show up?"

"Yes it did, and I'm delivering it to our experts while I'm in Arizona. The rest of the information you requested is being compiled right now, but won't be available for another week. I'll have it overnighted to your home if that is OK with you."

"Call first and see if I'm still here. If not, send it to the office address and I'll make arrangements to get it later. Thanks, Ms. Timmons with a name in the middle." No information – shitfuck.

"You're welcome, Harry Mickey Shorts," and she was gone, getting the upper hand on me again.

To top it off, when I got off the phone, young Bunny said, "Sorry, Harry, but I have to go and sit at an open house. With my mom's dinner party tonight, I won't be able to take that tour we talked about today."

Go ahead and fill in the blanks: s_i_f_c_.

"No prob, Bunny. I'll catch you later in the week to give you the keys and some cash incase anything happens while I'm gone. Sound good?"

"Sounds perfect, Harry," a big smile to go with it. Mel shook his head, looking like he could just puke.

Hard to believe, but the day didn't get any better from there.

Listen kiddos, before something else goes wrong, why don't I cut my losses with end of chapter period

Chapter 59

The rest of that week went by in a blur, right up to Tuesday morning when I boarded the big bird for Florida. I was as anxious as a little squirt on the night before Christmas waiting for Santa to bring me a shiny new bike. I was losing it altofuckingether, and my activities during that week showed it.

My final gym work slowed to a maintenance mode while my body craved more punishment. The school kids had midterms, so my throwing was down to a minimum, too. I was left searching for partners to toss the ball around with, and my hands had blisters from all the balls I was hitting off the batting tee. Major nutjob at work.

Thursday night was kiddie night, and Sherry actually hung around instead of vacating the premises like she normally does. Brianne was her teenager know-it-all self till she saw the goodies I got her, then she shrieked like a six-year-old. Max's birthday had passed, and I gave him the new baseball glove he wanted that I had ordered. It was better than anything I had right through high school. He's got some talent, and the right tools are important when you're learning. Plus, I love the little guy to bits.

"You spoil the shit out of those kids" was the thanks I got from my lovely ex. I knew she appreciated what I did for them and allowed me to spoil them a bit. I appreciated her for it.

"Yeah, I do. But it's fun doing it, and the look on their faces is worth a million bucks to me. You can deal with it later 'cause you're the real tough one. I'm just their push-over loveable old daddy."

It hurts when she hauls off and punches me in the arm.

The case wasn't exactly progressing swimmingly either.

da bushes

Tom's headaches had returned, which was a symptom of overdoing it, according to the head doctor he was seeing. "Sorry Harry, but I'm restricted to the house and no computer work at all. The stuff I have for you is close, but not quite done. Give me a few weeks to screw my head on straight and finish it up. I'll get word to you when it's done."

"No problem," I said, which seemed to be a common phrase for me of late. "Take your time and get better, and don't worry about the info. Whenever is soon enough."

"You're all right for a washed up old coach, Harry," wisecracked Tom with a hearty laugh that was good to hear.

"Keep it up and I'll come up there and whack you upside the head myself, shit-for-brains," I threatened with a laugh. "You take care, Tom, and I had better see your sorry ass out at the Schooner games come around April or May, kiddo."

"Yes sir, coach. I be there, coach," and he was gone. I knew I'd get what he promised as soon as he could physically get to it. In God and Tom Westbrook Jr. you can trust.

Spent the weekend packing for my trip, doing some light lifting in my home gym. Late Sunday afternoon there was a knock at the door and I wondered who it could be, since I wasn't expecting anyone. Pleasant surprises are always nice to get, and Sandy and her homemade lasagna was as good a surprise as I could have wished for. She and I had been missing each other since our grocery soiree.

"Well, well, what have we got here. Little Miss Homemaker seems to have been busy in the kitchen, I see."

"Harry, it's cold as a witch's tit in a brass bra out here. Shut up and let's get inside before this lasagna turns to ice and me with it."

"We can't have that now, can we?"

Bounced up the stairs and I opened a bottle of wine to wash down the grub. Luckily, I had some garlic bread in the freezer.

"How about a drink to start your engine, Sandy? The wine needs to breath, or so I've read, and anyway, it's early to go directly to dinner."

"A drink would be nice, Harry. Surprise me."

"That would be pretty hard to do, don't you think?" She got it without any coaxing from me and smiled that knowing smile I had seen before.

A coupla Absolut Gimlets over crushed ice sounded as if they would hit the spot, and Sandy was pleased with the choice. Turned into a couple for each of us, with a Harry Chapin/Van Morrison mini-concert to complete the mood, which also met with Sandy's approval. We did what came naturally and we both enjoyed the hell out of it, both of us leaving our inhibitions at the door.

The wine was out of breath and the lasagna was well aged at nine when we finally got around to it. Just two consenting adults eating dinner by candlelight who happen not to have any clothes on. Does make for some interesting and entertaining dinner conversation. If you haven't tried this one in the privacy of your own home, please do so with my hardiest endorsement. But perhaps it would be best to do so when the kids are staying over at a friend's house.

Dinner will never be the same again.

And for your information, Harry did have a surprise or too left in his bag of tricks. One goodie before dinner and one for after dinner, which was better than any dessert I've had in a long while. Amazing what you can do with an ordinary can of whipped cream and a bunch of grapes when you let your imagination run kinda wild.

I was ready for Florida.

I was ready for end of chapter period

Chapter 60

Richie Collins was headed down to Florida early to work with the Schooners marketing crew and just happened to be on the same flight as me Tuesday morning. Turns out he did lots of photography work in the summers and was a natural when it came time for the individual and team photo shoots. He was making it pretty tough to let him go if the baseball side didn't pan out.

What pissed me off was the fact that he got a window seat and I was in the middle of two maniacs who were deathly afraid of flying. I mean white-knuckle, head buried in the pillow afraid of flying, with little whimpering sounds for affect. If I could have, I would have jumped out of the plane just to get away from those two bizerkos. One of those "life sucks" episodes we all get shoehorned into at times. It was ten in the morning and I was still tempted to drown them out with alcohol. I resisted, but it was painful.

Once we took off and got safely in the air without either of my seatmates having a coronary, I switched seats with the gal next to Richie and renewed our Schooners conversation. He had given our talk some serious thought and wanted to bounce a few things my way. I wasn't holding my breath for any earth-shattering revelations, but a scrap of anything could only add to the mish-mosh I now had. I let him talk.

"It wasn't what you asked, Harry, it was what you didn't ask. You didn't want my opinion on who could have done this, if someone actually was trying to sabotage the Schooners. Or whether I thought someone or multiple people were behind it. That surprised me when I ran our conversation back in slow motion."

Interesting concept – "ran the conversation back in slow motion" – and I figured I'd take a flyer and see what he meant by it.

"What do you mean 'slow motion,' Richie?"

"It's how I analyze something that intrigues me. I try and reconstruct the conversation almost word for word, give meaning to the pieces that need emphasizing. You only asked what happened to the team and me. We discussed that at length, but the natural progression was to get my opinion on who, how or why. You didn't and I'm wondering why not. So, why not?"

"You seem to be the thinker here. What's your theory on it?"

"Well, Harry, you either already know the answer to those questions and need proof, or you have some of it and you're trying to fill in the blanks to get the other answers you need. My guess is it's the second one and you're holding your cards real close to the vest for now. Take in what you can get, don't let on where you're headed. Close?"

Smart sonovabitch, isn't he? Coupla ways to handle this, none of them good. I could piss him off with a "fuck-off, Richie" and pretend I didn't give a shit about his input or help. Or I could try a bold-faced lie and say I didn't have a clue who, how or why, if there even was something to it. Lastly, I could always claim I had forgotten how to speak English and leave with an "adios muchachos." I chose the dumb Harry routine.

"I'm just a two-bit coach trying to get a handle on what happened last year to help us win this season. Nothing more, nothing less."

"OK, I'll tag along on that ride for awhile, Harry. But if you were doing anything more than that and you happen to need a hand someday…" with an open-ended finish that gave me plenty of leeway one way or the other. A real smart sonofabitch, it seems.

In this case, saved by the food. I'm gonna munch on my rather appetizing looking rubber omelet and sausage patty, and you can munch on end of chapter period

Chapter 61

We landed without further discussion and I missed Charlie and his purple chariot right about then. Come to think of it, I missed Charlie period. You just start getting to know somebody and they seem to fade from view. Charlie was OK in my book and I hated not having our little reality talks now and again. I did miss the service, too.

The ride to the complex was non-eventful, but I could tell there was an invisible wall between Richie and me at the moment. No need for that shit to exist.

Thought I'd break the ice and get us back on track. "Hey, I'm stepping up here and maybe I'm a tad nervous. It's been awhile and I'm not sure what I'm gonna find at the end of the rainbow. Cut me a yard of slack and we can get back to your question later, OK?"

"No sweat, Harry. Maybe we're both a little nervous, and there is plenty of time to rehash old shit later on. Who you bunking with at the complex?"

"They have me in the coaches' wing with the kid bullpen catcher with the bum knee. I'm guessing new kids on the block get stuck together – tag we're it. Who you got, you know?"

"Yeah, I lucked out. They put me in the 'hole in the wall' single since I'll be pulling double duty on the field and with the back office marketing guys. I may be cutting my own throat agreeing to double dip while I'm down here. The P.R. guy had it last year, but he's renting a place this year. Your clothes closet is bigger, but I can come and go without disturbing anybody else if I'm up late. Give me three weeks and I'll tell you how lucky it turns out to be."

"You'll do fine, kiddo – have some faith. We be there, so let's boogie."

You can boogie on down the road to end of chapter period

Chapter 62

Harry Mickey Shorts just can't be happy, can he? Here I was in beautiful sunny Florida, feeling like I belonged. At least that was what I was trying to talk my brain into believing, having a mediocre amount of success so far. A wise man once told me to accept what you're given, finagle the rest till ya got what ya need. Accept Harry, for just once accept, will ya?

The coaches rode into town between the first and fifth of February, and organizational meetings started on the seventh. Doc got in early, and he and I renewed our conversations, a somewhat wary approach from both sides. Little by little we maneuvered till we got to the information sharing point and each side gave a bit. I think we can get on the same page and be useful to each other. I've gotten more confident the gaps will slowly fill themselves in, and Doc has had something to do with that. I have to trust somebody on the staff side, and he's gonna be it.

Bobby and Jerry had gone home just before I got into town to finish up some business stuff and prepare for the long haul of the season. Too bad, 'cause I was looking for some compatriots to do a little damage before we got down to serious body torturing. Cruised by the sports bar where I had met Dana hoping for a miracle, but the '69 Mets were no where to be found, and neither was Dana. Ah, the memories.

Lest I digress, the 1969 New York Mets won the World Championship and were called the Miracle Mets. In the future, I'll try not to use New York sports history for the less fortunate in the crowd.

Anyway, organizational meetings turned out to be boring as hell. I know this shit and a half day on what signs we were gonna use during the season was pure hell to endure. Coach Curran was cool about it, letting Punch go on forever, since it's his responsibility. I heard it took a whole day last year, and I would have quit before I could have put up with that much shit. Thinking twice, to play ball I would have stayed, but I would have made the afternoon living hell for Punch. And if you doubt my ability to do so, you haven't been paying enough attention, my buckoes.

The first few weeks down here I spent half my time preparing to be a coach, the other half remembering how to be a champion-caliber baseball player. I had a major problem when we started spring training workouts – I was toiling on both sides of the fence. Jerry and Bobby came into camp early, which helped, and we worked out every afternoon after the organizational meeting broke up. Darkness stopped us most days. That and my fuckin' aching 31-year-old broken-down body.

When you're a player, you gear up mentally for each day's activities, knowing what to expect, and your body reacts to the stimulation. Drills are the worst part of early camp; they are monotonous and work you harder than you are mentally or physically ready for. Preparation doesn't matter – you can't voluntarily push yourself to the point one of these sadistic demon conditioning coaches can.

I had responsibility for the catchers and made sure we broke our asses every day. Steiner was ready for spring training, but the third string kid came in expecting to coast for awhile, then go back to Single A when we broke camp. He was in for a rude awakening, and I had no problem introducing him to said awakening. He learned more in a month than he had in his entire playing career to date. Who teaches these kids, or better yet, who doesn't teach them on the way up? This kid missed the boat somewhere along the line.

Of course, I should not be one to speak such unkind words. A boatfull of baseball talent is a terrible thing to waste – you can go and look it up in Webster's Dictionary under Shorts, Harry M.

It was going to be my responsibility to right this wrong, and I broke the kid's proverbial balls unmercifully. Even Steiner got in on the act and rode him like a champ, but that was OK. He has the skills and could back it up on the field. The kid will be better off for it – he'll just hate my guts for life.

The other side of the show nearly broke me. Conditioning drills in the Florida sun was a bitch on wheels from day one. My sorry ass was dragging so low for the first two weeks, I had raspberries on both cheeks. I couldn't figure which Harry was more beat – Harry the coach or Harry the player. Hold the presses, Harry Shorts even turned down a night at the sports bar due to the fact that my body wouldn't let me get out of bed. That, without a doubt, qualifies as beat to shit and back.

Even thinking about it makes me need a rest, so end of chapter period

Chapter 63

Early March, the routine was pretty well established, with the pitchers and catchers getting their work in early. That gave me the opportunity to work on special drills, like pitch-out/throw-down combinations, and bunt coverage. Sounds mighty exciting, doesn't it, boys and girls?

When the team starts to drag a bit, the organizational shit kicks in, and today was picture day. Richie was doing more and more promo/marketing stuff, and if I was a betting man, I'd wager a bob or two on his moving to that side of the Schooners before too long. The young kids we added will probably push him out of the utility role, and I know he's not gonna want to drop down a level in the organization. I've watched him and it's probably for the best. Nice kid, but not higher level pro material.

The team gathered that morning, and I got surprised by "The Speech." Why I hadn't heard about this before I don't know, 'cause I wouldn't have missed it for anything. Teddy got the players together last year on picture day and gave them his first annual "da bushes" speech that will go down as a classic. It was now time for the second annual rendition, I guessed.

"Now guys, you all have the dream, and that dream is to be a major league baseball player. And it truly is a noble dream, let me assure you. To get there, though, you have to pay your dues here in the minor leagues, 'da bushes,' as they are called. I'm not totally sure why they are called 'da bushes,' but they are. So you are here in 'da bushes' for a reason."

It was difficult to sit there and not break out laughing as he went on for five more minutes talking in circles about "da bushes" and the greats of baseball, who had traveled these same roads before us. He saved the best for last.

"And while we are here to prepare for the season ahead of us, there are distractions we must overcome. They are here at the ballpark and they are everywhere when you go out at night. I'm talking about those groupies that tempt you to go home with them, distracting you from your duties to the club and your teammates. Stay away from them and 'da bushes' that can only lead to trouble. Stick to 'da bushes' we call minor league baseball, and not 'da bushes' in other places. Do I make myself clear, guys?"

In unison, thirty-five guys said with straight faces, "Perfectly clear, Mr. Trundle." When he left the room it took twenty minutes to calm everyone down and stop the hysterical laughter that erupted with his departure. They all gathered around me and presented me with the first annual "Master of da bushes" trophy, which I will treasure always. Quite fitting an award, as you already know.

The other coaches just hid behind end of chapter period

Chapter 64

On picture day you have guys scattered all over the field. The weatherman cooperated for a change, the sky was crystal clear, with temps in the mid 70's. The theory is to get shots of every player with some part of their gear in view and at least one action shot. The pitchers are shown in some variation of a wind-up pose and the catchers in a crouching position, etc., etc., and you get the rest. We finish off with the portrait shots and the team photo. You can't believe how long this shit can take.

I spotted Richie with the guy shooting the coaches over by the first base dugout. After my player shots were done, I sauntered over to do the coaching thing. As I got closer, I saw Punch with his arm around some fan who must have been in his eighties if he was a day. They were laughing it up, and the photo guy was snapping shots for the yearbook. All at once I stopped dead in my tracks and almost shit myself. There was Punch with his arm around this old guy, and a bunch of people milling around in the background. When you concentrated on the front two people, Punch and the old geezer, the background was kinda blurry. But there it was, framed perfectly for me to see.

It was an identical match to the photo that had been bugging me. Punch with his arm around some old geezer, and when you focused in, there, barely recognizable in the background crowd, was the piece to the puzzle I had been searching for. It was identical to the photo hanging in Punch's house, with Punch, his father-in-law, and the mystery guy in the background. I could see it clear as day. I knew it was in the picture, and somewhere in the recesses of my brain, I had known it was important. I also knew it would come to me sooner or later.

Now I was sure of the who, and had the how pretty well figured out.

Somehow I was confident the pieces of information Ms. Timmons and Tom Jr. would give me, coupled with Doc's input, would put the whole operation into perspective, and I'd have the why as well. Little did I know the final piece of the puzzle would come from the most unlikely of sources.

It was Saturday and I was feeling high as a kite with the revelation of earlier today. Got the boys rounded up and we hit the sports bar for a night of fun. Sunday morning was always free time for the players and coaches. We planned on carousing till the wee hours, drinking tons of suds and pursuing "da bushes" as our general manager so aptly labeled them. The newly crowned Master was leading the charge of the light-headed brigade.

We were a-hootin' and a-hollerin', having a hell of a time, when I heard a voice from the past behind me. "Fancy meeting you here, big boy" was all she said.

I didn't need to turn around to know who it was, but when I did, Dana was standing there looking as pretty as a picture, grinning from ear to ear. I wasn't quite sure what to say, so I grabbed her and gave her one of those "boy am I glad to see ya" kisses. Took us awhile, so I guess she was glad to see me too. Didn't stop the boys from continuing their hootin' and hollerin', most of it now directed at me.

"What the hell are you doing here? Shouldn't you be in Arizona?"

"That run ended, and we are moving the production to Washington for a two-week engagement. I'm still understudy for the lead and picked up two other roles that get me on stage about every third performance."

"If you're going to Washington, why are you here in Florida?"

"I didn't get a chance to get back here and pack the rest of my clothes and stuff. When you left, I stayed in Phoenix till now; I'm just passing through to collect a few things. I leave for Washington in the morning. By the way, a Ms. Timmons stopped in to see me after one of the performances and seemed to know you. You're not sneaking around behind my back, are you, Harry?" brought out that smile I had learned to love.

"Got a gal in every port ready to help me forget the likes of your kind, sweetie pie."

da bushes

"Oh, screw you, Harry. Let's get out of here and you can get your jollies by helping me sort through my undies."

"I'll be getting my jollies, but you can bet there is only one pair of undies I'll be sorting through," I said as I squeezed her a little closer.

"If that's a promise, you're on, big fella," and we were off to be jolly together.

And you guys and gals are off to end of chapter period

Chapter 65

Dana was gone by seven the next morning, and I was on the field by eight. Another memory to carry me through those dark and cold nights. Don't worry, people, I wouldn't be feeling sorry at all for Harry, if I were you. I'm sure you aren't.

Tom Westbrook called and left a message for me at the team office. After breaking my butt in the baking sun all day, it was a surprise to get the message, but a pleasant one. I had been thinking about Tom recently and planned on calling him to see how he was doing. Actually, I wanted to see how he was physically, and also see if he had made any progress on the research that he was doing.

Last thing I heard, his headaches had stopped him from proceeding any further, and I wondered if they had started up again recently. Can't say I wasn't at least a little bit worried about him. Head smacks can be real dangerous shit.

The number on the message was for the insurance agency office, which confused me. Why would Tom be in his dad's office and leave that number for me to get back to him? You would think he'd be at home recuperating. Strange. But as you have seen, strange can be good.

"Tom Westbrook, please. It's Harry Shorts returning his call." I recognized Nancy Westbrook's voice but thought better of chasing that one right about now. Plenty of time to pursue later on.

"Tom Westbrook. Can I help you?"

"Mr. Westbrook, it's Harry Shorts. I got a message from Tom Jr. to call him at this number. Is he in?"

"Harry, thanks for calling back. Tom Jr. didn't call you, I did. Tom is back in the hospital and I was just about to leave and head over there. You just caught me…."

da bushes

"Excuse me for interrupting, Mr. Westbrook, but I thought Tom was on the mend. What happened?"

"He was still getting those headaches and they were getting a bit worse. When he had a bout of blurred vision the doctor readmitted him to the hospital for observation. Stubborn as he is, he didn't want to go. But after I promised to send the material he had gathered for you right away, he gave in. That's the other reason I called, besides letting you know about the hospital."

"Mr. Westbrook, are you giving me all of it? Is Tom in any danger?"

"No, Harry, we don't think so. The doctor just wants to keep a closer eye on Tom and figured he could do it better in the hospital."

"That's not good, but better than I feared. You scared the shit out of me, Mr. Westbrook. Ah, sorry about the language."

"We've all been through a lot of shit, Harry. Better days are ahead of us. Anyway, I wanted you to know I sent the package overnight; you should see it tomorrow. Don't know what was in it, but Tom was adamant you get it right away. He said to tell you he wasn't done, but it was the best he could do under the circumstances."

"Be sure and thank him for me and tell him I'll call soon. I'm coming up to New York shortly; I'll make it a priority to see Tom while I'm there. You can tell him that and tell him to count on it."

"He'll appreciate that, Harry. We all appreciate what you have done. I'll tell him when I get over there," and he was gone.

Things start going good and somebody turns around and hands you a half a shit sandwich for dinner. Man, I'm tired of the ups and downs of this roller-coaster ride.

Maybe Tom's info will right the ship, but for now I need end of chapter period

Chapter 66

It rains in Florida for about twenty minutes almost every day. Everything dries quickly, but the humidity just hangs there, making life miserable for a bunch of guys running around in the heat. The next day was one of those all-day soakers that occurs occasionally, a welcome sight for a beat-up old has-been. No day off altogether, as the staff needed to begin finalizing our plans on who we would take north. Cutting guys bites the big one.

The mainstay of last year's team was here and intact, but the reserves will change to some degree. Unfortunately, Richie looks like he is destined for the world of sports marketing from here on in. Actually, he is spending lots of time on that side of the house down here and setting himself up for the coming year. Smart kid, doing what he needs to do.

By lunch we had pared it down to a few battles, one in the outfield and one in long relief. The team from last year was so good there wasn't much room for new guys to break in. All we need is for the players to stay healthy and we are gonna cruise.

Harry the expert giving you the scoop of the year. Bet the ranch on the Schooners – that is, if you happen to be of the betting persuasion.

I picked up the package from the Westbrooks and took it back to my room with a coupla hot dogs with the works. A beer would have gone great, but I settled for a root beer instead. Close but no cigar, kiddo. The info from Westy was obviously unfinished, but the guts were in there. When I was done going over what he was able to put together, if I was reading it right, I had the makings of a slightly fucked-up ingenious mind using his expertise to manipulate a bunch of kids. Most of the how was now in the bank and it was just the why I needed.

da bushes

It would come.

It was also obvious it wasn't a one-man show that I was dealing with.

Time to pow-wow with Doc and run my theories by him. He told me he had a few of his own, and hopefully we will be somewhere on the same page.

The players have to use wall phones in the hallway, but coaches get their own phone in their rooms. Mine rang as I was getting ready to split. Since the kid coach wasn't there, I figured I'd see who was calling. I'm kind of curious like that.

"Hello, Harry, it's good to hear your voice" was all Ms. Timmons said.

This must be a test.

"And equally nice to hear yours, Ms. Timmons."

Two can play the same game.

"Mr. Trundle would like to know if you would be available to come up and see him tomorrow. Would you be able to get away from training for a day?"

"The man has the pen, Ms. Timmons. When he says jump, I'm in the air waiting for the signal to come down. When does he want to see me?"

"The plane will pick you up at 8:00 a.m., if that is convenient, and Charles will meet you at the airport. You will be back for bed check, if that is the correct term. Wouldn't want you to miss bed check, now would we, Harry?"

"That depends to a large extent on who's doing the checking, Ms. Timmons."

"You do have a point there, Harry. And by the way, Tom Westbrook said not to worry about visiting with Tom Jr. on this trip – he understands. We will see you tomorrow then?"

"I'm looking forward to it, Ms. Timmons" and was able to get off the phone first for a change, leaving her to ponder.

Playful, isn't she.

I'm off so it's end of chapter period

Chapter 67

The G-Men were waiting for me. We took off at eight on the dot as planned. The purple bird was a bit more at home in Florida, with a few canary yellows and a pinkie around to keep it company. Still butt-ugly, though.

While we flew, I had time to review my talk with Doc the night before. Tom Jr.'s information fit right in with his overall theories, the few new pieces he contributed complementing my view very well. Living in Arizona and being able to snoop around out there proved to be very valuable.

How I was going to approach Randy was less than obvious in my mind. I wanted to give him the full picture, but hated to lay it all out without being able to prove the whole shebang. Doc and I put together a game plan, but it wasn't going to produce immediate results, and I needed time to implement it properly. Randy would have to buy into it and endorse it totally or it wouldn't fly. There was a big risk factor, with disaster written all over it if we had misjudged the culprits or their methods.

If we were right, we would be able to flush them out with some help from a few select Schooner players. But if we were wrong, we were fucked big time.

No guts – no glory.

I spent the rest of the flight reviewing the team roster decisions and the main player nucleus that would form the Schooners for the coming season. With the talent we had, it was a fun job. Even better was the fact that they were all good guys and a blast to be around.

The middle of the infield was set with Bobby "Cat" Hoffman and Howdy McDuff ready to dominate, probably moving up to Triple A

da bushes

next season, if not earlier. Dee Smith was back at third base, and the big kid Bradford was gonna man first. He was smacking the ball like hell. His total fear that came to my attention right away earned him the nickname "Bugs" immediately. A strategically placed caterpillar or similar bug was worth ten minutes of merriment for all. Pete Sanchez in left and Scoot Munoz in center were as good as advertised and carried whoever played right – the "weak" spot if there was one. Donovan Jonathan (D.J.) Smalley was born to hit the long ball and did it regularly as the designated hitter.

The team was held together by the fine catching crew, led by yours truly, with Steiner as backup.

Rusty and Smokes Randolph anchored the pitching staff once again, with Bill "Dong" Wong and Barney making up the best starting four any minor league team has ever seen. Add three better than average middle guys, Slam Wilson to close, and the team was unbeatable in my eyes. Not even Herbie could fuck up this staff if he tried – and, as you know, he doesn't try. It was a true pleasure to sit back behind the plate and watch them work their collective magic.

The rest of the team was good, not great, but complemented the accumulation of minor league stars that pointed the Schooners to a league championship. If I weren't aware of what happened last year, I'd say there wasn't a thing in the world that could stop them.

Maybe not a thing – a who, or a couple of whos to be more exact.

I must have dozed off at some point, because the wheels hit the ground before I knew it. I would say I'm running about a quart low in the sleep department right about now. I'm gonna see Charlie; you're gonna see end of chapter period

Chapter 68

"How ya been, my man? It's been awhile, hasn't it?"

"Why, yes it has, Harry. I can't complain too much and I gets paid not to go 'round complaining anyway. So, I've been good, I guess."

"You always know the right thing to say, don't you, Charlie? Mr. Trundle in a good mood after coming back from Europe, or am I in for trouble?"

"I hear Paris wasn't a pretty sight, but London always makes Mr. Trundle come home in a good frame of mind. Nobody seems to know the secret, but it never fails."

Interesting. I wonder what it is about London that cheers him up like that. Have to mention it to Ms. Timmons next time I see her.

"Well, I'm only here for the day, and I'd hate to rain on his parade if he's in a good mood. You gonna drive me back tonight?"

"Yes sir, Harry. Wouldn't miss it for the world."

"Oh, go to hell, Charlie. Let's make sure the cool ones are ready for the ride to the airport. You never know, I may need a few. And by the way, you were dead on with the smile."

"I'll see what I can do, Harry. And I usually am."

We pulled up to Trundle Industries, and I'd have to say I was quite disappointed. Ms. Timmons was no where in sight. Some guy met me and rode up in the elevator to Randle's office. Couldn't decide if the elevator door or my escort had more personality. Or perhaps I was just being pissy 'cause Ms. Timmons wasn't there to meet me. Need to get a grip, I think.

It's a business meeting, Harry. Get in and get out with the facts leading the way. Why the hell should I be nervous? Randy probably knows everything I know, and maybe more. He always seems to. But

da bushes

what if he doesn't?

"Mr. Trundle, it's good to see you again."

"Come in, Harry. Can I get you something? I assume you have already eaten."

Actually, I had forgotten to eat lunch, but I wasn't hungry at all. The G-Men had some stuff on the plane and offered me lunch or a snack, but I declined. Sometimes my mind gets one-tracked and all else becomes secondary. I was zeroed in on this case and the meeting with Randy, couldn't focus on anything else. There's always time for eats later on.

"I'm fine, Mr. Trundle. I hope your European meetings went satisfactorily?"

What the fuck is satisfactorily, you idiot? Just be yourself and talk to the man. And stop talking to yourself. Yes, Harry.

"I wasn't looking forward to that particular trip, and as expected, it started off very poorly, but ended up on a high note. Thank you for asking, Harry. Now, tell me where your travels have taken you."

Everything I had rehearsed on the plane went out the window, and I was at a loss on how to get started. Perhaps Randy saw my hesitation and helped out.

"Harry, we have had frank discussions before. Whatever you tell me is going to be OK, so just be yourself, not like one of my asshole executives that tell me what they think I want to hear. I want the truth and I want it straight. Now, tell me where we are."

Man is good. He is very good.

For the next forty-five minutes I led Trundle through the entire investigation, recapping the parts we already discussed, presenting the new theories in detail. Doc as a resource and co-theory guy helped, I think. Also, Randy accepted as fact the information gathered by Ms. Timmons and Tom Jr. that supported my results. I didn't hold back any punches and gave him the total picture, whether he liked it or not. It seemed to go well until I was done, and he didn't say anything.

OK, Harry, let's decide. Either say something or sit there and wait. Which one?

After what seemed like a damn eternity, he finally opened his mouth.

"How about a cold one, Harry?"

A cold one?

"Ah, ah, ah, sure Mr. Trundle. If you are having one, I'd be happy to join you" I guessed was the right thing to say.

"Becks I believe is your choice, isn't it, Harry?"

"Why, ah, yes it is."

"Have you been to Germany and had their version by any chance?"

"Ah, no I haven't."

One more "ah" and I'll declare myself mentally fuckin' incompetent to speak to another human being. Words, Harry, try using words.

"It's better, but not worth the trip. Here you go, Harry. These steins are from some German baron and are about a hundred years old. Tastes the same as out of the bottle, but impresses the don't-know-any-betters I have to deal with at times. Cheers."

We clinked the hundred-year-old steins like they came from Wal-Mart and tossed down a healthy mouthful. Foam mustaches all around. Randy was a normal guy when he let his guard down, and I think I was being treated to a side of him very few people saw. Comfortable wasn't usually Mr. M. Randle Trundle's style.

"You have done very good work, Harry. We could probably confront these individuals right now and be done with it. But I'm told you have worked very hard down in Florida; you've earned time on the field. I wouldn't take it away from you. Go on back and have some fun. Your plan to draw them out is chancy, but sounds like it's worth a try. If it doesn't work, I'll get them anyway. Just honor one request, will you?"

"I'll try, Mr. Trundle…I mean Randle. What is it?"

He told me and I understood completely. It wouldn't be easy to do, but I'd try my best to find a way.

End of chapter period

Chapter 69

Ms. Timmons was right. I was headed back to Teterboro by late afternoon and would be back in Florida in time for a little carousing with the boys. Disappointed again not to have seen the fair maiden, but I'll get over it.

I called the Ebil's office, but the troops were gone for the day. When Mel goes anytime after 3:30 p.m., Bunny splits pronto. Dedication isn't one of her strong points, but I enjoy her other fine points when I can. It's my contribution to keeping the younger working generation happy and content. As we have said before – what a guy I am.

Charlie was kinda quiet on the way to the airport, which definitely wasn't his normal M.O. Getting him to shut his mouth for two minutes is more like it.

"What's with you, Charlie? Cat got your tongue?"

"The St. Paulie Girl instead of your usual is my mistake, Harry. I allowed someone else to prep the car, didn't check everything out before I picked you up. It won't happen again, I promise."

What a shmagook – pisswater beer would be OK, as long as it was cold. Or at least not totally warm. I could tell that wasn't what was really bothering him. Trained private investigators can do that, you know. Also, I am the consummate bullshit artist and can't be fooled by any amateur.

"Nice try, Charlie. Now, what really gives?"

"Mr. Harry, I don't know what to make of the goings-on around here the last half a year or so. First things get kinda out of whack, and then you show up. Mr. Trundle is all worked up, and Mr. Fredericks, who'd been with him for more than twenty years, is gone, and nobody knows why. Ms. Timmons is traveling everywhere now. She was always at Mr. Trundle's side, but only when he was local. And his interest in that ball team – he didn't never speak about it to me before. I just don't know, Harry. Maybe I should just keep my stupid mouth shut and drive."

Jump back Jack, as they say.

"Charlie, who is Fredericks?"

"Mr. Trundle's Number One man – always was. Went to his school, I think. He's as close a friend as Mr. Trundle has, or had."

"Any idea what happened?"

"I think I've said enough, Mr. Harry. Sorry about your beer – I'll make sure it won't happen again."

I got the feeling the conversation was over as far as Charlie was concerned.

"Charlie, friends trust each other, don't have to worry about what they say to each other. You understand?"

"I hope so, Harry. Thanks."

The rest of the ride was me, Paulie and my thoughts. What did Fredericks do to fuck over Trundle and where was Ms. Timmons off to all the time? And what the hell does any of that have to do with me and my investigation? Man, I hate being in the dark, and just when I thought I had this fuckin' thing tied down. Déjà shitfuck vu all over again.

I told him to keep his head down and thanked Charlie for the ride. Got on the plane wondering what was gonna happen next. That's the problem, I didn't have a clue.

"Hang on to your hat, Harry, there's a storm brewing down the coast and we may hit some pretty tough going" was my greeting from G-Man #1 as I boarded. "Drink perhaps?"

"You guys concentrate on flying, I'll help myself to the bar. Drinks plural is more like it. And the weather, don't worry. Perfect ending to a perfect day."

Flight from hell, you don't even want to know about, so end of chapter period

Chapter 70

The rest of March flew by like we were standing still. Players get ready and then they want to get the show on the road. Spring training is too long for the guys who have the team made. You spend the last two weeks jumpy as hell, trying not to get hurt. For the last few cuts, it's never long enough.

"If I only had one more week...." is the standard last man cut lament.

The coaching staff was ready, and we went about our business like last year never happened. How could anybody fuck with a bunch of kids like that, then just go about their business like it didn't happen? When I get done with them, they will believe – oh, how they will believe.

Coach Curran was still riding my ass harder than most and I'd had just about enough. Last week in March, I decided it was time to put an end to it.

"Coach, we about done with this 'ride Harry's ass' shit?"

"If you're asking, then you know it's time. How about from here on in we kick some ass together, just like old times."

"Mr. Curran, exactly like old times." We never discussed it again. The pupil had learned another valuable lesson from the teacher.

The new marketing manager for the Bayport Schooners interviewed the coaching staff and several players for an edition of the local Bayport newspaper. It was for a special edition on the upcoming second campaign with lots of promise and fanfare. Learn from your mistakes and all that typical bullcrap. He did a great job of profiling the talent that would be on display, downplaying last year's folderoo.

The byline made me proud: Richie Collins, Marketing Manager – Bayport Schooners. Good things come to good guys every once in awhile.

Doc and I discussed my trip to New York when I got back. We went about the business of preparing for the season and the end to the "Collapse Case," as I had named it for my files. All the names for my cases mean something to me and are undecipherable to the untrained masses. Just in case, I have another computer file with all the names and what they mean. Brain surgeon I'm not. Practical I am.

I have to admit, I'm even getting a severe case of the heebie-jeebies waiting to get the hell out of Florida, ready for the season to start.

Harry Mickey Shorts – minor league baseball player/coach. Pretty damn impressive if you ask me.

In the words of another famous Harry, Mr. Chapin – "Life is like a circle," and I'm living proof.

Life is also like end of chapter period

Chapter 71

Junior's brain works in mysterious ways. The bus we use for our road trips is a "money's no object" top of the line model, with TV's and VCR's and enough heads to handle an army on leave. The problem is the outside of the bus – it's painted to look exactly like an old Schooner. He loves this monstrosity and uses it in all the PR shoots the team does. From what I can gather, it caused a major blowup with the old man when Jr. had it painted. Randy likes low key and fought like hell to stop him from making a spectacle of the team's name. He lost, and I know from experience he doesn't like to lose.

We were tooling down Route 81 in Pennsylvania in the four-wheeled Schooner, signs showing Harrisburg twenty miles away, headed for a three-game series with the Harrisburg Senators. Steiner's stoked to play his old team, the guys riding him real good. I'll have to make sure he starts at least two of the three games.

Two and a half months into the season, nine games up on the Harrisburg Senators, and we were buzzing everybody in sight, same as they did last year. A sweep would finish them by the All-Star break, which was coming up after this series, and we have four guys on the team for sure. I'm still playing pretty well, but getting the kid into the action a lot more. Baseball on this level really is fun.

Sky high is the only possible way to describe the team's attitude, and I was riding pretty high myself. I knew it was almost over, but what a run it had been. A HMS Life Flashback: What a run it could have been if only…but there's no room for regrets. My life and I'll live with the cards I dealt myself. There's still a coupla hands left to go.

No signs of anybody getting that tiredness that took over last year, and only one minor injury so far this year. Maybe last season was a freak thing and I'm not gonna be able to prove anything. The suppositions I had coming into the season still existed, but nothing seems to be evident in the team clubhouse or on the field to prove them out.

Tom Westbrook was real, and I just know I'm gonna get the bastards sooner or later. He, or they, will slip up and I'll nail em. I owe it to Tom Jr. and Randy.

The G.M.'s wife traveling with us on the bus was fuckin' absurd and had made it real uncomfortable for the players. What in the world was Teddy thinking about? Guys read or slept, with the occasional whispers and laughter from a group of guys in the back of the bus. Me, I avoided any eye contact with her like the plague.

Our last night together still had me thinking, and I knew there was something she said that was critical. I couldn't put it together with what I knew so far, and that bugged me. It was obvious she was on the verge of doing something that would rock their boat, big time. I needed to talk to her to find the thing that was eating at me. I hoped it wasn't her!

We cruised into the city of Harrisburg and pulled up to the Harrisburg Hilton. The Trundles do know how to take care of their employees, since we always went top of the line in everything we did. The Hilton would do nicely. It was only a few minutes to City Island's Riverside Stadium where the Senators played their games. I hear the city's mayor did a great job of revitalizing this town; the ballpark and City Island were both top notch.

When we got settled in, I wandered down to the bar for a few. The players were headed to some sports bar for a burger and fun, but I had another agenda to deal with.

Punch was sitting with Doc at a table, just off the bar, exactly as Doc and I had planned. When Doc saw me, he waved me over, and I sat down. At about the same time, the bartender called over to Doc and told him he had a phone call.

Doc said, "Sorry guys, but I have to see a man about a horse. Save me some peanuts in case I get finished early enough to make it back."

"See ya, Doc," I said as he walked away. The bartender gave me the thumb's-up, and I nodded in recognition.

"Long ride, huh, Punch?"

"Funeral procession is more like it. The players normally handle these trips pretty well, but this one was bad news. What's their problem?"

At first I thought he was kidding and I smiled. He didn't smile back.

"Well, Punch, maybe they were a little uncomfortable with Mrs. Trundle on the bus. Can't exactly fart in the G.M.'s wife's hair, can ya?" Did it as much to see on whose side he was standing, as well as how he could handle Harry's crude sideshow.

"Harry, you shouldn't speak like that about Teddy or Mrs. Trundle. Have a little more respect, will you?" sounding as if I had hurt him deeply.

Fuck him and his respect. Jeannie could handle herself in more ways than one. Personally, I could only vouch for one of those "ways" right now, and vouch for it quite well, I might add. But I had no fear that she could handle herself in a down and dirty with Junior when the time came. Might be fun to watch, too.

"Didn't mean to show any disrespect, Punch. I was only indicating the guys' unease with her on the bus and their inability to be themselves. They are only kids, you know," I said, with a bit too much emphasis on the "kids" for his liking.

Punch sat back in his chair and eyed me up and down. He was about to say something, but changed his mind at the last second. He took a sip of his drink instead and waved for the waitress to bring another round.

Doc made his entrance exactly as I had anticipated, surprising Punch, and immediately hit him just as hard on the subject of the bus ride. Not as crude as my approach, but equally as obvious. The emphasis on the "kids" was clear as a bell and meant to put him on the spot.

He didn't like it and was getting pretty worked up.

"You guys are taking the side of the goddamn 'kids' as you call them. Teddy is the general manager of this team, and he can do whatever he wants, whenever he wants, and no kid is gonna say squat about it. We'll do whatever it takes to...." He caught himself and stopped mid-sentence.

A huff and a puff and he blew the bad men down.

"Calm down, Punch. We're all coaches here, and of course management can do anything they want. Nobody is trying to claim anything different," I said.

Doc smiled the conspirator's smile.

What I wanted to say was "Gotcha, ya prick."

What I will say is end of chapter period

Chapter 72

The Harrisburg Senators were a formidable team in the Eastern League over the last coupla five years or so. A dramatic grand slam in the bottom of the ninth inning won them another championship a few years back, making it four in a row. They were a team that you had to pay attention to.

We had been for a short spell, and now it was time for them to pay attention to us again.

Opening game of the series – we had our pitching staff primed for the kill. Rusty has been unhittable the last three times out and totally geared up to strut his stuff. The whole team was chompin' at the bit, and even the coaches were on edge anticipating something special. Smokes was set for game two, and the Dong-man will finish out the series. Three aces up our sleeve and we're gonna showcase them all.

Steiner wanted at them, but he agreed I should start game one. The main thing you need to guard against is getting too high, hype it away. Keeping your pitcher within himself, focused batter by batter, is the catcher's primary function in a game as big as this one. I do it well, I might add. I bet you figured I'd say that. You're right!

Coach Curran got the team together before we started the game and reminded us why we were there. To finish, he said it all – "Last year don't mean jack shit. It's our time now; let's show 'em why we're the best." We roared out of the dugout like our asses were on fire.

Cat lined the first pitch to center and stole second on the next pitch. Howdy rapped the next offering into the left-center gap and hustled it into a triple. Before the inning was over, we scored five times, and the stadium was dead silent. It was all over but the shouting, and the Schooners were pumped. Rusty shut them out for six innings on two infield hits, and we were up eleven zip. So as not to forget, I had two hits and knocked in three runs, in case inquiring minds were wondering.

The beginning of our master plan was put into motion in the middle of the seventh inning. Rusty and Doc were huddled together at the end of the dugout with Scootch when we finished our at bat in the top of the seventh. Little by little the rest of the team got wind of their conversation.

"Coach," Doc said, "Rusty is done for the day. He's been feeling tired and kinda rundown the last week. Scootch and I both think it would be best to be careful for now."

Coach Curran looked at Rusty in disbelief, just nodded his OK. We ran our middle guys the next three innings and won 12-1 going away. Game one for the good guys, and big. Message delivered – loud and clear.

Doc and Rusty played it perfectly, and we felt bad for the rest of the team, but that couldn't be helped. Rusty and Smokes were in on it for now, with me and Doc controlling the way it went. So far, so good. There was no backing out now. We had a plan, and it either worked or we were in for some trouble. Using Rusty and Smokes was chancy, but we had to make it as real as possible to succeed. I had my fingers and toes crossed.

The Hilton bar was jumpin' after the game, and super pumped would be a safe description for the players. The coaching staff was trying to play it cool, but big wide smiles were in evidence across the board. Me, I was sky-high, smiling from both sides of my mouth, with just a hint of concern under the surface. Doc's assurance that "we have it under control, Harry, stop worrying" didn't quite soothe my nerves. I was worried about the guys.

Game two the next night was more punishment for the Senators, with lotsa whoopin' and a-hollerin' for the Schooners. Seven nothing after five innings, a granny by D.J. in the top of the sixth made it eleven-zip. Smokes was stoked and firing bee-bees. He had struck out eleven in five innings, with Steiner handling him like an old pro and chipping in a two-run homer to boot.

Time for step two in our plan. Bottom of the seventh, Smokes is taking his warm-up tosses, when he stops and moves to the back of the mound. He bends over and looks like he is sucking in air and having a hell of a tough time doing it. Scootch heads for the mound in his usual slow-as-molasses way, and Doc sprints past him to get to Smokes first. The kid does an Academy Award job of "I'm feeling kinda woozy," and we get him to the clubhouse pronto – the "we" being me and Doc trying to keep the asshole from laughing out loud along the way. There goes his trip to Hollywood – he's lucky I didn't smack him one on the side of the head.

The coach and Scootch are trying to get somebody ready to go in and pitch, while the rest of the team is on the bench in shock. Looks like we had everybody thinking the same thing. Teddy was hanging over the railing yelling for somebody to tell him what the fuck was going on.

I think I heard him yell, "What the fuck is going on?"

In due time, my good man, in due fuckin' time.

Mini-rally by the Senators in the midst of the confusion was too little, too late, and we won 11-4. Everything was moving along according to plan, with a two-game convincing whomping of the Senators gravy on top. Doc and I got Smokes and Rusty together that night and had them tell Coach Curran they were really beat. We suggested they go ahead to the All-Star game the next day. Also gets Smokes the fuck outta here before he blows it.

Coach bought it and Teddy reluctantly went along. You could tell he was flustered and decided to split town himself and go up to New York a day earlier than planned. Good to get rid of the schmuck, but ruined my evening celebration plans with Mrs. G.M. Oh well, plenty of time for that when we get back to Long Island. Unfortunately, I won't be able to get her to help me figure out what it was she said to me that was so critical.

The guys got it together the next afternoon, and we were able to sneak by the Senators 5-4 for a three-game sweep. Dong wasn't himself and got knocked around a bit, but Barney came in and went five shutout innings for the win. Slam fanned the side in the ninth, and we were cruising into the second half of the year twelve games in front.

Doc headed to Arizona to meet with a guy and get the last piece to the puzzle, while I headed to New York to see Tom Jr. and clear up a few loose ends. He had been admitted to the hospital for a checkup before he went back to work for his dad. You're headed to end of chapter period

Chapter 73

"Why don't you get your fakin' sorry ass out of bed and let the real sick people of the world have this room? Glad to see ya, bud."

"Harry, in the words of a famous bard – go fuckith thyself for thyne own pleasure."

"Good one, Tom. You must be thinking with at least half your brain to come up with that little ditty."

Tom Jr. looked good and would have looked even better if the thirty pounds he had lost jumped back on his bones. I knew there was a reason I was still worried about him.

"Really, kiddo, how you doing? You getting out of this place soon?"

"Doctors want to review my test results tomorrow, and if they like what they see, I'm outta here. The headaches are all but gone, and I've been up and moving around pretty good. I'm hoping it's a go for tomorrow. But fuck that, tell me about you and the guys."

"Tom, it's all I thought it would be and more. I'm having the time of my life and actually doing some good for the team too. That kid is gonna be a good catcher one day."

"That's great! What about the stuff we have been working on. Where are you on that?" Tom asked.

"Hooked up with Doc and we are two-teaming 'em. Had to enlist a coupla guys to help, and it's working out OK, so far. Trundle wants to play it out just like I laid it out for him, and that's what we're gonna do. We put the first part of the plan into action during the last series in Harrisburg, worked like a charm. Doc went to Arizona to get confirmation on the last piece of info we need and then we nail 'em to the cross. You done good, Tom, real good. The research you did put me on to the method they used and solidified our suspicions on who was involved. Mr. Trundle knows what you did for us and, as you know, he doesn't forget."

"Harry, I couldn't give a rat's ass. Just promise me that when it comes to hammer time, I'm in the general area to have a go at them nails. I deserve at least one good swing."

"Kiddo, you'll be swinging away with the rest of us. I gotta split. You need anything?"

"I'm cool, Harry. Thanks for stopping by. I know you have lots on your mind and a million things to do up here. I appreciate it, man."

"Oh, stop that shit. Do me a favor and say hi to your dad for me. And get the fuck out of here and do something useful for a change, will ya? I can't be worrying about you and catching rat bastards at the same time, now can I?"

"Get out of here, you asshole. I'll see you out at the park soon. And be careful?"

"Bet on it, chief."

Bet on end of chapter period

Chapter 74

"Bunny, I thought I told you to lock the door. You didn't do it, and now look at the crap that can just walk right in here."

"Hi to you to, Mel babe. How they hanging?"

"Lower than turtle balls, as long as you asked. What the fuck are you doing here? Big star comes home to break balls, I guess."

"Big star my ass. A 31-year-old player-coach for a Double A team in Bayfuckinport, Long Island, ain't star material, my man. But just knowing you're thinking of me does my heart good."

"Shove it, Harry. What do you want?"

"I missed you, Harry," Bunny chimed in finally. "You haven't even invited me to come out and see you play. My feelings have been hurt."

"Bunny, my dear, you are always welcome. Why don't I pick you up for Saturday's game and we can get some dinner afterwards. Sound good?"

"It's a date," she blushed.

I came to my senses finally and did what I had come to do. A few new messages of no consequence and junk mail to throw away. Figured I'd try my luck with Ebil and asked, "Heard anything on Trundle Industries lately, Mel?"

"Like what?"

"Anything at all. I've been concentrating on playing and haven't been in contact with them much recently." No sense in putting words in his mouth.

"The stock took a hit right after you left for Florida, but it rebounded to a new high in May. Some European deal went sour and they needed a new manufacturer for one of their companies. It was fixed and nothing more was said."

No help, but glad to know everything was cool.

"Good enough. I'm outta here. See ya Saturday, Bunny; how's 10 o'clock sound?"

"I'll be here in the office, Harry. I'm looking forward to it. And thanks again."

I walked over to my place. As I got to the top of the driveway, Sandy was bending over to get something out of the back seat of her car. When she straightened up and turned around I was right in front of her. She just smiled that smile and said, "Get the other bag, Harry, and come in. It's déjà vu time again."

And what a déjà vu time it turned out to be.

All at one time now, end of chapter period

Chapter 75

Rusty and Smokes weren't scheduled to pitch in the Double A All-Star game since they threw in the Harrisburg series. As planned, they got treatment for tiredness in their throwing shoulders from a clinic in New York. While there they also complained of an all-over fatigue. Planned, as in I had them request it as part of my master scheme to flush out the rat bastards we were tracking.

In actuality, they couldn't have been healthier, and loved playing undercover agent. Smokes convinced Rusty they were the next Mission Impossible team. Vivid imagination coming from that dude's brain.

Cat and Howdy were brought into the fold before they left for the All-Star game; they signed up right away. Punch was with them, acting as the Schooners' representative to the All-Star coaching staff. They both started, and as rehearsed, begged out after two innings with symptoms identical to Rusty and Smokes. Punch didn't know what to make of what was going on and left for New York as soon as the game ended. The boys played their parts like old pros.

The tricky part was being able to bait the trap without jeopardizing the Schooners team as a whole, and the individual players themselves. We didn't plan on going public, so everything hinged on us being able to force the hand of a few individuals who had laid low for over a year now. We weren't dealing with a bunch of dummies; there was a lot at stake. What happened to Tom Jr. still loomed large in my mind.

Doc and I had enlisted the four musketeers as accomplices, but didn't want to risk adding anyone else to the plan. It was make or break with what we had, and we were in deep already – there was no going back now.

I was still stuck on one very important point and had racked my brain over and over trying to make some sense of it. The attempt to scuttle the Schooners last year was deliberate, well-planned, as well as very risky. After going to all that trouble and almost succeeding in bringing down the franchise, why haven't they followed up? A winning year and everything they did would seem to go down the drain. Unless that's what they wanted. But why? The old adage is when you have them on the run, bang 'em into the ground. There's something wrong with this picture, and I'm not focused in. Damn, I hate this shit.

Hopefully, Doc will come to the rescue when he gets back tomorrow. Unless something out of the blue comes up, we are ready to move to the next part of our plan. The end is in sight, if all goes well, and nobody spills the beans early.

Gotta get to the park early, so it's sack time, and end of chapter period

Chapter 76

We were due to start the second half of the season the next night, and I met Doc at the ballpark at noon. We were the only ones there that early, so we decided to stroll out to the bullpen to get away from the early arrivers.

"I don't know how you figured it out, Harry," Doc told me, "but you were dead on. The guy I had check it out found all the information we needed through a contact in the company's human resources department."

"That's all we needed to finish this up, Doc. Great work. How about the small seek and search mission we talked about?"

"I have a cousin who dabbles in getting into places he shouldn't be – he was able to take a peek at the place last week. He got a sample and I have it with me. Do you want to have it analyzed?"

"I don't think that will be necessary, Doc. Just having it will be enough to turn the bastard, I'm sure. Once he spills his guts, the others are dead meat."

"Your call, Harry. I'm gonna love seeing the look on his face when you confront the fuck. I still can't figure out how you did it, though. What was it that pointed you to him?"

"There was something somebody said to me that was buried in this thick head of mine; I knew it was important. It finally came to the surface, and that's why I had you check out that stuff. It just kinda popped into my head for no reason, other than it was there."

"Well, it's good it did. When do you want to nail the peckerwoods?"

"We better do it soon. I can't guarantee the boys will hold up for too much longer. I also don't want to include anybody else, and if it's gonna look like last year, the rest of the team would have to follow suit. No, let's kick some ass and get it over with. Tomorrow before the game is gonna be it. He folds like a cheap suit and the rest of them will fall like dominoes in a row."

"You know I have tons of faith in you, Harry, but what if he doesn't crack and holds it together? Without him we can't go after the others."

"Don't worry, Doc. We made arrangements for a very special guest tomorrow to do the honors. I can tell you for certain he won't hold up under the pressure when the sheriff comes to town."

"OK, Harry, it's your show. Do I get to watch?"

"Front row seat, Doc, right next to me. Be sure and bring your best gloat with you 'cause it's gonna come in handy."

We went out that night and started off the second half with a bang. Cat and Howdy sat out to keep the trick going, and Dong came back strong to throw eight shutout innings. The last place team played like one, and we romped by nine runs. Yours truly had two hits and I'm hitting .307 for the year with eleven homers and 31 RBI's. Not bad for a P.I. masquerading as a ballplayer, if I do say so myself.

Before I forget, not that I'm prone to forgetting or anything, RBI is Runs Batted In in baseballese. I don't give two shits about the proper pronunciation, the "'s" belongs on the end of RBI's. Now, get up and write or call ESPN and hound them until something gets done about it. I don't ever want to hear "he had 23 RBI for the week" again!

The general manager was nowhere to be found, so I headed home to Manhasset after the game. That was kinda strange for him not to be at the game. Teddy gets to most home games, and after what happened in Harrisburg, you would have thought he would have been there. Odd, don't you think?

No G.M. meant no way to know what the G.M.'s wife was up to. Probably better that way under the circumstances. Tomorrow's gonna be a wild day, and I have to get my shit in order.

Prepare yourself is what I was taught, and I always do.

End of chapter period

Chapter 77

Doc came in about twenty minutes after I did. We made ourselves look busy by having Doc work on my shoulder. Scootch was in early too, and sat down to bullshit with us. I could tell Doc was nervous by the way he was attempting to tear my arm from my shoulder.

"Just a little easier, Doc, if you don't mind. It's a little tired, but I think I'll keep it for now unless you have a better one to replace it." He laughed and that seemed to calm him down a bit.

Punch ambled in around one o'clock looking for Cat, who had asked him to come in for a little extra hitting today. In actuality, I had Cat ask him to get him here when nobody else would be around. As planned, Cat was nowhere to be found. What we hadn't planned on was Scootch being here this early. No problem though, as it turned out. When Punch showed up, Scootch got up and left without saying a word. Not the best of buds, I presume.

"You guys see Cat today?" Punch asked us.

"No, Punch, we haven't. You supposed to meet him here this early?"

"Yeah, he wanted to hit some and asked if I'd watch him. He thinks his bat speed is down and wanted to see if I could spot anything mechanical. Where is the little shit?" he said, annoyed as all hell.

Promptly at 1:10 p.m., as planned, the mystery guest came stomping into the clubhouse, followed by two rather large and imposing fellows. The kind you say "yes, sir and no, sir" to, and don't dare piss off for fear of your life.

Punch turned when he saw us looking at the men approaching, and his mouth fell open when he recognized the man leading the group.

"Hello, Paul, it's been awhile, hasn't it? How have you been? And how's Roberta?"

"Um, ah, I ah – fine I guess, Mr. Trundle. I've been fine, and Roberta is fine too." Talk about your bumbling idiot.

"That's good, Paul. And again, I'm sorry for Roberta's loss. Her father was always a good man and a credit to Trundle Industries." You got the feeling he was talking in the past tense and not just because he was dead. There was something else intended that Doc and I already knew, and Paul was about to find out.

"If you have a minute, Paul, there is a matter I would like to discuss with you. Perhaps we could adjourn to the meeting room for a little privacy."

"Sure thing, Mr. Trundle."

Randy led the way, the walking buildings following Paul into the room. Doc and I trailed along and shut the door behind us.

Punch noticed Doc and I when he heard the door close. "Guys, Mr. Trundle and I are meeting in private...."

"It's alright, Paul, I've asked Harry and Eddie to sit in on our meeting."

Took me a second to remember Eddie was Doc's real name. Wondered who else was here that I couldn't see.

Punch was beginning to sweat even though the air conditioning was pumping in enough cool air to keep us all comfortable. Trundle can do that to you. I'm sure the gorillas didn't help any.

"Paul, I have a rather large problem that needs attention and should be rectified immediately. I have some material here that I would like you to read. After you have finished, we can discuss the contents and other issues that go along with it. Would you do that for me, Paul? It would be most helpful if you could assist me in understanding this material."

The information Randy was referring to had been extracted right off the Internet. It also included a combination of data from the research Tom Jr. gave me, plus Ms. Timmons' staff's documentation. I'm no scientist, rocket or otherwise, but this stuff was explosive shit.

Randy handed Punch a piece of paper he had extracted from his leather folder and asked him to read it to himself first, and when he was comfortable with its contents, read it aloud to the rest of us. I was sure I knew what it said since I had prepared it myself and sent it to the big guy for this occasion.

Punch took the piece of paper and read it to himself. Any attempt to say anything to Randy or anyone else in the room was met with a "Just read it, Paul" from Randy as a direct order from on high.

POISON - a substance, natural or synthetic, that causes damage to living tissues and has an injurious or fatal effect on the body, whether it is ingested, inhaled, or absorbed or injected throughthe skin. Poisoning involves four elements: the poison, the poisoned organism, the injury to the cells...cause, subject, effect and consequence.

A poison is a substance capable of producing adverse effects on an individual under appropriate conditions. "Appropriate conditions" refers to the dosage of the substance that is sufficient to cause these adverse effects... capable of inducing weakness and paralysis... and Synthetic toxins are responsible for most poisonings. "Synthetic" refers to chemicals manufactured by chemists... The physical form of a chemical – solid, liquid, gas vapor...ingestion is the most common route of exposure to toxic chemicals...a poison in a liquid form can be absorbed by ingestion or by inhalation or through the skin...

The amount of chemical to which a person is exposed is extremely important...administered at a dose that will 'cause the toxin to accumulate in the tissue and consequently the elimination of the chemical is not completed within 24 hours...eventually the toxic threshold is reached and injury will develop.

CURARE is a skeletal-muscle-relaxant drug belonging to the alkaloid family of organic compounds ...acts as a neuromuscular blocking agent to produce flaccidity in striated (striped) muscle... preventing nerve impulses from activating skeletal, or voluntary, muscles… sources include various tropical American plants (primarily Chondrodendron species of the family Menispermaceae) …in anesthesia produces a profound relaxation…quickly reversible action…Curare also is used in cases in which a state of profound relaxation or even immobility is desired…

CURARIFORM DRUG, any of various drugs that interfere with the transmission of stimulatory impulses from nerve to muscle… used to induce muscle relaxation in surgery… in fatal doses death is 'caused by respiratory paralysis…

A look of astonishment was etched on Punch's face. We would see that look again before long.

He had read all he needed to read, dropped the paper on the table, and buried his face in his hands. A broken man – end of chapter period

Chapter 78

We just waited.

Trundle stared at Punch with a look of disgust.

Finally, after what seemed like forever, Punch lifted his head and turned toward Trundle. The tree-trunk twins never took their eyes off him for a second and were ready to pounce if he even twitched a muscle.

Trundle still stared.

Me, I did what I was told to do per Randy's instructions before we entered the room. "Just sit there and keep Doc quiet. I'll handle everything" was what Randy had said.

When I thought we were gonna go on like this forever, Randy pointed to the hulk on the left and asked him to get Mr. Tennly some water. He then turned his full attention to the matter at hand.

"I surmise we can dispense with the reading of the document out loud, Paul?"

"I would appreciate that, Mr. Trundle" as he took the water.

"Then let us proceed. For Harry and Doc's sake, recap for us your involvement with Trundle Industries in the past, and also your involvement with last year's Schooner team problem. Do not assume anyone other than you and I know any of the details.

"And Paul, the complete story please," Randy said.

"I'll try to do my best, Mr. Trundle," Punch said with a sigh.

As background, Punch gave us the Reader's Digest version of his baseball career. After a mediocre nine years in the minors, he caught on with his original organization as a bullpen coach. Slowly he worked his way to hitting instructor and hung around the minors for nineteen years. During that time, he was going to school and working in his father's business in the off season.

His dad owned a pharmacy.

At the age of fifty, he hung them up and got a job at PharmCo. Inc., an Arizona pharmaceutical company near his home. It was part of a conglomerate – Trundle Industries. Twenty-five years experience working at the corner drugstore and his years of studies earned him a choice spot in the company working on a government project.

From the Schooners perspective, the rest is history. Black history as it turned out. First things first.

"I was working in the 'High Profile' wing supervising one of the government projects at the time," he started. "I had been dabbling on my own for about ten years and that assignment was perfect for me. That's where I met Roberta's dad, who was the project manager. He had been with the company his whole life, took a liking to me, and brought me in under his wing. His health had been failing and he was getting ready to retire. He brought me in on the project with the idea that I would take over for him."

"What was the focus of this government project, Paul?" Trundle interrupted.

"Mr. Trundle, I believe that was a NTK project."

Doc looked at me and I shrugged. NTK, whatever the fuck that was, never came up in any information I was given.

"Paul, there are no NTK projects at that company, haven't been since you left. What was it?"

I guess Randy saw the confusion on our faces and helped out. The twin-tower boys couldn't give two shits; they concentrated on Punch.

"NTK, Harry, was the company's code for a project whose details were on a 'Needs-To-Know' basis. If you weren't involved, you didn't need to know it existed was the theory. It's common practice."

"Thanks," I said for both me and Doc.

"Go on, Paul. What was the scope of the project?"

"We were working for the government trying to perfect a masking agent. It had been ongoing for some time when I came into the project. My assistance helped them turn the corner, but ultimately the government's interest gave out and we lost the funding. We only needed another year and we would have had it."

da bushes

"Masking agent for what?"

"Poisons."

"What happened then?" Trundle asked as if he didn't know.

This is where I got a little fuzzy. From what I gathered, the next we see of Punch is him being hired by the Schooners. Why I still don't get.

Everyone but Randy jumped when his cell phone went off. Punch almost went to see his dad permanently, and he had to gulp the rest of his water to keep from heaving.

"Yes," Trundle said into the phone. "Don't let him do that. I have the bird – I'll be right there."

"I apologize, gentlemen, I have to attend to an emergency. Paul will not be continuing with the Schooners. Harry will assume his duties as of this moment."

News to me, boys and girls.

"Paul, you will go with these two men and stay where they take you until I send for you. Do not diverge from those instructions. Have I made myself perfectly clear?"

"Yes, sir," Punch whispered, head down.

"What has occurred in this room stays among us for now. We will resume where we left off very soon. Any questions?" Nobody blinked and Trundle was gone.

I was a hitting coach and Punch was getting his ass hauled out the back door for places unknown. This was getting very interesting with more to come, I promise.

Gotta get ready for tonight's game and keep Doc cool. So cool your own jets with end of chapter period

Chapter 79

Teddy showed for the game with Jeannie in tow. She had on this yellow jumpsuit number that she wore the first night I stopped by on my journey home. It's light and airy, and if I remember correctly, as she wears it, touches nothing but skin.

It had been awhile, and seeing her again brought out the horny toad in me. What, you're surprised? Just because she happens to be the wife of the general manager for the team I work means I can't do the horizontal watussi with her on occasion? Go down to the local Blockbuster and rent yourself a life.

The G.M. stormed into the clubhouse and started right in. "Where the hell is Punch? Hey Curran, where's that dumb-ass hitting coach of yours?"

"He won't be able to make tonight's game, Teddy. I believe I heard he wasn't feeling well enough to come out."

"You believe you heard he wasn't feeling well? You don't know? Didn't you speak to him? Who runs this club anyway? Do I have to do every goddamn thing around here?"

Coach was getting red and was about to explode; he had put up with Teddy's shit for two years. The asshole had pushed him too far.

"Hey, I took the call," I lied to save Coach. "Punch won't be coming out tonight and hopes to make it tomorrow. He's gonna see if he can get something for it tonight."

What the fuck does that mean? Doc looked at me like I had three heads, but luck was on my side. The team's music to hit the field started, and the guys ran for the door like Dr. Death was on their asses. Teddy gave me a look and shook his head.

"Another time, Shorts," he barked, and stormed out.

da bushes

"And the horse you rode in on," I answered, just low enough so he couldn't hear me.

The phone in Coach's office rang and he went in to get it. "Go on out, Harry, I'll be right behind you," he said.

As I started for the tunnel door, Coach yelled for me to come back into his office. "It's for you, Harry. You can take it in here – I think she said her name was Ms. Timmons."

Will wonders never cease?

"Harry, it's Ms. Timmons. Mr. Trundle would like to see you in his office tomorrow morning at nine. He is planning on concluding the meeting you attended today, and all parties involved will be present. May I send Charles for you?"

"That would be great. We have a game tomorrow night at 7:30, so I have all day. I'm due here at 3:00 p.m. to get the early hitters through their workout before game preparations begin."

"That shouldn't be a problem, Harry. Charles can take you back when your meeting is finished. Would 8:00 a.m. be appropriate?"

I wanted to tell her me and her all night long would be appropriate, but settled for "Eight would be fine, Ms. Timmons. Thanks for your help."

"You're welcome, Harry. We'll see you tomorrow. And don't worry, Paulie Girl won't be visiting you again," she said as the phone disconnected.

Damn her. How does she know everything all the time? Come hell or high water, I'm getting that babe's first name so I can do the ultimate one-up and hang up on her. Count on it.

We kicked ass on Erie, and it looked like nobody was gonna catch us the way we were playing. When we get Cat and Howdy back on the field, and the aces throwing again, it'll be like taking candy from a baby. Man this is fun – did I already say that?

I didn't play and made every excuse to get on the field to catch a glimpse of the vision in yellow. When the game ended I got a small wave that meant no dice for tonight.

Have to be soon, sweetie, have to be soon.

Have to be end of chapter period

Chapter 80

Eight sharp and Charlie had the purple chariot idling in the driveway. I can tell you, I was glad this day was finally coming, and the people that did this would be getting what they deserved. I just didn't know what Randy was gonna do to them.

"How you been, Charlie?"

"Good, Harry, very good. The wife just got back from seeing her grandkids again and she is happier than a kitten in a yarn factory. She's happy, I'm happy."

"That's good, Charlie. Gonna be a long day, I think. You pulled the Harry detail for the day I hear."

"Be worse things I could be doing. And by the way, the lady with the smile left a few minutes ago. How you and she be getting on these days?"

"Every once in a while, Charlie. It's how we like it, suits us both fine. No harm, no foul, as they say."

"You the man, Harry. Let's head downtown. Eats in the bag. Enjoy."

"Thanks, Charlie. My usual – you the man, too."

I tried to envision how this was gonna go down but was drawing a blank. I never would have thought something could have been more important than what we were doing when Trundle split on us. Man can surprise you for sure.

"What's the old man like, Charlie? You seen him since yesterday?"

"I picked him up from the heliport and took him to the office straight away. The man wasn't in a talkative mood. Barely got a 'Thank you, Charles' from him as he flew out of the car. Something big was up, I can tell you that."

"Some heavy shit going down, Charlie. Good idea to keep your

da bushes

head down for a few days. Do you know if Ms. Timmons is in today?"

"Haven't seen her but her car was in the garage when I left this morning. That usually means she is in."

"Thanks Charlie, and the grub's great as usual. I'm gonna miss you when I split."

"Me too, Harry."

We were quiet the rest of the way in with the traffic kinda light for a weekday morning. I got to Trundle Industries by 8:45 with no sign of my favorite guide. Guess they figured I could find my own way by now. You just can't get good help these days.

The receptionist pointed me toward the conference room down the hall from Mr. Trundle's corner suite. No reason to spill blood in his personal conference area. Let the working masses deal with the clean-up when he is done. I must have been early 'cause I was the first one there.

"Harry, how about some coffee?" could only have come from the voice of the darling Ms. Timmons. "Come on down to my office. It's early. The meeting has been pushed back to 9:30 due to Mr. Trundle's schedule. He is due here any minute and has to deal with one issue before we get started."

"We?" I inquired.

"Mr. Trundle has asked me to sit in and witness the meeting as the official corporate representative for Trundle Industries. All corporate business decisions require two corporate officers present to make it legal per the company's charter. I will be acting as the second officer."

"Something going to happen that involves Trundle Industries that I don't know about, Ms. Timmons?"

"You never know, Harry, you just never know."

"Ms. Timmons, Mr. Trundle is in the conference room and would like to see you," came over her phone intercom.

"You'll have to excuse me, Harry. I'll see you in the conference room" as she hurried by. I think it was Chantilly that trailed after her.

With nothing else to do, I took a look around her office. Smaller digs than I would have expected, but a lot of bread was spent furnishing it. There was also an obvious lack of clutter one would have expected for a person as high up as Ms. Timmons. She either was a compulsive neatnick, or somebody else kept the paper trail for her.

Computer was locked and I didn't have time to fool with it. That was where the rubber met the road, I'd bet – if I was a betting man.

"Mr. Shorts, would you follow me to the conference room, please? The meeting will be starting fairly soon," which really meant get your ass out of my boss's office, in executive assistantese.

It was time to get down and dirty with the dirty ones. Been there, done that, and nobody plays in the mud like Harry M. Shorts. Except maybe Mr. M. Randle Trundle, as I was coming to find out.

I'm gone to my meeting and you're gone to end of chapter period

Chapter 81

As I entered the conference room I pulled up short and wondered if I had lost my way. Couldn't be though, as Ms. Timmons' executive assistant had brought me to the door.

"Come in, Harry. We will be done in a minute. Have some coffee – it's over on the credenza," Randy offered

"Hello, Harry," Tom Westbrook, Senior said as he waved to me from the other end of the conference table.

"Hey bud," came from Tom Westbrook, Junior, seated next to his dad.

"There we go, Tom. Just sign this last one, and we are done with this matter for now. Congratulations on joining Trundle Industries. And you, go play golf and have fun," he directed at Tom, Sr.

Before I could get a word in, Tom, Sr. was up from the table, out a side door, and gone. At the same time, the pair of human monuments came in, Punch sandwiched between them. From the look on his face and his drooping shoulders, I don't think he was planning on making a run for it.

"Harry, come down here and sit next to me. If you wouldn't mind, Tom, why don't you make yourself comfortable on the couch over by the window? Gentleman, please escort Paul, or Punch as Harry calls him, to the seat at the other side of the table. We'll fill in the other chairs as we go."

Everyone sat as instructed, the big fellows hung out along the back wall close to Paul. It was clearly Randy's show to direct.

"Now, where were we before we were rudely interrupted yesterday? And for everyone's edification, this meeting is being taped, with Ms. Timmons serving as second officer as per our charter."

All looked at Ms. Timmons and tried to figure out where the mics were. I'd rather just look at Ms. Timmons, so I continued to do so.

"Paul, I trust you had a comfortable evening?"

"Yeah, I mean yes, sir – under the circumstances."

"Good, now please continue where you left off yesterday. And if I might warn you, other individuals will be joining us as we go along. Do not, and I repeat, do not address them in any manner. You will restrict your comments to the matters we are discussing and direct them to me at all times."

Looking somewhat confused, Punch nevertheless said, "Yes sir, Mr. Trundle." It would appear Punch had a come-to-Jesus meeting with himself last evening and he done seen the light.

"You were about to tell us about masking agents and how that dovetails with what you had been doing prior to your employment at Pharizon. Please proceed."

"My dad had been a pharmacist his whole life and I worked with him since I was a boy. That and my love of plants drew me to the job at Pharizon. My interests as I got more experienced had gravitated to working with hybrids, and I had been experimenting with all kinds of plants, including growing a form of Chondrodendron in my greenhouse in Arizona. It's Curare to the common person to simplify things."

Doc's secret spy had gotten us a sample from the green house and Trundle had it in his possession at this very moment. What you call proof of the pudding, you might say. Punch didn't know it, but Trundle would have sprung it on him if he denied growing it.

"The masking agent project was a natural extension of my personal interests. I envisioned incorporating that aspect with my own hybrids and making a fortune by selling the end product to Pharizon for mass production. I could retire and continue my work at home, in my own greenhouse, with the funds to do as I pleased."

"Get on with the Schooner part of the story, Paul, if you would" showed Randy's impatience with Punch for the first time.

"OK. One day I was approached by Roberta's dad with a proposition. I had met Roberta after starting at Pharizon through her father, and we got married about two years later. He wasn't just my boss then, he was

da bushes

also my father-in-law, and we had gotten to like each other quite a bit. We were in my den when he dropped this bombshell in my lap. I just sat and listened to what he had to say, kinda dumfounded."

He was looking a little white at this point in time and asked for some water. The largest water boy in the world got him some.

Punch was drinking his water as the conference room door flew open and Teddy Trundle burst in, pissed as all hell. "Why was I ordered to come in here at this specific time without any knowledge of what...." He stopped in mid-sentence, looked around the room, and surveyed the people seated around the conference table. His eyes shifted from his father to me, finally settling on Paul Tennly.

He just stood there at a loss for words.

He could have said end of chapter period

Chapter 82

"Theodore, sit down in the chair in front of the large gentleman by the credenza," came a directive from Randy.

I never saw the Hulkmeister move from where he previously stood, but he was in front of the credenza when Randy spoke.

"Please do as I have instructed now, and don't say another word until spoken to. If you do, you will regret it dearly."

Interestingly, Ms. Timmons hadn't said a word nor blinked an eye the entire time we had been in the room. She just observed as the second officer as per corporate charter dictated. As I was sure she had done a whole lotta times before.

Teddy was about to run his mouth again, thought better of it, and stopped before any words came out. He sat where he was told to sit.

"Go on, Paul, and please disregard that small interruption."

Teddy's eyes were boring a hole right through Punch. The whole room was a bundle of tingling nerves as he started in again.

"Carl, that's Roberta's father's name, laid the whole plan out for me. He was to be the front man on a bid to purchase a minor league baseball team in the Double A Eastern League that would become available the following month. There was only going to be one other bidder, and his group was to be a surprise second one. The money was all behind the scenes and he would be listed as the owner, with silent partners. I was to be the hitting instructor – I'd be back in baseball again."

"Paul, did Carl give you any indication who the silent partners were?" asked Trundle.

"It was the weirdest part to the whole thing. Carl was beside himself with joy. He told me the president of Pharizon himself had come to

da bushes

him to ask him to be part of the team that was going to put in a bid on this minor league baseball franchise."

"Did he mention any other silent partner during the conversation?" Randy prompted.

"No, just the president of Pharizon. He was so thrilled that the president wanted him to be part of the team, personally make the offer, and that I would be back in baseball, he didn't ask any questions. He said yes right on the spot, and actually forgot to ask what he would get for fronting the offer."

I hadn't said a word up to this point, but I knew a bombshell was about to hit the table. That important conversation hidden in the back of my brain that I finally remembered had tipped me to the answer. It was confirmed by Doc and the human resources person at Pharizon.

"Who was that person, Paul?"

"Why, you know who it was, Mr. Trundle, it was Teddy Trundle, your son," Punch said matter-of-factly. "He was the president of Pharizon."

With that Teddy jumped up, pointed at Punch and yelled, "You fucking bastard, I'll kill you for that."

A hand the size of a catcher's mitt grabbed Teddy and slammed him back in his chair. Stunned, he didn't try to get up again.

"Teddy, I told you to sit there and not speak until spoken to. Do not force the gentleman behind you to hurt you in order to get you to comply with my wishes," Randy said in his calmest of voices.

The important piece to the puzzle that I had struggled with and couldn't put my fingers on had finally come to me in a flash. I could see Jeannie's eyes that night as she said, "We were both reasonably happy in Arizona, him being the boss running Daddy's pharmaceutical company…." At that instant I pulled the whole operation together.

"Let's all take a deep breath and then we can continue. I'm sure we won't be interrupted like that again," said Randy.

We will be interrupted by end of chapter period

Chapter 83

Order was restored and everyone was seated again, including Teddy. He was sitting there seething, knowing there wasn't a fuckin' thing he could do about what was about to go down. And what was going down was him and what was left of his life, as he presently knew it.

"Let us continue, Paul, if you would. What happened to the plan that was laid out, as you understood it? Take your time, Paul," urged Trundle.

"I don't actually know what went wrong with the plan, to tell you the truth. Roberta's dad presented the offer to the league with the complete proposed outline from franchise inception to inaugural game. It was guaranteed to be a slam-dunk. Our inside information was supposed to give us exactly what we needed to get the nod. Someone screwed up is what happened."

A daddy-to-son look-me-in-the-eye occurred, the son blinking first.

Addressing the group again, Randy went on. "That would be correct, Paul, but we can come back to that later. When your group didn't get the franchise, what did you do next?"

"Well, Teddy was furious and said some very nasty things about what he was gonna do about it, and how he would get that fucker. I didn't know who he was talking about at the time. I found out later on that it was you, Mr. Trundle, that got the franchise. The saddest thing is I think it killed Roberta's dad; he had his heart set on being part of that team."

It was all Teddy could do to keep from jumping across the table and strangling Punch with his bare hands to shut him up. Well, maybe the man-mountain behind him had something to do with it, I would imagine.

"I am sorry to hear that, Paul. Carl was a good man. What happened next?"

"Nothing happened next is what happened. We went about our business just as Teddy told us to. He said it wasn't over yet, we would have our chance later on."

"What did he mean by that?"

"I didn't know when he told us originally. It was about a year later that he was named the general manager. He asked me to quit Pharizon and join the team as hitting coach. That's when he laid out the details of his plan, told me I was the person to help him do it. I guess he knew of my work in the government project."

"What did he ask you to do specifically, Paul?"

"He asked me if I could manufacture a product that would help him sabotage the team without anybody finding out about it. I assumed he meant using the masking agent we had perfected, or almost perfected. He wanted them to play badly and start to lose precisely when he wanted them to."

Randy looked very disturbed at this statement, even though he knew all of it, the details I had given him matching Punch's comments. He looked right at Punch and said, "Paul, I've known some men who have done some very bad things in their lives and thought nothing of it. How could you do this?"

Punch just sat there looking down at the tabletop, afraid to look up or open his mouth.

Randy shook his head in disgust. "Go on," he said.

"I said sure, I could do it. The masking agent I was perfecting was foolproof. I could combine any substance, in any form, and you would never be able to detect the poison later on. I must have been crazy to agree to do it – but I did."

"What exactly did you do, Paul?"

"Integrating it with the normal baseball activities would be the best way to introduce the foreign substance and not draw any attention was what I figured. Having the resources at hand in Pharizon, I was able to produce vitamins and salt tablets with a low enough dosage to use on a daily basis, build up the toxin level slowly. We had to wait until it got warm enough to make sure the pills would be used every day. Doc gave me the daily supply of good vitamins and salt tablets. I exchanged my pills for his, and gave them to select players at regular intervals. I controlled their toxin levels on a daily basis."

"Is that the only method you used?" Randy interjected.

"No, it wasn't," Punch continued. "The rubdowns Doc handled were with the normal liniment we had on hand. When I scheduled the outside people to do rubdowns, I gave them the liniment laced with the toxic substance and the masking agent. Looked and felt the same, but it had the effect of introducing the poison into their system directly through the skin. They used special gloves I provided from Pharizon that protected their hands from the substance.

"Lastly, I brewed my herbal tea from plants I had grown in my greenhouse that I had been experimenting with for the last five years. I had hoped to publish my derivative work with Curare someday, but I guess that won't be possible now. I told the players it had extra minerals that would help heal them. Actually, tasted pretty good, if you ask me," he said quite proudly.

Everyone in the room was quiet when Punch finished speaking. Trundle, Senior stared at Punch for a minute and then shifted his glare to his son, who still hadn't moved or said a word. Me, quiet as a field mouse, I wasn't gonna say boo until spoken to by the guy in charge.

Finally, he spoke. "That is an ingenious use of the work that could have been very beneficial to Pharizon, and to yourself, Paul. It is a shame you wasted it. Now tell us, was this plan all yours, or did someone direct you to do this?"

"Teddy and I discussed it, and we came up with it together. I told him what I could do, he decided exactly what we would use and how."

"To your knowledge, was anyone else a part of this?"

"Well, I don't know for sure, Mr. Trundle. Teddy was the only person other than Roberta's father that I spoke to about the team, or our plans."

"Very well. Teddy, do you have anything to add at this time?"

Not a word.

"Harry, may I see you privately for a minute in my office? The rest of you will stay put for now. Ms. Timmons, will you accompany us, please?"

da bushes

Directing his words toward the giants squared, he said, "Please see everyone stays comfortably in place. Mr. Westbrook may move about, but the rest should remain seated."

When we were seated in his office, Randy spoke directly to Ms. Timmons. "Upon his entering the room, all hell may break loose. Are the proper precautions in place?"

"Yes sir, they have been attended to. I took care of them personally. What would you like to do with Paul and Teddy after we are concluded?"

"I personally took care of that. Harry, when this is all said and done, you and I will sit down and discuss where we go from here. Your assistance in handling this matter has been invaluable. Just stick close to me for now, OK?"

"Yes sir, boss. You can count on it."

"We will begin again in a minute" after end of chapter period

Chapter 84

A squirt and wash of the hands and we were back in the conference room, all in our assigned seats. Randy was still holding court.

"Most disappointed is probably the least I can say about your involvement and actions in this whole affair," Randy started in, directing his comments toward Punch. "How you could do something so unthinkable to these fine young men who wanted nothing more than to follow a dream – it's inexcusable. And you, who had been in the game for so long and understood what they were up against in the best of circumstances. I'm appalled. Your father must be turning in his grave."

He sipped from the crystal glass before him, then continued, "Teddy, I'm ashamed to call you my own flesh and blood. Not just for what you did, but for stabbing me in the back as well. Did you actually think you could beat me at my own game? How foolish."

Teddy said nada word, which is more than he should have said. What he did was defenseless.

"Now, which one of you will tell us who the brains behind this debacle was? Teddy, you may speak now."

He wasn't sure what to do or what his father knew. The look on his face said he was about to shit himself. Honor among thieves, and all that. He continued to remain quiet.

"Just as I expected. Paul, I don't believe you actually know who it is, do you?"

"Well, no, I don't know of anyone else, Mr. Trundle. Just Teddy, that's all."

"Fine," said Randy. He hit a button on the console in front of him and spoke to his executive assistant, I guess. "Send them in, Martha."

Just like in the movies, all eyes in the room were riveted on the

da bushes

doors to the conference room. When they opened, a tall, rugged-looking man entered, followed by two guys wearing detective badges in the breast pockets of their suit jackets.

Randy was right – all hell broke loose, and Tom, Jr. had to be forcibly escorted from the room.

The detectives stepped in front of the guy, and the hired muscle made sure everyone else in the room sat back down and behaved themselves. I was being a good boy, so they didn't have to worry about me. Ms. Timmons was behaving as well. Thought you might want to know.

"Hello, Joseph. Please have a seat at the head of the table. We saved the place of honor for you."

He sat and we waited for the man to explain what the hell was going on. Me, I hadn't met him, but I knew who our visitor was.

"For the group's sake, let us put all bullshit aside. We will now get down to the heart of the matter. The two gentlemen standing by the door are detectives Crowley and McGraf from the NYPD. They are on vacation, and at my request have been entertaining Joseph for the past two days."

We all looked at the two detectives in unison. Nice looking guys, but I'd bet you don't fuck with them without living to regret it.

"That," as he pointed to the other end of the table, "is Joseph Fredericks, who until recently was my friend, and anointed by me as the all important Number One here at Trundle Industries. We worked together for over twenty years. I trusted him with my company on a daily basis, acting as me in all company business when I wasn't there. Joseph is no longer a part of Trundle Industries."

It was clearly evident Teddy was familiar with Joseph, as was Ms. Timmons, for obvious reasons. While not having met him previously, I felt I knew him through the information I had in my possession.

"The remainder of the story, as they say, goes like this," Trundle continued. "Joseph was the mastermind behind the original plot to win the franchise, and with that failing, sabotaging the team's success. He remained behind the scenes at all times. Working through Teddy, he recruited Carl to make the bid, and brought you, Paul, into the picture both times."

Randy looked around the room at each person for emphasis.

"Joseph is the estranged son of Roberta Fredericks, since remarried, now named Roberta Tennly. He used Roberta's father, his grandfather, and Paul to get what he wanted. He used information from Trundle Industries, and me personally, to try and steal the bid for the Schooner franchise. That's why he was a Number One, and not me. He just wasn't good enough, and that's why he failed."

Teddy slumped in his chair, accepting defeat.

Punch was in shock, shifting his attention from Randy to Joseph and back again several times.

Me, no big deal, since I uncovered all of it and confirmed it with Doc's assistance. I couldn't rest until I discovered why Randy canned Fredericks' ass like he did. Trundle found out from a league source who had backed the other offer, and it was Joseph Fredericks.

"Do you have anything to say for yourself, Joseph?"

"No, Randle, I believe you've said it all. The only thing left is what you are going to do about it?"

"I'm glad you asked, Joseph. Here's how the deal will go down:

"As of this morning, Tom Westbrook, Jr. has assumed control of Westbrook Insurance Agency from his father, and the agency was purchased by Trundle Industries. This purchase will be funded by the three of you.

"The players from last year's Schooner team will each receive $100,000 for pain and suffering inflicted through your wrongful acts. The three of you will provide those funds.

"The coaches from last year's Schooner team will each receive $100,000 for the same reasons. Again, funded by you.

"Kizmet Inc.'s fees and expenses incurred while investigating this matter will be paid by the thee of you, plus a bonus of $100,000 for a job well done.

"Roberta Tennly and Jeannie Trundle will each receive a lump sum divorce settlement of $2.5 million, plus all real estate holdings currently jointly held. They have filed for divorce this morning, by the way, and neither of you will contest.

da bushes

"A scholarship fund in the amount of $1.0 million will be established in Carl's name to be distributed to Arizona students, funded the same way."

Randy sat back and took another sip from his crystal goblet. He assessed the reaction of the three pathetic dickheads before him and found them to be soundly beaten men.

"Documents have been prepared and will be signed by each of you before you leave this room today. You will agree and you will sign the documents. Questions?"

Without waiting for an answer he went on.

"Good. Next item would be what happens to the poor excuses for human beings before me. You will be transported to Arizona immediately, where you will live together in a modest three-bedroom ranch under house arrest for the next five years. The three of you will work at Pharizon in the cafeteria under strict daily supervision for the sum of $10,000 each per year, which you will use to pay all your bills. To ensure compliance, tracking bracelets will be provided free of charge. Any deviance from this plan will result in extradition to New York, where Detectives Crowley and McGraf will process the charges in this sealed envelope to the fullest extent of their powers. I would of course assist them, with extreme pleasure."

Trundle let that settle in for a minute.

"And, oh, by the way. The stipulations stated above have left the three of you absolutely penniless. That includes all offshore accounts, and my people are very thorough, as you well know."

Three nods, we were done.

"Ms. Timmons will see to the details," and Trundle left, having concluded this matter for good.

You can conclude end of chapter period

Chapter 85

M. Randle Trundle looked drained, as evidenced by the lack of color in his face and the apparent lack of strength in his posture. The man had a very tough morning on the back end of an unsettling year of utter confusion and uncertainty.

"Can I get you something to drink, Mr. Trundle?" inquired Ms. Timmons. "You look as though you could use one right about now."

I'd have to agree with her assessment. He didn't though.

"No, let's finish this business so we can all get on with our lives."

He turned his attention to me and asked, "What do you think of this morning's fiasco, Harry?"

I composed my thoughts for a second and then replied, "There was a moment when I wasn't sure how it would turn out. Fredericks coming into the room surprised everyone other than you, and it threw everyone into a tizzy. The detectives were a good safeguard on your part, not to mention the World Wrestling Federation tag team you employed."

"Yes, I felt some muscle and authority might be necessary. Joseph had been a problem of late, and we couldn't have any altercations in the room. He was the last piece to the puzzle, as you said before. WWF tag team – I like that one. The boys will be amused as well."

"May I ask a few questions to clear up a coupla points I'm a little hazy on?" I asked.

"Sure, Harry. Fire away."

"First, what was so urgent that required you to leave our meeting with Punch at the Schooners complex? It seemed odd to both Doc and me as well. And second, what set Westy off like that today?"

"Sorry not to have gotten back to you myself, Harry. I did have a very good reason to leave so quickly. It seems Tom, Jr. was about to go

da bushes

ballistic, a term you have used before, I believe. He was at Trundle Industries with his father to discuss the sale of the agency with my lawyers when he came upon a photo that unraveled the mystery of the person who attacked him at the train station. It was necessary for me to hurry back to the office to diffuse a potential explosion from occurring."

"You mean the feeling that the image of the attacker in the station window was tucked away somewhere in his brain was actually real?"

"Yes, it surfaced when he saw the same image through a conference room window wall at Trundle Industries. It was a recent photo of Joseph Fredericks in England, on a foxhunt. It was just a passing glance as he went by the room, the clothes and angle of the view rattling his memory, and it surfaced. It was Joseph who attacked Tom, Jr., and he wanted to tear the office apart to find him. I was needed most urgently to quell the situation."

"I'll be damned" came out of my mouth without me knowing it.

I do know it's end of chapter period

Chapter 86

When I came back down to earth, we discussed the rest of the morning, and I relayed to them how I came to know about Fredericks. Roberta had worked with Carl for a few years and used her married name. Pharizon's human resources department, through Doc's contact, provided the confirmation, and I had the last bit of information I needed.

Trundle had stuck it to them in spades and his generosity toward Kizmet Inc. and yours truly was way beyond what was necessary. I tried to tell him that with "You didn't need to go to that extreme," but he wasn't hearing any of it.

"Confidentiality and good work need to be rewarded. You deserve every penny of it, Harry." He reached into the top drawer of his desk and handed me a pen and a standard employment contract of two lines. It read:

> Trundle Industries extends the amount of $50,000 annually to Kizmet Inc. as retainer for future services rendered on their behalf.
> Agreed:_____
> Harry M. Shorts

"Sign on the line above your name, Harry. You are hereby on retainer to Trundle Industries, and to me personally, for future considerations. I may never need your help again, but if I ever do, I know I will be able to trust you. That is very important to me, Harry."

Ms. Timmons had been observing our conversation the entire time and chimed in at this point. "Harry, all contracts of this nature are lifetime agreements broken only by mutual agreement. Mr. Trundle and

da bushes

yourself are the only two individuals who have that power."

"Ms. Timmons will give you the first annual installment as you leave today if you agree to our arrangement."

"Mr. Trundle, consider Kizmet Inc. retained," I agreed.

"Good, Harry, I truly hoped you would agree. Now, a few more items and I'll let you go. I would assume you are beat after all this."

"Sure, Randle. What are they?"

"First, Jeannie has gone to Europe, and will be there for several months traveling and tending to some Trundle Industries business. She will be working with Ms. Timmons directly and also doing some things for me personally. I am very fond of her, Harry, and perhaps it would be best if she were able to distance herself from this episode in her life completely. Do you see any problem with that in any way?"

Jesus H. Christ, the man does know absolutely everything, doesn't he? And I mean everything!

"Perhaps that would be best, Mr. Trundle. It may not be the most pleasant part of the conclusion to this mess, but I don't see any problem with it."

Probably wouldn't have worked out anyway, I tried to convince myself. Randy hadn't been wrong yet, and I needed to trust someone in my life right about now.

"Good. Secondly, and this is a question, Harry. Have you had enough fun yet?"

I knew exactly what the question meant, and had been anticipating it for some time now. The problem was I didn't have an answer, or at least not one that I was happy with.

"I can't tell you how much enjoyment I have experienced playing with the Schooners these last few months. Not too many people get an opportunity like this once in their lives, never mind twice. But I know I was just biding time, and there are other players who need the chance to move up if they are to improve. From what I hear, I did too good of a job with the kid in Florida and he's tearing up Single A. Plus, Steiner is ready to be the number one catcher and has busted his butt to get there."

I didn't want to do it, but it was the right thing to do. Don't always give a fuck about the right thing to do, surely didn't want to give a fuck now.

Ah, hell.

"It's time I moved on, Randle. We both know it and I just have to accept it. I did my thing here, and we got results. End of story."

Trundle smiled like a father who approves of what his child had learned, and for another reason as well. "Not quite end of story yet, Harry. Ms. Timmons, if you would, please."

"Harry, in anticipation of this moment, we have put a few things in motion on your behalf, as well as the Schooners' behalf. The 'kid' as you call him has been recalled from Single A, and will be here for Saturday's game. Steiner will assume the primary catching duties upon your retirement following Saturday's game. And finally, any fan attending the game on Saturday wearing shorts will be let in free on our newest Schooner promotional day – 'SHORTS DAY' – in your honor, Harry."

Trundle was still smiling, and Ms. Timmons was right there with him.

Me, in fear of the tears thing, I'm running for end of chapter

Chapter 87

I didn't want it to, but Saturday morning came. I was feeling down knowing that it was gonna be over, but up knowing I had proved that I could play this game. Not just to myself, but to the people who play it for a living. I really did belong. For that I will be forever in M. Randle Trundle's debt.

Charlie pulled into the driveway with the purplemobile for what was to be the last hurrah, at least this time around. Who knows if we will get to ride and eat grub together in the future? We did have a time or two, though.

As I came around the corner, Charlie got out of the car to open the door for me – in shorts. "How are you, Harry? Beautiful day for a ballgame, wouldn't you say?" he laughed, with a grin the size of Manhattan.

"You old sonofabitch. You coming to the game today?"

"Harry, I wouldn't miss it for the world. Let's get Miss Bunny and be on our way."

We did, and we were. And it was a beautiful day for a ballgame. The park was filled with standing room only, setting a new Trundle Stadium record. Believe it or not, just about every damn one of them in shorts. The guys gave me a hell of a ribbing, and I ate it up, asking for more. When the music hit, they scooted out onto the field and I stayed behind for my own little surprise. Finally dressed, I headed out.

Stopped at the end of the tunnel to make sure my fly was zipped, then stepped into the dugout and trotted out onto the field in my custom made purple shorts. The fans caught sight of me, stood all at once, and began a chant of "Harry – Harry." I almost lost it right there.

Trundle himself was sitting in the owner's box behind the first base dugout with Ms. Timmons, who looked beyond dynamite in shorts and matching tank top. Sherry and the kids were with them, the little guys yelling up a storm. Big Mel was there right behind them with his whole clan in tow. Bunny was jumping up and down, causing quite a spectacle for the guys around her – she didn't even notice she was having so much fun.

My man Charlie beamed with pride.

I had all I could do to stop myself from breaking down right there on the field. Luckily, Coach Curran came over and told me enough of this shit, let's get to work. "And Harry, it was my pleasure," he said, extending his hand.

When it came time, Mr. M. Randle Trundle jumped over the fence and came out to throw out the first pitch. He removed the jacket to the pinstripe suit he was wearing and took a few steps onto the field. Then he stopped, reached down, and grabbed the front of his pants with both hands. Just like tear-away basketball warm-ups, his pants came off in his hands to unveil a pair of pinstripe shorts matching the suit he had been wearing. Needless to say, the place went wild, and he ate it up.

My legs were shaking so bad I don't know how I got myself behind the plate. Trundle wound up and fired a strike that would have made Smokes proud. He came in and shook my hand as I tried to give him the ball. "No, you keep it Harry," he said.

I looked at it as he walked back to his box and saw what he had written on it: "To Harry M. Shorts – you bet your ass you belong. Randy."

The Schooners won the last game I played in, and while I didn't get the winning hit, I did get two doubles to finish at .311 for the year. Now it was time.

Epilogue

The Schooners, under the direction of Coach Curran, went on to set a new league record for regular season winning percentage and swept their way into the finals of the Double A championship.

Rusty and Smokes threw shutouts in the first two games of the finals. A four-game sweep of the Harrisburg Senators gave the Bayport Schooners their first Eastern League Championship. They were truly a team for the ages and were written up in all the local papers as one of the best Double A teams of all time. The national wires caught wind of it and it played for a few weeks across the country.

Cat and Howdy got called up to help the Triple A team in their playoff finals and played pretty well. Rusty, Smokes and Slam went along for the ride, but didn't get any action. All five of them will be mainstays at Triple A next year.

Rusty won the Most Valuable Player award for the league.

Richie was named Assistant General Manager for the following season, as well as head of all team marketing and promotional activities. He will be helping the person in the newly created position of General Manager and Field Manager – Coach Curran.

Harry M. Shorts got his championship ring at the team's year-end dinner, and a standing ovation from the Schooner players and coaching staff when he went up to receive it from Mr. M. Randle Trundle. He got a high-five from Randy and a big hug from Ms. Wendy Timmons.